---- ★ ----

My eyes had no time to adjust to the gloom. Feeling my way down the spiral stairs, I grabbed the iron handrail on the inside wall and hoped for the best. I dashed out the side door, around to the wall and over it, swinging my feet onto the grass a few feet from the blue tarp.

The body of a young man lay on the tarp, dark streaks of blood smeared all over his khaki shorts, his Hawaiian shirt and the tarp itself. He lay on his stomach with his head turned to the right and his right hand raised as if he had been trying to suck his thumb. His left arm extended behind the body and down, palm up. His face was waxen, but even so I recognized him immediately.

It was Froggy Quale.

I forced myself not to touch him, grab him up and start CPR or something, because it was obvious that he had been dead a long time.

---- ★ ----

Previously published Worldwide Mystery title by
MARIA HUDGINS

DEATH OF AN OBNOXIOUS TOURIST

Death *of a*
Lovable Geek

Maria Hudgins

WORLDWIDE®

TORONTO • NEW YORK • LONDON
AMSTERDAM • PARIS • SYDNEY • HAMBURG
STOCKHOLM • ATHENS • TOKYO • MILAN
MADRID • WARSAW • BUDAPEST • AUCKLAND

For John and Betsy MacKenzie

Recycling programs
for this product may
not exist in your area.

DEATH OF A LOVABLE GEEK

A Worldwide Mystery/March 2010

First published by Five Star.

ISBN-13: 978-0-373-26704-0

Printed in U.S.A.

Acknowledgments

I want to thank my Sisters in Crime friends, especially Teresa Inge, Sally Parrott, Cindy Lane, Donna Nichol, Lori D'Angelo, Linda Bux and Phyllis Johnson for their unwavering support in the release of my first novel and in the development of this one.

Thanks also to Tricia Dyer for her help with the Scottish dialect and current Scots culture.

To my critique buddies, Amanda Flower and Sally Parrott, my good friends Brian and Marie Smith, and to Peggy Becouvarakis, who traveled through Scotland with me and made learning Scottish history fun.

To the bookstore owners who have given me a chance to present my work to their customers. And a special thanks to Island Bookstore in Duck, North Carolina; Broad Street Books of Ghent, Norfolk, Virginia; Mystery Lovers Bookshop, Oxford, Maryland; Borders in Virginia Beach; and Barnes and Noble, Hampton, Virginia.

I'm forever grateful to my friends and family who have attended signings even when they already had a copy of my book and showed up to support me whenever I needed them.

And to Deni Dietz, my tough but loving editor whose advice I always heed, hugs.

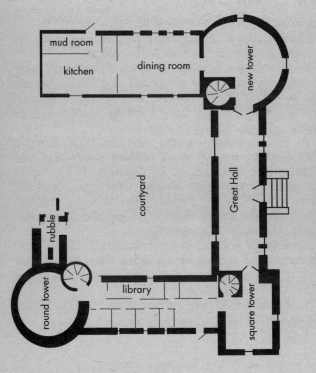

mud room

kitchen

dining room

new tower

courtyard

rubble

Great Hall

round tower

library

square tower

Ground Floor of Castle Dunlaggan

CAST OF CHARACTERS

Dotsy Lamb—History professor from Virginia, she's come to Scotland for an archaeological dig.

Lettie Osgood—Dotsy's friend and traveling companion, she's here to research her ancestors.

William Sinclair—Owner of Castle Dunlaggan.

Maisie Sinclair—William's wife.

Dr. John Sinclair—Brother of William, he's an archaeologist and director of the dig.

Fallon Sinclair—John's wife.

Tony Marsh—Archaeologist, John's second-in-command.

Amelia Lipscomb—Guest at the castle, she's a TV news reporter from Brighton, England.

Brian Lipscomb—Amelia's husband.

Alf and Eleanor Downes—Castle guests from Texas.

Robbie MacBane—Farmer, musician and landlord of Van Nguyen and Froggy Quale.

Van Nguyen—Froggy Quale's roommate and the dig's media man.

Graham Jones—Site manager at the dig.

Joyce Parsley, Tracee Wagg, Iain Jandeson, Proctor Galigher—College kids at the dig.

Chief Inspector Coates—Policeman in charge of the murder investigation.

Boots—Castle handyman.

Christine—Kitchen helper at the castle.

Wanda and Winifred Merlin—Castle guests from England, aka "the weird sisters."

Gone but not forgotten:

Froggy Quale—Graduate student, on-site spore and pollen expert at the dig.

Roger Sinclair—Father of William and John.

Lady Rebecca (Becky) Seton Sinclair—Wealthy, much-divorced actress, Roger's second wife.

Fenella MacBane Sinclair—Roger's first wife, William and John's mother.

ONE

FOR THE LIFE OF ME, I couldn't think why a perfectly good Super Bowl ticket would be lying on the back stairs of a castle in Scotland. But that's where I had found one, and I had it in my pocket now, waiting for a lull in the conversation to bring it up and find out if anyone else knew anything about it.

We, the guests and residents of Castle Dunlaggan, gathered in the library every evening after dinner for coffee, and tonight there were six of us: William Sinclair, our host; Dr. John Sinclair and his wife, Fallon; Tony Marsh; my dear friend, Lettie Osgood; and me, Dotsy Lamb. A wood fire crackled in the fireplace. I sat in an armchair on one side of the hearth, my trip journal in my lap and a small glass of Drambuie on the table beside me.

Lettie, perched in the armchair on the other side of the hearth, studied her road map of Central Scotland and the Highlands as she had done every night since we got here. From my vantage point, Lettie was represented by a few tufts of random-length red hair, two red-nailed hands and a couple of short legs, crossed at the ankles and swinging gently an inch or two above the rug. The rest of her was obscured by several square feet of map.

"Any catastrophes on the road today, Lettie?" Dr. John Sinclair asked, his tumbler of single malt Scotch sloshing as he tacked away from the sideboard. John was the director of the archaeological dig I was lucky enough to be participating in, my college in Virginia having been so kind as to give me a couple of weeks off at the beginning of fall term, but not kind enough to pay for the trip. John was also the brother of William Sinclair, owner of the Castle Dunlaggan at which we were staying.

"One small one," Lettie said, crunching her map into her lap. "I told the man at the rental place, I said, 'I can either shift gears or I can drive on the left side of the road, but I can't do both at the same time. I need an automatic.'"

"I'm not surprised that he didn't have one. We Brits and Scots are keen on shifting our own gears," John said.

"And putting roundabouts in all the intersections, so you have to go backward around your own elbow to make a turn," Lettie added.

Fallon Sinclair, John's wife, scanned the floor-to-ceiling books along one wall and beckoned to Tony Marsh to join her. Tony was John's second-in-command at the dig and, so far, my favorite of the bunch. He was knowledgeable about Scottish history and about archaeology in general, but not priggish. John Sinclair was just knowledgeable. Fallon pulled out a small book and, eyebrows raised, handed it to Tony.

"Dotsy, here's the very book for you, compliments of the Sinclair family library." Tony leaned across a dictionary stand to hand it to me.

A thin volume entitled *Macbeth and the Early Scottish Kings,* it looked like no more than one evening's bedtime reading. In the past year I had dug up all the information I could find on Macbeth. The real Macbeth, not the murderous villain invented by Shakespeare. A simple question from one of my students had prompted me to research the Scottish king and discover that little had been written about him compared to all the other Scottish kings. After a few online inquiries, I had concluded that no one in Scotland wanted to talk about him. As soon as I find someone doesn't want to talk about something, I do.

"Thanks, Tony," I said, taking the book from him. "Do I have to check it out if I take it to my room?"

Tony and I both turned to the burly, ruddy-faced William

Sinclair who seemed confused by my question, but Tony clarified it. "Is this a lending library, William? Does Dotsy need a reader's ticket?"

"Nae, just take it," William said.

"Speaking of tickets, can somebody explain this?" I dug into my skirt pocket and drew out a small, rectangular strip. "I found this in the stairwell of the round tower before dinner."

Tony leaned over the back of my chair and took the strip for a closer look. "Super Bowl?"

"Super Bowl," I said. "The ultimate American football game. It's our equivalent of the World Cup finals."

Fallon Sinclair took the ticket from Tony. "But what you call football isn't what we call football."

Lettie said, "What you call football, we call soccer."

John took the ticket from Fallon. "There's a diagram of the stadium on the back. Row ten. Section one hundred ten." He angled the ticket under the beam of a desk lamp. "It looks as if this would seat you near the middle of the field."

"On the fifty-yard line. I've already checked it," I said.

"How much would a ticket like this sell for?" Tony asked.

"Thousands."

"Thousands of dollars?" Fallon took the ticket back from John and studied it, almost reverently, I thought. "This may be a memento. Someone's keepsake, don't you think? I mean if they paid thousands to attend this game, they wouldn't simply throw the ticket away."

Tony turned to William. "Have any of your recent guests been the sort to have attended an American Super Bowl game?"

William took the ticket. "Not that I can recall," he said.

"Look at the date," I said. "This isn't a keepsake. This is a ticket for *next February's* Super Bowl."

William passed the ticket to Lettie. Now, six people: John, Fallon, William, Tony, Lettie, and I, had left our fingerprints on the ticket.

TWO

A HALF MILE FROM Castle Dunlaggan, Van Nguyen danced in full view of the road. The window of his second-floor room wide open to the wind sweeping in from the moor, he improvised as wildly as the cord to his headphones would allow. A strand of his long black hair escaped from its restraining rubber band, and he smoothed it back with one hand while shifting the mouse connected to one of his computers with his other hand.

One whole wall of the room was stacked solid with electronics. Two monitors flashed a series of photos while two others, with their screen savers morphing from one geometric form to another, stood by. Multiple layers of shirts hung from a peg on the back of the door. Socks, T-shirts, and jeans lay on a shelf above one of the two single beds, intertwined with electric cables, bungee cords, and CDs. Van stopped dancing long enough to click on a few choices from the bank of photos on one of the active screens.

Outside, near the road that ran past, a young woman in an anorak and with a camouflage hat pulled down low over her face watched the window from behind a scrubby Scots pine. She stood on the concrete slab of an old roadside shelter, a remnant of the days when milk in stainless steel cans was picked up by a truck before dawn. Van came to the window, and the girl stepped back a bit, putting more pine between herself and him.

Van plucked an air guitar and tossed his head backward. He sang, a bit off-key, "'Cause I got cat class an' I got cat style!"

His desk light flickered. He pulled his headset off and turned toward the desk. The light flickered again, in unison with the ringing of his cell phone. He yanked the phone from its cradle and said, "Hello."

A pause, then, "He's not here."

After another short interval, Van said, "He's probably at the camp, hanging out. I guess you've already tried his cell phone?"

Then, "Yes, ma'am."

And a few seconds later, "Maybe he went to the—what do you call it? The loo?—and left his phone outside."

Then, "Yes, ma'am. I'll tell him to call you."

While Van finished his phone call, the girl studied the road in both directions and peered across the meadow toward the Castle Dunlaggan with its dark towers and turrets piercing the night sky. She hitched up her shoulders and walked off, southward, down the road.

BESIDE A DRYSTONE WALL some thirty yards from the northwest corner of the Castle Dunlaggan, a blue tarp lay crumpled. Thin fingers of fog crept up the valley, across the field and into its folds as dew collected on its surface.

From under the blue tarp, a laughing horse, a novelty ring tone on a cell phone, whinnied again and again.

THREE

I WAS DRIFTING OFF to sleep when Lettie tapped on my door.

"Psst! Dotsy."

I padded to the door. Lettie, wrapped in a blue robe, pulled me into the hall. Her face was smeared with some sort of green goo, another one of her age-reversing miracle creams, I supposed.

"I hear a strange noise," she said.

We stood silent for a few moments before I heard it, too. It was a sort of rhythmic clanking sound, like metal on something non-metal. The walls in the stone hallway, I knew, could play tricks with sound so I walked to the north end of the hall with Lettie, trembling, attached to my left arm. I heard nothing from that end. At the south end of the hall, I carefully pulled on the door to a winding staircase and listened again.

The sound was louder here and coming up from below. That stairwell led up to the third floor and down to the first. Possibly below ground as well. The noises stopped. I turned to Lettie and chuckled. Her hands clasped tightly under her chin, she wore a comically exaggerated expression of fear on her green face.

"What is it?" she asked.

"No idea."

"Are you going down there?"

"Absolutely not."

It started up again. *Clink, shush, clink, shush.*

"I'll never be able to get to sleep, now," Lettie said. "Even if it stops, I'll be listening for it to start up again."

"We can ask William about it in the morning. For now, I'll lend you a book on Neolithic flint that's guaranteed to put you to sleep."

AT 6:00 A.M., I started up the spiral staircase to the bathroom on the third floor of the round tower. My room was actually closer to a bathroom at the southern end of the hall, and there was another, a half bath, on the ground floor beneath it, but those two were generally occupied in the morning, and I hated to wait in the hall with my towel and soap, like some summer camper.

To get to the top of the round tower, you had to start at ground level then climb the narrow stone stairs that wound up the turret within the tower, like a straw in a glass. The only light came from the occasional arrow-slit window and a wall-mounted bulb which popped and went dark as soon as I flicked the switch. I had my flashlight, my towel, and my roll-up travel toiletry kit with me.

At the foot of the stairs, I paused. This was where I had found the Super Bowl ticket yesterday evening. On the third step. I had racked my brain to think of a reasonable explanation for a yet-to-be-played Super Bowl ticket to be lying, fresh and un-trampled, on the steps of a castle in Scotland, but I hadn't come up with a thing. If this were a castle where public tours traipsed through, I could understand it. But Castle Dunlaggan was a bed-and-breakfast, catering to the sort of people who like to go off the beaten track. To my knowledge, there had been no American guests but Lettie and me for the last week or so at least, and if that ticket had been lying there more than a day, I would have found it earlier.

The landing at the base of the stairwell adjoined a large, round room, currently used for storage, and a door leading outside to a small stone stoop in the inner courtyard. Last evening, I remembered, I had left my boots and trowel on the stoop because the boots were too muddy to bring in. I stepped out and checked them. The mud was still damp. I plopped myself down on the stone and began to work away at the mess with my trowel because I had to wear those boots again today.

It certainly hasn't taken me long to make myself at home in a castle, I thought. *Here I sit, in my pink bathrobe and slippers, cleaning mud off my boots in the morning sun.*

The open courtyard had once been a completely enclosed quadrangle, but the north wing had crumbled a few hundred years ago. It had once joined the round tower on the northwest to the kitchen and servants' quarters in the east wing, but now it went only a third of the way across before tapering down to rubble. I stopped scraping my boots for a moment and breathed in the morning air. The sun, rising over the kitchen roof, had not yet reached the ground in the courtyard, so the grass was still covered with dew.

Banging the boots against the stone a couple of times, I placed them inside the door and climbed the stairs. The room on the second floor of the tower was circular like the one below it, but this one was nicely furnished as a bedroom. Until yesterday, the two women Lettie and I called "the weird sisters" had been staying there. I had heard William dragging their luggage across the front drive and the car doors slam last night shortly after I'd gone to my room. This morning, the bedroom door stood open.

On the third level, I flung my towel over the shower curtain rod, hung my toiletry kit from the light beside the mirror, and looked out a narrow window while I ran the water to heat it up. I could see the old drystone wall that ran northward between a dew-covered pasture and the back lawn. On the pasture side of the wall lay a bright blue tarp that I couldn't recall seeing there yesterday.

In the distance, Christine, a local teen-ager who helped in the kitchen, crested a small hill and slogged across the meadow on her way to work. I imagined that her shoes and socks were getting soaked. I checked the shower's water temperature again.

"Crikey! Oh my Lord, oooh!"

I dashed back to the window in time to see Christine jump the wall and fly across the lawn toward the kitchen. I turned off the water and ran out to the stairs. My eyes had no time to adjust to the gloom. Feeling my way down the spiral stairs, I grabbed the iron handrail on the inside wall and hoped for the best. I dashed out the side door, around to the wall and over it, swinging my feet onto the grass a few feet from the blue tarp.

The body of a young man lay on the tarp, dark streaks of blood smeared all over his khaki shorts, his Hawaiian shirt, and the tarp itself. He lay on his stomach with his head turned to the right and his right hand raised as if he had been trying to suck his thumb. His left arm extended behind the body and down, palm up. His face was waxen, but even so I recognized him immediately.

It was Froggy Quale.

I forced myself not to touch him, grab him up and start CPR or something, because it was obvious that he had been dead a long time. The arms and legs looked stiff, as if rigor had already come and partly gone.

Fighting back the urge to scream, "Why?" toward the skies, I looked around and tried to think what I should do next. Run inside and call the police? No, undoubtedly Christine was doing that. Stay right here? I probably should. Cover him up? No, you're not supposed to touch anything.

On closer inspection, I realized that the tarp had only recently been pulled back. I could clearly see that the dew-dotted part of the tarp was absent from a wedge-shaped area next to the body. It seemed logical to assume that Christine had pulled the tarp back, made her gruesome discovery, screamed, and ran.

On top of the drystone wall, a sheet of notebook paper, folded and tucked envelope style, lay dry and untouched by the dew. After raising five kids, I know a note when I see one. Paper folded exactly like that used to fall out of my kids' book bags by the dozens. I still wonder how they got any school work done. In my experience, a particularly treasured note might stay in a book bag or tucked into a math book for months. The temptation to pick it up and read it was strong, but I resisted.

Froggy wasn't his real name, of course. I tried to remember what he'd told me his real name was. Dylan. That was it. Dylan Quale. He was our pollen and spore expert at the dig. Why they called him Froggy was obvious. He looked like a frog. He had a round face, a wide, thin mouth, and wide-set eyes accentuated by big, round horn-rimmed glasses. His straight brown hair covered his ears and made him look as if he didn't have any ears. If I had been his mother I would have advised a different haircut.

Why would anyone kill a harmless kid like Froggy? The others at the dig, mostly college students, generally regarded him as a geek. A nice geek, but a bit of an outsider. Robbery. That's the only reason that came to mind.

I spotted something written on the palm of his left hand. I knew better than to touch the body, but by kneeling at the edge of the tarp and leaning over, I was able to see. It reminded me of the way my kids used to write important things like phone numbers and school assignments on their hands, never thinking that it would soon rub off.

It looked like "alloi." I leaned a little farther and tried to move his thumb. It was cold and stiff. There was a lowercase "h" in front of the "a," and I decided the "i" might be an "l." "halloi" or "hallol." It meant nothing to me.

Something was wrong about his shirt, but I couldn't put my finger on it. The shirt was red with white tropical hibiscus all over it. Not the sort of thing I'd seen Froggy wearing at the dig site, but then I hadn't seen much of his wardrobe. I'd only met him four days ago.

Maisie Sinclair, William's wife, rounded the corner of the east wing. Maisie, with her pleasantly weathered face and unruly hair, was our hostess, chief cook, housekeeper, you name it. She gazed across the lawn, wiped her hands on her apron, and tramped across the grass toward me. When she was close enough to peer over the stone wall, she recoiled sharply. "Oh, my Lord!" Her fist flew to her mouth. "D'ye ken who it is?"

"Dylan Quale. From the dig."

"John needs t'be told."

"Should I go in and find him?"

"Nae, the police told me—I did the callin' because Christine's gone daft—they told me to let no one else come out here, and anyone who was already out here had to stay 'til they get here."

"Very well."

"He's young. No more than a lad," Maisie said, still not looking straight at the face.

"He graduated from college last spring," I said. "That would make him about twenty-one."

William Sinclair, in a tweed jacket and blue shirt, open at the neck, had donned Wellington boots for the trek across the wet grass. He groaned and hid his mouth with both hands when he saw the body.

"The police told me not to let anybody leave the house," Maisie told him.

"Isn't that one o' the lads from the dig?" William asked, ignoring Maisie's comment.

I confirmed that it was. "This tarp," I said, "is like the ones we use at the dig."

"It's like all blue tarps," William said. "They're everywhere. There's one in the car park by the kitchen door right noo."

Saying that she needed to see to the other guests who were by now in the dining room waiting for breakfast, Maisie headed back to the house. A few minutes later the first police car, siren blaring, wheeled into the parking area. Behind it was a white emergency van. Two uniformed officers in lime-yellow vests and checkerboard caps ran across the lawn ahead of two paramedics bringing stretcher and gear.

The paramedics did a quick check and one said, "Don't move him. Doctor'll be along in a minute."

I would have liked to dash back to my room for something more appropriate than my pink robe and satin slippers, but I didn't have the nerve to ask. William and I stood back while the officers drove stakes and rolled out yellow crime scene tape.

Two men in tweed jackets approached. One, a rugged, gray-haired man, proved to be the doctor. He went immediately to the body and pronounced it dead. The other, a short, bald man with sunglasses, greeted William. They shook hands.

"Nasty business, eh?"

"Oh aye," said William.

The short man adopted a deferential posture, head forward, and stepped back. I gathered, by their stances, that he and William knew each other. They stood side by side, facing the body. The new man heaved himself over the wall, walked around the tarp, and signaled to one of the uniformed officers. With a snap of his forefinger in front of his eye, he indicated it was time for them to start taking pictures.

William introduced me. "Mrs. Lamb, this is Chief Inspector Coates. Duncan Coates."

"Are you the one who found him?" Coates asked. His demeanor changed completely as he addressed me. All I could think of was what my grandmother used to call a "bantie rooster," meaning a little man who struts to create an illusion of great size.

I explained that it was Christine who had made the discovery. "My apologies for not being properly dressed." I drew in my robe and tightened the tie belt. I was showing more cleavage than I normally expose strangers to.

"No problem." Chief Inspector Coates averted his eyes and nodded toward the body. "Any idea who it might be?"

"It's Dylan Quale," I said. "He works—worked—at the archaeological dig down by the road. Have you seen it?"

"John Sinclair's excavation?" Coates asked.

William and I nodded.

"I haven't been by there recently, but it's the same one he's been working on for several years, aye?"

William affirmed that it was and said, "I've seen this lad around there, I ken, but I dinnae ever actually meet him. Not that I recall. Mrs. Lamb can probably tell you more."

"The kids called him Froggy," I said. "He was a recent graduate of Worcester University but he was going on for a doctorate there. Quite a remarkable young man. He was only about twenty-one, but he was already considered somewhat of an authority on spore and pollen identification. That's why John asked him to join the dig this season."

Coates's neck and jaw muscles tightened. "What does pollen have to do with this dig? You mean like tree pollen?"

"Yes. Or any kind of pollen. Or spores, like from ferns and mosses, you know. We examine the soil at different depths as we dig down to earlier and older material." I used my hand like a trowel to illustrate. "Froggy could look at a soil sample under a microscope and tell you what kinds of plants were around at the time that soil was laid down."

"You work at the dig, too?"

"Yes. I'm the oldest member of the team. Most of them are college kids, you know. Most are from Worcester University, because that's where John Sinclair teaches. Dr. Sinclair invited me to join them after I had consulted him several times about some matters of Scottish history. I teach ancient and medieval history in the U.S."

Chief Inspector Coates reached into his inner jacket pocket but drew his hand out empty, as if he'd planned to write that down, then thought better of it. He nodded toward the body. "Did he get along with the other kids? Any conflicts?"

"I couldn't say for sure, but I don't think so. I've only been here a few days so I don't know any of them that well, but I think he got along with the others. It's just that they…"

"They what?"

"Most of them thought he was a bit of a nerd, I think. They liked him okay but he wasn't considered cool."

"Did he have any special friends?"

My voice caught in the back of my throat. I may have been the closest thing he had to a friend, myself. And I'd only known him three days. I shook my mind away from my memories of the afternoon we'd spent together with his microscopes and specimens.

"He had a roommate. Van Nguyen. He and Van had a room at a farmhouse between here and the dig site."

Coates's hand moved back to his inner pocket. He pulled out a notepad and wrote the name. I had to help him with the spelling of Nguyen.

"Oh, aye. They took a room at the MacBanes', dinnae they?" William said to me, then turned to Coates. "The MacBanes have a couple of extra rooms to let. Bed-and-breakfast, like. I've seen the lads walking over there in the evening."

"Do all the kids from the dig stay at bed-and-breakfasts hereabouts?" Coates asked.

"Nae, most of them stay at a camp they pitched beside the road, doon there." William pointed roughly to the southeast, but from our vantage point, the castle blocked the view of the fields and road between here and the dig site. "Well, I'm sure you'll be goin' over there to talk to them, so you'll see the camp for yourself. Bit of a mess, it is."

"Van and Froggy stayed at the MacBane house because Van is the media man for the dig," I said. "He makes the slide shows, presentations, does all the photography, and keeps the computers running. Most of Froggy's work involved the microscopes and fixing and staining specimens. Both he and Van needed a regular room to keep their equipment out of the weather."

"We'll be needing to set up an incident room close by, sir," said Coates. "Do you have a small room we could use? If not, we can bring a mobile unit round and park it. I suppose we could put it at the back of your parking area."

William looked toward the castle. After a minute, he said, "The bottom level of the round tower isnae being used. We've stored some old furniture in it, but we could move it."

William and Chief Inspector Coates drifted into a lengthy analysis of what the police required, and the round tower's access to electricity and water. I asked if I could leave.

"Stop by the incident room when we get it set up and give us your formal statement," Coates told me, by way of dismissal.

MY ROOM, WHICH I HAD cautioned Lettie not to call "my cell," had one long window that overlooked a sheep pasture. The window was set in a granite wall so thick that an armchair placed in front of it was completely contained within its alcove.

I stood at my window for a long time, remembering Froggy.

Two days ago we had sat together in the finds shack, a shed that housed artifacts and whatever equipment we couldn't allow to get wet. Froggy had set up a plywood bench with a binocular microscope and a regular microscope plugged in to a power strip that also fed a scary mare's nest of other cords.

Froggy let me look at mushroom spores through the binocular scope. He showed me some dormant fern spores, and some others that he had germinated in a Petri dish by keeping them moist for a few days. These, he called fern gametophytes. The spores, he explained, came out of those dots you find on the undersides of fern leaves. If they germinate, they produce eggs and sperm which can beget a new fern.

Through the microscope, Froggy had taken a photo of a perfectly heart-shaped fern gametophyte, a patchwork of tiny green cells magnified 40 times. He had pointed out some specific cells with names I could no longer remember, then grabbed a pen and wrote across the bottom of the photo. "To Dotsy. Love, Dylan."

He had handed it to me with a wide grin and said, "Will you be my Valentine?"

I turned from the window and spotted a book on my bedside table. Picking up the book, I drew out that same photo. Then I sat on the side of my bed and let the tears roll.

There was a knock at my door, and I assumed it was Lettie but I was wrong. Amelia Lipscomb, another castle guest, said, "May I come in?" Amelia radiated a sensuous beauty even in the morning. Had we been in the same generation, I could have been jealous of her, but since we weren't, I was merely envious.

"Is it really Dylan Quale?" she asked.

"I'm afraid so. Do you know him?" I blew my nose into a tissue.

Amelia ignored my question and went on. "Is it suicide?"

"No. It was murder."

"How do you know?"

"I'm sorry, Amelia, but I've promised not to talk about it until everyone has given statements to the police. How did you know him?"

Amelia scanned the room with the practiced eye of a news reporter. "I don't know him but I know his mother."

My heart thumped against my ribs. His mother. Someone had to tell his parents. "Have you called her?"

"The police have to do that," Amelia said. "I'm not even supposed to know that it's Dylan, but I forced it out of Maisie."

"Right."

Amelia was a reporter for a TV station in the south of England. Brighton, I thought they had said, on the north coast of the English Channel. Amelia, with her full, sultry lips and great cheekbones, might well be assumed to be simply another pretty talking head, but she wasn't. According to her husband, Brian, she was a tiger after the truth. Brian had told me about Amelia's exposé of a medical director who had "harvested" himself a secret stockpile of transplantable children's organs without bothering to get parents' permission. She had single-handedly solved the mysterious disappearance of the loose-lipped husband of a Sussex inquiry judge. It turned out that the couple sometimes indulged in politically unwise personal activities.

She had a mildly irritating habit of pursing her lips between sentences. This morning she wore a green shirt with jeans and gold hoop earrings. Always a solid-color top. It occurred to me that I had yet to see her in anything other than a solid color above the waist, and that a TV reporter, to be ever ready to go before the camera, might shy away from camera-hostile patterns.

Amelia's gaze settled on the fern gametophyte photo I had left on the bed. She sidled over and picked it up. "How odd. What is this?"

It felt, to me, like an invasion of my privacy and the hair on the back of my neck bristled. "It's a picture Dylan took with his microscope. He gave it to me a couple of days ago." I could think of no reasonable way to avoid telling her, and actually there was no reason not to tell her except that I resented her asking.

"Love, Dylan," she read. She laid the photo back on the bed and pursed her mouth twice. "Did Dylan and John Sinclair get along all right?"

What an odd question, I thought. Out of the clear blue. "Sure. As far as I know."

Amelia must have noticed the puzzlement on my face. "Sorry," she said, "it's just that Dylan's mother told me he'd been paid rather handsomely to attend this dig. I wondered if he got a grant, himself, or if John got a grant for him. Money for this sort of thing is tight, you know."

I glanced pointedly at the door.

"I'd better let you go downstairs before Maisie stops serving breakfast," Amelia said, took the hint, and left.

I grabbed my blood sugar monitor and did a quick forearm test. Amelia was right. I did need to get some breakfast. At the basin beside my nightstand, I washed my face and breathed in the sweet cottony scent of my face towel. It took several splashes of cold water to lessen the redness around my eyes to the point where I thought makeup could handle the rest.

Another knock on the door. This time it really was Lettie. "Oh, Dotsy, it must have been awful for you. Did you know that boy?"

I told her about Froggy and she listened.

"I saw Christine, poor thing, she was hysterical," Lettie said. "Maisie was hustling her upstairs as I was going into the dining room."

"Who else was at breakfast?" I asked.

"Tony Marsh was there and so were Amelia and Brian Lipscomb. Fallon Sinclair was there, but not John. She said he wasn't feeling well and she told Tony he'd have to take care of things at the dig today because it looked like John wouldn't make it over there."

"How did you find out about Dylan?"

"Maisie came in after she got Christine settled down upstairs and she told us. She said the police had told her not to tell anybody anything, but they also told her not to let anybody leave the house so she had to tell us a little something, you know, so we'd understand why."

I heard another knock at the door. It was William Sinclair, still slogging about in his Wellies. "The police need to look through all our cars," he said apologetically. "They asked me to collect car keys and to tell you it's all right if you go out and watch them."

While Lettie slipped into her room next door for the keys to her rental car, I said, "Has John been told yet?"

"Aye, I went up to his room and told him." William lowered

his eyes and coughed self-consciously. Lettie emerged from her room and handed him her keys.

As William turned to leave, Lettie pulled me back inside my own room and shut the door. "Oh Dotsy! What are the police going to do to me? There's a big dent on the fender from where I ran into a sign post yesterday!"

"Why should the police care what you do to a rental car?" I said. "And how will they know if you did it yesterday or someone else did it last month?"

"Oh. What a relief."

Sometimes my friend Lettie doesn't think things through before she speaks.

FOUR

"THEY'VE BROUGHT IN more police. Four squad cars out there, now." Lettie let the curtain fall and brought her fresh cup of coffee to our table.

I loved the dining room at Castle Dunlaggan. The morning sun danced on the green and red Sinclair tartan of the rug and chairs. The walls were white stucco with heavy, dark, oak ceiling beams and wainscot. Today, Maisie had placed a bowl of creamy white hydrangea blossoms on each table.

I tossed my orange juice into my face in response to a loud shout and a thud from the parking area. Lettie and I rushed to the window. Beyond several guest cars parked next to the building and the police cars parked willy-nilly behind them, two uniformed men wrestled Brian Lipscomb into a spread-eagle stance and shoved his hands against the top of a blue BMW.

"What the hell?" Lettie said.

I heard the screen door of the kitchen slam and guessed that Maisie had heard the ruckus and had gone out to investigate.

After the police patted Brian down, they let him stand up straight and take his hands off the car. Brian appeared to be explaining something at great length. One policeman took a handful of keys from his jacket, and Brian pointed to a particular set. They moved around to the trunk of the car.

"Is that the Lipscombs' car? The BMW?" I asked.

"Yes," Lettie said. I can always count on Lettie to know things like that. She has a phenomenal memory for details. "Here comes the detective."

"It's Chief Inspector Coates," I said. The little rooster planted his feet wide apart, and Brian continued his explanation of whatever it was, gesturing frequently at the trunk. The officer with all the keys stepped forward and unlocked the trunk. Brian pointed to something inside.

Coates lifted out what appeared to be a stack of papers, handed them to Brian, and waved a finger toward the driver's-side door of the car. As the men searched the front and rear seats, Coates escorted Brian, still carrying the stack of papers, around the back of the building.

"What's going on?"

I turned from the window to find Tony Marsh standing behind me. "The police and Brian Lipscomb have been having a sort of… well, I don't know what it was, but it seems to be over now."

Tony drained the last bit of coffee in the urn into a cup and joined us back at our table. "I'm so sorry about Dylan, Tony," I said. "How is John taking it?"

"I think he's in shock, as I am." Tony stared at his cup for a long time in silence. When he looked up, I noticed that his eyes brimmed with tears ready to spill over. "This is hard to accept. Who in the world would…" He choked on his words. "Everybody liked Froggy! He was brilliant. He had so much ahead of him."

Tony shook his head slowly and stared at his cup. "Who could possibly want to kill him? Why?"

There was nothing I could say to that. I waited a minute, then said, "Have his parents been told?"

Tony didn't seem to process that question right away, but at length he said, "The police asked John if he wanted to be the one to call them, but he said no, he'd rather they did it."

Maisie came in from the kitchen. "They've almost got the interview room set up. Whenever you're ready, they said, you can go round and give a formal statement. Chief Inspector Coates'll go out to the dig site and the camp and tell all them clingin' bairns what the situation is. After that, he'll let us all do whatever we've got planned for the day."

"Including going to the dig?" I asked.

"I suppose so," Maisie said.

"Are you going over there then, Tony?"

"As soon as they let me, yes."

Maisie looked down at our table. "I need to know what ye'll be wantin' for yer suppers. Ye'll be eatin' here, I suppose?"

We all nodded.

"We're havin' rabbit and salmon. Dessert will be raspberry tart, I ken."

Although the Castle Dunlaggan was a bed-and-breakfast, Maisie always offered dinner as an optional extra. This far out in the country, guests often found themselves too far from town, or too exhausted after a day's hiking to eat anywhere else in the evening. But Maisie's evening meals were so fine that word had gotten around to the locals. As long as they called ahead, she could usually accept more diners, and it wasn't unusual for us to have four or six people from a nearby village eating with us.

"Is your salmon fresh?" I asked.

"Still swimmin'. Boots is doon at the river noo."

WITH A LITTLE TIME to kill, Lettie and I explored the great hall. It ran the entire length of the south wing from the square tower to the new tower, the new tower being the accepted name for a tower that was round but had to be distinguished somehow from the other round tower which already had dibs on the name. The floor in the great hall was inlaid with three colors of marble in a geometric pattern. The granite walls, lit by the morning sun slanting through tall, bare windows, were covered with antlers, swords, guns, claymores, helmets, and coats of arms.

Directly across from the front entrance were a tile-lined fireplace at least twelve feet high and wide and, incongruously, two cannon balls as big as bowling balls, one on either side of the hearth. This was not a woman's room.

Lettie gravitated toward a particularly painful-looking suit of armor in one corner.

"Ouch!" I said. "Did you ever wonder what knights wore under their armor?"

Lettie ignored the question. "I'm afraid my imagination was running away from me."

"How so?"

"I was thinking about those noises we heard last night," she said, "and I was wondering if this castle has a ghost. Most castles do, don't they? Assuming there is a ghost here, maybe he or she comes out at night and puts on the armor and clunks around, pretending to be a knight of old." Lettie clunked around, stiff-legged, to show me what she meant.

I looked at her, refusing to laugh while I searched for a snappy comeback. I couldn't think of a thing. "A ghost in armor would make a sort of *creak-clank* sound, I believe. What we'd heard last night was more of a *clink-shush*."

To my great relief, Lettie laughed first.

CHIEF INSPECTOR COATES led me to a table and chair along the wall of the interview room. They had already moved out most of the stored furniture and had set up a large rectangular table in the center with computers and folding chairs. Cables and cords running from the table to a couple of wall outlets, I noticed, needed to be taped down before somebody hurt himself.

Coates gave me paper and pencil. "Write down everything you remember, from the time you heard the young lass scream until our men arrived. Everything. When you've done, don't leave. I have a few questions to ask you."

My recollections ran to three pages. As I turned them in, Coates ended his phone conversation and motioned me back to my chair. He pulled up another one in front of me for himself. "Can you tell me anything more about this Van what's-his-name? Quale's roommate?"

"Not much," I said. "He's a tall, nice-looking kid, an electronics wizard, they say. He's in the U.K. on a fellowship. At Cambridge, I believe. Most of the students here are from Worcester University, but I'm almost certain Dylan told me that Van goes to Cambridge."

"Asian kid?"

"Asian-American. He's from Seattle, Washington, I seem to remember hearing, but you'd better check on that. I think his grandparents came from Vietnam."

"Anything else? Does he speak good English?"

"Of course. He's third-generation American."

"Who else did young Quale hang around with?"

"I don't know," I said. "I'd only known him a few days. He seemed to spend most of his time at his microscope. By the way, did you notice the writing on the palm of his left hand?"

"No, but the forensic examiner will. He'll have it in his autopsy notes, I'm sure."

"Yes. Well, I just thought it might be important."

Coates gave me a look that said, in no uncertain terms, "I'm in charge of deciding what's important." As he checked back through a few pages of his notes, his jaw muscles clenched and unclenched repeatedly.

Then he said, "We need background information on you, Mrs. Lamb. Your home is…?"

"Staunton, Virginia, U.S.A."

"Occupation?"

"History instructor." I gave him the relevant addresses and phone numbers.

"Married?"

"Divorced."

He glanced at me as if to say, *I'm not surprised,* and jotted something in his notes. "Where were you yesterday between noon and midnight?"

So Froggy had been killed yesterday. I had already guessed that. "I was at the dig site until nearly five. Then I came back here, showered, dressed, and went down to dinner at about six-thirty. We always have drinks before dinner in the new tower, next to the dining room. After dinner, I visited the library. Lettie Osgood, John and Fallon Sinclair, William Sinclair and Tony Marsh were also there. I returned to my room at about ten and went to bed."

"Was Maisie Sinclair with you in the library?"

"No, she was in the kitchen, cleaning up from dinner, or I assume she was." I wondered how I could have said that without sounding as if I suspected Maisie of not being in the kitchen. All I meant was that I hadn't personally seen her in the kitchen.

"John Sinclair and Tony Marsh were in the library with you the whole time you were there?"

"Yes."

"When you showered before dinner, Mrs. Lamb, did you use the bath on the third floor above us here?"

I was impressed. Chief Inspector Coates was already well up on the layout of the castle. "Yes, I did."

"Did you look out while you were up there? What I mean is, did you look at the area where the body was found this morning, and, if so, did you see a blue tarp?"

"I didn't look out, as far as I can recall."

"You didn't look out, or you don't recall whether you looked out or not?"

"I didn't look out…as far as I can recall," I said as nicely as I could. "There is one other thing, sir. It's not important, I'm sure, but on Wednesday, I believe it was, Dylan and I had a long talk in the finds shack at the dig. About his work. He showed me how he identified spores and pollen grains. He gave me a photo he'd taken of a heart-shaped fern, an embryonic fern, and he signed it 'Love, Dylan.'"

Coates looked at me blankly.

"I mean, I know it's not important. I simply wanted to tell you so you wouldn't think I was holding anything back."

His look progressed through patronizing all the way to "You poor, pathetic, deluded, old thing."

Tony Marsh came in and handed a sheet of paper to a uniformed man at one of the computers. The man handed it back to him and pointed toward us. Tony brought the paper over and handed it to Coates. "It's the list of workers at the excavation that you wanted," Tony said. "I've put notes beside the ones who aren't students and explained what their job is or why they're here."

"Very good," Coates said.

Thankfully, I was dismissed.

FIVE

I FOUND LETTIE IN her room, poring over a city map of Inverness. Lettie's justification for coming to Scotland with me was to do research on her ancestors. She loves to travel, but has no interest in archaeology and even less in wielding a shovel on her vacation, so the ancestor hunt provided her with an adequate excuse to come with me. Lettie's husband, Ollie, isn't much of a traveler, but he encourages Lettie to go places, particularly, I believe, when she goes with me. Ollie told me once that he trusted me to get Lettie out of any jam she might get herself into.

Last summer, however, we had gone on a group tour of Italy and it was I, not Lettie, who had nearly gotten into more trouble than I could extricate myself from. It wasn't my fault that two members of our group got killed, but I was the one who got us both mixed up in it. Lettie said that when she got home, she found that Ollie had already packed himself a bag and bought a plane ticket to Florence.

"Chief Inspector Coates is on his way over to the dig," I told her. "He told Tony and me to give him an hour to talk to the kids and get them organized for interviews before we come over."

"So he thinks the kids don't know about the murder?"

"I reckon."

"I bet they already know, Dotsy. Someone's bound to have heard the sirens."

"The real question is, did any of them know about it yesterday? Did any of them know about it when it happened?" I had to shiver at my own words. "Lettie, would you go to the cellar with me? Let's see if we can find out what was making those noises last night."

"It'll be dark down there."

"We have flashlights."

"How do you know it was coming from the cellar? Are you sure there is a cellar?"

"No, but this is the best time to do it because we know Coates is at the dig. I'm not sure I could explain it to him."

Lettie looked unpersuaded.

"Or, we could do it tonight after they've gone—when it's really dark."

WE PAUSED ON the landing at the first floor. This stairwell gave access to the various levels of the square tower and the west wing. A nail-studded wooden door guarded the steps leading belowground. Lettie and I switched on our flashlights and descended to a small sort of alcove littered with garden and lawn equipment. Three old tires leaned against one wall. There was an exterior door which was locked, but a small, barred window allowed me to look out and see another flight of steps leading up to groundlevel. That little window, though caked with dirt, let in a bit of light.

A doorway joined the alcove and a small room beyond, but the stone flooring ended at the threshold. I took my flashlight in and played it around the room, while Lettie stood in the doorway emitting a continuous stream of objections to our being there.

This room was about fifteen by twenty feet and empty except for a brass headboard, a dozen or more old picture frames, and some more tires. A light bulb topped by a conical reflector hung from the ceiling in the center of the room. It worked; I snapped it on and clicked my flashlight off.

"Stay by the door, Lettie."

The plain dirt floor was packed hard everywhere but one

corner. There, away from the clutter lining the walls everywhere else, was an oval of tilled dirt, about two by three feet. Recently tilled. As I scanned the four walls again, it looked obvious to me that the clutter had been shifted to clear out this space. I really didn't want to stick my hands down into that dirt, but I had to.

"Do you see anything I could dig with, Lettie?"

"Dig with? There's a shovel out here. Don't people sometimes dig with shovels?"

I jammed the shovel down with my foot and removed a gallon or so of dirt, then felt around and tried another spot. After several test holes, I knew there wasn't anything like a body underneath. At a depth of about a foot and a half, I hit hard-packed soil. The tilled area wouldn't have been large enough for a casket, but a body, not in a casket but tucked into a fetal position, might have fit. I could have missed a small box or any number of small items hidden in the dirt, but I could find nothing. Without actually removing the dirt and sifting through it, I'd done the best I could for now.

"Listen, Lettie." I used my foot to push the shovel into the dirt one more time. *"Clink-shush?"*

Lettie was fed up with me. "Please, Dotsy. Let's go!"

"One more minute. Put this shovel back where you found it."

There was another room. An opening in the center of the wall to the right of the door from the alcove had apparently had a door in it at one time because there were halves of hinges on one side. I walked through and found that the other room was about the same size as the first. I used my flashlight again and spotted a long fluorescent bulb suspended from an overhead beam by a couple of chains. It proved to be a low-wattage bulb, emitting little more light than my flashlight. Odds and ends, about three feet deep, obscured one wall, and against another, rows of wooden slats formed three wide shelves. I swept my beam along the shelves. Why were they all empty when there was so much junk on the other side of the room? Rooms collect junk either all over or in a few spots, not jammed up along one wall while three shelves on the other side remain perfectly empty.

Lettie sighed impatiently and added a little squeak.

My light found a dark, furry lump in the doorway and I knelt to touch it. It felt slightly damp and looked like spongy peat moss, but it smelled like mildew. I'd seen a bit of the same sort of material scattered on the slatted shelves. Beside a pile of spilled nails, I spotted a brown paper bag and slipped the strange mass into it.

"Let's go, Dotsy. I hear someone coming."

"One more minute." I felt sure Lettie did not actually hear someone coming; she just wanted to leave.

Back in the first room, I walked along the wall to the right of the tilled oval and directed my beam along the perimeter of the empty picture frame at the front of the stack. A heavy layer of dust covered all but one small spot about as wide as a hand. This frame had been moved recently.

LETTIE LEFT FOR INVERNESS with a sputter and a lurch but, for the first time ever, she got away from the castle without actually killing her motor. I tramped across the sheep pasture with my trowel and the insulated bag that held my emergency supply of little orange juice cartons.

By trekking diagonally across the sheep pasture and a field of barley, I cut a quarter mile off the distance between the castle and the dig site. Lettie had offered to give me a lift but for some strange reason, I had told her I preferred to walk.

I thought about the kids at the dig, searching my mind for anything like tension or conflict that I might have noticed so far. I hadn't even talked to most of them individually yet. There was one girl, Joyce Parsley, who I suspected had a crush on Froggy. Joyce appeared to be an outsider, a square peg, like Froggy. She tried too hard to fit in, to be cool, with predictable results. It made her look even dorkier.

As I approached the site, I counted three squad cars parked in the mud beside the tent. A few kids were outside, sitting on the ground in a conversational circle.

"Did you hear about Froggy?" one of them asked me.

"Yes," I said. "I'm staying at the castle, so I was among the first to know."

"No shit. Did you see him?"

I perceived a definite hunger for lurid details and wanted no part of it. I changed the subject. "What's going on now?"

"The police are interviewing us one by one. We're not supposed to talk to each other about…you know, until we've been interviewed," a small redheaded girl said. "We've already been interviewed, but they—" she swept her arm around, indicating a dozen or so kids who were working in isolation on various parts of the excavation "—haven't."

I pushed through the tent flap and got stopped by Graham Jones. Graham was third in command. John Sinclair, the director, spent most of his time doing PR, but worked with Tony Marsh to map out the overall plan and analyze the finds. At least once a day, John and Tony walked together around the site and took stock. Tony coordinated things, like a general contractor on a building site. Thanks to Tony, the backhoe showed up when needed, bag lunches were delivered by a local caterer at noon, and digging proceeded in a logical sequence.

But Graham, a wiry, no-nonsense Welshman, was the nuts-and-bolts man. If you found a suspected piece of pottery, no matter how small, you showed it to Graham, and he decided whether it should be bagged and tagged or tossed away. Graham double-checked the readings when a new worker was on the surveying equipment, and it was Graham who condemned the unfortunate to the dreaded mattock, a heavy-duty sod-busting tool, whose use was the rough equivalent of swinging an anvil.

"You've already been interviewed?" Graham asked the question in the tone of a funeral director.

"And given my formal statement. The whole works."

I saw three centers of activity inside the tent. At two folding tables sat two students, each being questioned by an officer. At a third table in the far corner sat Van Nguyen, Chief Inspector Coates, and a uniformed woman who was taking notes. I had the definite feeling I shouldn't be in here at all.

Graham pushed on the tent flap and looked out. "The lunch van just pulled up. Is Tony outside?"

"I didn't see him."

"Lovely. Leaves me to handle everything. I can't be gopher for these guys and take care of things outside, too." He peeked out again. "Do me a favor, Dotsy. Take care of lunch outside. You can send a couple of kids in here to pick up the soft drink cooler."

At least I had a job I was competent to do: feeding youngsters. I directed the caterers to lay the bag lunches on a tarp beside the finds shack and sent a pair of idlers into the tent for the cooler full of drinks. "We're dining al fresco today, folks," I said. "Sorry, no chairs, no napkins, no salt."

"We didn't get our tea this morning," groused one. Several others glared at him.

Before I came to the U.K., I thought that tea time was a ritual still followed only by little old ladies in hats. Wrong. The young, the old, the construction worker, the hip-hop star, all require tea twice daily to sustain life.

The kids, more subdued than I'd ever seen them, sat on the ground's few grassy patches, avoiding the worst of the mud. One student, Joyce Parsley, didn't come over for lunch at all. She wandered around the south end of the excavation alone, her canvas hat pulled down low, her hands jammed into her jacket pockets. I started to go to her, but thought better of it. It didn't seem like the thing to do right then.

As I crammed the lunch trash into a large garbage bag, Graham Jones came out and called a couple of students into the tent for their interviews. He thanked me for supervising lunch and asked, "You want to work on the old wall this afternoon?"

"The eleventh-century wall? That one?" I pointed to a trench in the southwest part of the dig. "You betcha." Telling me to dig out an eleventh-century wall is like throwing Brer Rabbit into the briar patch. Macbeth was king of Scotland from 1040 to A.D. 1057. This wall, if we had dated it accurately, had been built at or the near the time when my main man was king.

I grabbed a foam kneeling pad and walked to the wall, but before I began I looked around the whole site. It was beginning to look like a Lego city with its squared-off trenches and pits hollowed out to various depths. They had started out, three years ago, to explore the remains of a Neolithic campsite dating back some six thousand years, but in the process they found a stretch of drystone wall which, based on its depth, would have been built in the eleventh century. Then, while digging to see where that wall went, they ran into the foundation of a fifteenth-century church. Now, we were trying to expose as much as we could of all three without destroying the other two. Not an easy task.

I sat on the pad and tried to imagine the Stone Age hunter-gatherers knapping flint, perhaps telling stories and laughing, around the campfire a few feet away from which we had now pitched our meeting tent. I could see an eleventh-century Scots woman, in homespun wool and soft-soled leather shoes, stirring a cauldron over an open fire. Which side of this wall was the inside and which was the outside? Inside and outside of what? A fort? A homestead? Which side of this wall would a cooking fire have been on?

I turned to the church foundation, such as it was, behind me. It would have been Catholic, of course, and built in a time of opulent French-style manor homes, castles and constant warfare. A century in which four Scottish kings were crowned, but not one died peacefully in his bed. For the first time, I saw this place in layers of time, with overlapping ghosts.

Joyce Parsley trudged by. She had been walking clockwise laps around the perimeter of the dig since before lunch. I spoke to her, but she merely glanced my way, not answering. I wondered when she had last seen Froggy.

When, in fact, had I last seen Froggy? I had stayed at the dig until nearly five. I had sat with him inside the tent at morning tea, but I couldn't recall seeing him after that. Had he been there at lunchtime? I couldn't remember. Too bad Lettie hadn't been with me; she could have told me exactly what he did, when he left, and whether he'd eaten all his lunch.

Where, between here and the MacBane house, or between here and the castle, could Froggy have been attacked? Where could it have happened without someone noticing? There were no large trees this side of the woods. The woodland was a possibility, I thought, because a densely wooded area stretched the length of the sheep pasture south of the castle. Between the dig and the woods, there was a corner of a barley field and some moorland.

Froggy might well have gone to the woods in the afternoon. The ferns and mushrooms on the forest floor would have been like spore heaven to him. He could have been attacked in there without anyone seeing, but how would his body have gotten from there to the other side of the castle? The thought of someone dragging his body, or a tarp with his body in it, across the entire pasture was ludicrous.

Perhaps he had gone to the castle for some reason and been attacked there. Near the car park sat a barn and several other outbuildings with farm equipment, an old truck, and some baled hay lying around. Almost always, you could see at least one person, usually more, working around that area. Maybe Froggy happened upon something he wasn't supposed to see.

Could he have been killed at the MacBane house or at the dig? Or at the kids' camp along the road between the house and the dig? Did it happen before or after dark? Was he killed behind the castle, where Christine found him, or was he brought there from somewhere else? If the latter, was he dragged or carried? Could he have been brought around in a car, wrapped in the blue tarp? Why?

I couldn't imagine any of those scenarios succeeding in broad daylight, and I couldn't imagine it after dark either because, by evening, the castle was full of guests having cocktails in the new tower and eating in the dining room behind the large windows on that corner.

But one thing above all didn't make sense: The simple fact was that in this part of Scotland, crime was so rare, many folks didn't even lock their houses or cars. I'd heard someone mention a homicide that happened more than a decade ago and miles north of here, on the shores of Loch Ness. It was still news.

The whole thing made no sense.

"You're not getting much done."

I jumped. Van Nguyen had sneaked up behind me. "Oh, Van, I'm so sorry about…Froggy. This must be awful for you."

"It's a nightmare. Look, Dotsy," he said, looking, not at, but beyond me, "can I talk to you? Sometime, I mean. Not now."

"Sure. But now's okay."

"I have to go." He walked on past me, jumped the fence, and left the site.

I turned back to the wall and considered where I should start. The soil appeared uniform in color and texture all around and felt dry now that the dew was gone. We hadn't yet reached the base. I knelt and ran the tip of my trowel along one of the rocks and pulled back a bit of soil. Continuing along that side for a few feet, I decided to go a bit deeper before moving my kneeling pad. My knees and back won't allow me to maintain that position long, so I turned and sat on the pad, curling my legs to one side and resting my left forearm in the coarse dirt. I scraped my trowel along the stone and felt the tiniest resistance.

Up popped a gold coin.

It took a few seconds to register. How many gold coins had

been found here already? None. Still as bright and shiny as the day it was lost, it was the diameter of a nickel but much thinner, and irregular around the edge. Before my hand began to shake, I held the coin on the tip of my forefinger long enough to see a bearded face on one side and to read the word "REX."

I had the presence of mind to mark the spot on the ground with my trowel before I dashed to the tent to find Graham. I folded the coin between the palms of my hands and forced myself to slow down and watch my step. This was no time to fall and drop the coin into a mud puddle.

Graham was still at his post inside the tent flap. I opened my hands wide enough for him to see the glint of gold and to be drawn out into the light like a kid smelling brownies in the oven. He took it from me.

Normally, Graham had a colorful, often profane, response to a good find but this time all he could come up with was, "My, oh my!" He turned it over and over. A tear trickled down beside his nose. He called out, "Tony!"

Tony Marsh, who had apparently returned within the last half hour, rounded the corner of the tent and took the coin from Graham's hand. "Show us where you found it."

I felt proud that I was able to point to the exact spot beside a loaf-shaped rock in the wall. "It was here, almost touching this stone."

"Don't do anything else here today. We'll rope this area off for now," Tony said.

"Do you think there are any more down there?"

"Don't know."

Tony took the coin away and Graham cordoned off an area about eight feet square around the spot. I spent the next hour telling and retelling my story until I had practically memorized the "Saga of the Coin near the Loaf-shaped Rock." Every student, it seemed, wanted to hear it for himself.

Within minutes, Tony Marsh himself was flat on his

stomach, working with trowel and brush in the spot which was to become hallowed ground. I was not good enough to dig there anymore.

SIX

"MR. MACBANE?"

"Robbie MacBane. And you be?"

"Dotsy Lamb. From the dig down the road." I had expected an elderly farmer, I suppose, and was taken aback by the impish red-haired guy eating a marmalade sandwich. He was probably in his early or mid-thirties. He met me at the door wearing a black tuxedo jacket with white shirt, bow tie, cut-off jeans, and black socks. No shoes.

"Oh, aye! You knew Froggy then, did ye?" Robbie hid his sandwich behind his back, as if he thought one shouldn't be caught engaging in such earthly delights as a PBJ so soon after the murder of one's tenant. He swallowed hard and motioned me in with a sweep of his empty hand.

"Yes, I knew him. This is so hard. I'm sure it is for you, too." I glanced around the hall and spied a stairway behind Robbie. "I'm looking for Van. Is he here?"

"Aye." Robbie pointed with his sandwich toward an out-building as Van rounded the corner of it and loped toward us. I admired the tall, clean-looking kid with shiny, waist-length hair that he kept pulled back in a rubber band. As he approached the house, I asked Robbie if the police had been there yet.

"They came, they went up to the lads' room, they took about a thousand pictures, they left. They'll be back later, they said."

"Did they take anything away?"

"Not that I noticed."

Van stepped onto the front stoop. "I didn't mean for you to

come here, Dotsy. We could talk anytime. Now, you've gone out of your way." Van was apologetic as he indicated the way to his room, up the stairs. "Or would you rather stay outside? Take a walk?"

"Your room will be fine. I'd like to sit in a real chair."

"I'm not sure you'll be able to find one under all the junk. I'm afraid the room is kind of messy." He paused at the top of the stairs and waited for me.

"I have four sons," I said. "I'm immune."

"Four sons?" Van's eyes widened. "Any girls?"

"One," I said, entering the room he and Froggy had shared. It rivaled my son Brian's room at its worst. Well, maybe not that bad; Brian lost a gerbil once and found it a month later, still fat and happy after living off the food scraps under Brian's bed.

"The police have been here. They just left. This is all their mess, really. The room was neat as a pin before they came," Van said with a straight face. "And Froggy's parents will be here soon. They're driving up."

"Oh, no. They're not staying here, are they?"

"God, I hope not. I assume they'll get a room in town." The town Van referred to was no more than a village and five miles north of here, but it had a small hotel or two.

Van's room didn't look dirty, but it was hopelessly cluttered. Electronic gizmos, speakers, computers, a fax machine, monitors, DVD players, tennis rackets, gym shoes, and miles of cables and cords. I could easily tell which side of the room had been Froggy's and which side was Van's because one side was stacked nearly to the ceiling with computer and video equipment and on the other, a couple of microscopes, little plastic boxes of glass slides, rolls of waxed paper and a stack of woven wooden baskets. On the desk beside one microscope stood two drinking glasses, each one inverted protectively over a mushroom cap. I felt my nose begin to sting from the sadness welling up.

Van lifted an armload of clothes from a ladderback chair so I could sit. "I feel sort of stupid," he said. "We don't know each other very well, but I don't know any of the kids at the dig very well, either."

"Oh, of course." It dawned on me. "You're from Cambridge aren't you? And the others are from Worcester University."

"I'm from Seattle, by way of Cambridge."

"How did you end up here, Van?"

"Dr. Sinclair's wife. She knows some people at Cambridge who recommended me when she told them her husband was looking for a media man. I've had to take time off from my research at Cambridge, but Dr. Sinclair made me an offer I couldn't refuse."

"He's paying you well, huh?" I said. "Was Froggy also being paid, or was this part of his course work at school?"

"Paid. The other kids aren't, of course. They're getting course credit for the work."

Van was interrupted by the ringing of his phone and the flickering of a desk lamp which he'd apparently rigged up somehow to the phone. Clever. I noticed a heavy-duty padded headset hooked around the stem of the desk lamp.

When the caller rang off, Van walked to the room's only window, a large one with a view of the road and of the Castle Dunlaggan nestled in the distance against blue hills. He pressed his arms and his forehead against the glass. "They think I did it, Dotsy."

He turned to me with fear in his eyes. "The police think I killed Froggy!"

"But why?"

"Well, for one thing, I was apparently the last person who saw him."

"That means nothing."

"And somebody told them they heard him and me arguing. Probably true, because he plays his Mozart so loud I can't hear my own music…at least I wear headphones." Van shook his head. "Never mind. Yes, we argued sometimes."

"Who told the police about the arguing?"

"I don't know, but Froggy and I liked each other okay, y'know? But, yeah, we argued sometimes, like guys do."

"I know." How well I know!

"And Froggy was wearing my shirt."

I felt my limbs go cold. "The red and white shirt with the hibiscus? That's your shirt?"

"Yeah. They asked me if we wore each other's clothes often, and I said, 'No, we never did.'"

"That's what I couldn't put my finger on this morning! I knew something was wrong, but I couldn't figure out what. The shirt was way too big for him."

"Froggy and I couldn't wear each other's clothes. I'm six-two and he is—was—about five-seven. Plus, I'm not into argyle vests and pleated pants."

As I LEFT BY the front walkway, Robbie MacBane, now wearing formal shoes and a well-pressed kilt with his tuxedo jacket, offered me a ride. He tossed a violin case into the backseat of an old Fiat. "I'm on me way to town. Me and my mates are playin' for a big dance."

In all likelihood, Robbie had been dressing in his formal attire when he discovered his kilt was wrinkled, so he ironed it while wearing his jacket, shirt, tie, and undershorts (unless it's true what they say about what Scotsmen wear under their kilts). When I had come knocking on his door, he'd slipped on his cut-offs before answering it.

There's a logical explanation for everything.

I SHOULD HAVE TAKEN Robbie MacBane up on his offer of a lift. By the time I got to the middle of the sheep pasture, my heart was racing; I had broken out in a cold sweat, and I began seeing spots before my eyes. Low blood sugar. I didn't even need to test it. Fortunately, there was a big boulder to sit on while I unzipped my insulated bag, pulled out a little carton of orange juice and jabbed a straw through its foil hole.

I had to rest a few minutes while the juice worked its magic. From the rock on which I sat, I had a perfect view of the castle. I made a mental note to bring my camera out here, preferably early, when the morning sun would light the new tower and south wing.

Two police cars sat in the parking lot, along with a truck that seemed to be always there, the Lipscombs' BMW, and John Sinclair's black Jaguar convertible. Fallon Sinclair dashed out the big front entrance. She scrambled through her purse as she ran to the Jaguar, lowered its top, and accelerated down the road, her light brown hair whipping around her face.

Soon after Lettie and I had arrived, William Sinclair had told us about the castle's history. I sat on the boulder now, recalling all I could. Castle Dunlaggan was built in the fifteenth century and rebuilt in the sixteenth, seventeenth, eighteenth, nineteenth, and twentieth. It had, over the centuries, been a fortress, a prison, a family seat, and a bed-and-breakfast. It was one of the few castles in all of Scotland with absolutely no claim to ever having given refuge to either Bonnie Prince Charlie or Mary, Queen of Scots. It had borne witness to the Jacobite Rebellions and the Highland clearances, not to mention countless wars and petty squabbles.

The front of the castle, which faced south, was mostly gray Aberdeen granite, except for the new tower (brick) and the square tower (sandstone). The west wing, where all the guest rooms were, was white stucco and granite, and the round tower, granite again. The north wing, having been cannibalized to repair other parts, was granite rubble and ruins. The east wing, completely rebuilt in the mid-twentieth century, had expansive modern windows set in mellow sandstone. It was a Rube

Goldberg castle in every style from the medieval to Charles Rennie Mackintosh.

Maisie Sinclair backed out the east door of the kitchen with a large metal bowl, the contents of which she tossed onto the compost pile behind the parking area. She bent over and picked something from her herb garden which was beside the compost pile, then straightened up and waved, not at me, but at someone to the east.

I saw that she had waved to Boots, the handyman, who was standing on the near side of the woodland where, I had heard, the Sinclairs had a shooting hut on a small lake. They owned all the land from about a half mile west of the castle to the public road on the east. I made another mental note to explore that woodland and the one across the field behind me when I got a free day.

The sheep in the pasture around me had all turned their backsides toward me. Sheep, being not the smartest of mammals, apparently think if they can't see you, you've gone away. Boots and Maisie, I was sure, could both see me if they looked my way, because, with my yellow shirt and sun shade and the sheep arrayed, butts inward, around me, I imagined we looked, from a distance, like a big daisy.

A long black car rolled down the road and around the circular drive in front of the castle. The right front door opened and a bald man with a long scarf got out. He strutted around the car and opened the opposite door for a woman wearing a large red hat which had to be readjusted immediately and held down with a white-gloved hand. *Uh-oh, new guests,* I thought. *That's all Maisie needs today.*

William Sinclair opened the big front doors and greeted the new arrivals as magnanimously as he had done for us five days ago. He extended a hand to the woman, who placed her own gloved one in it and…curtsied! Not simply a quick little bob, either. A full knee-to-the-pavement-meet-the-queen curtsy! The bald, bescarfed man bowed deeply and said something to William, who gestured toward the trunk of their car.

The new man lifted seven large suitcases out of the trunk. Seven. I would have loved to hear what William was saying as he picked up the first two and headed for the door. The red-hatted woman, the wife, I assumed, posed on the front steps while the man took her picture. Then she took one of him with his hand on the brass doorknob.

Lettie pulled into the parking lot in her tiny little rented Nissan Micra, a car so small they don't even market it in the U.S. I did worry about her driving that car around Inverness and the winding road between here and there. She had already had two accidents that she admitted to, and I feared there would be more. Lettie saw me as soon as she popped out, and she yelled, "Come on, I've got stuff to show you!"

SEVEN

LETTIE FAILED TO SEE the significance of the gold coin I'd found. She listened to my story politely, stifling a closed-mouth yawn that made her eyes water.

"That's nice, Dotsy. Do you think they'll let you keep it? I have a gold coin my grandfather gave me. I had it made into a pendant and sometimes I wear it with——"

"You're missing the point, Lettie! This has nothing to do with jewelry or the price of gold. This has to do with the fact that it was there, beside an eleventh-century wall. In undisturbed soil." How could I possibly make her understand? "Look. There were no coins, gold or otherwise, minted in Scotland before the reign of David the first, in the twelfth century."

"What did they use for money?"

"Nothing! They used the barter system. You know, one chicken for a sack of wool. They traded stuff."

"Oh." Lettie looked at me as if to say, "You don't have to bite my head off."

"Sorry, Lettie, I'm just trying to explain why this find is so important. In the eleventh century, when that coin was left there, this part of Scotland was practically no-man's-land. There were Vikings to the north, Picts and Scots were scattered around, but Scotland was hardly a country yet. Not like we think of a country, anyway. Few of them could read or write, so we know very little about them. That's why this dig is important." I paused for breath. "Where was that coin from, and why was it there?"

"I see," she said, but I don't think she did.

JOHN SINCLAIR HAD APPARENTLY recovered from whatever had been ailing him. I found him at the sideboard in the anteroom where we always had cocktails before dinner. He gave me a cheerful nod and lowered his tumbler of straight Scotch as he waved me over. "My girl, my girl! What can I say?" He hugged me, transferring his glass to his other hand before doing so, thank goodness, because a large schlopp of whisky flew out and onto the floor.

"Have you seen it yet?" I asked.

"Of course. Tony? Everyone? May I have your attention, please?" John put his glass down and raised both hands. "I have an announcement. Whether it's beginner's luck, or talent, or serendipity, or whatever, Dotsy Lamb has discovered a gold coin at our dig site that may turn everything we thought we knew about the Scottish Highlands in the eleventh century upside down."

I heard some applause and blushed modestly. John was exaggerating a tad, but archaeologists and paleontologists are, as a breed, addicted to hyperbole.

"I haven't had a chance to study it sufficiently, and I don't claim to be an expert numismatist," he continued, "but I've determined that the coin is Byzantine and that it was minted somewhere around A.D. 1050."

"Good," said Brian Lipscomb. "With all that gold, you can buy the next round, Dotsy."

The Sinclairs used an honor system for drinks. Spirits, mixers and a couple of wines were put out in a silver tray on the old oak sideboard each evening so we could serve ourselves. We were supposed to write our names and our consumption on the tablet of lined paper they left beside the tray. Maisie always put a stack of paper cocktail napkins on each end of the sideboard and in several other spots around the room, but some people, most notably John Sinclair, dripped all over the wood, anyway.

I fixed myself a gin and tonic.

It was an oddly uncomfortable time, and I wished we could get on with our dinner. Tony Marsh, standing by the wall, had been excluded from the limelight. It seemed inappropriate for any of us to be laughing and applauding with poor Froggy in the morgue, barely cold, and then there were the new people, introduced to us by William as Alf and Eleanor Downes of Houston, Texas. They knew nothing about any of this.

The Downeses were way overdressed; he, in a tuxedo, and she, in a long black sequined job that looked as if it weighed a ton. Eleanor's champagne-beige hair was anchored on top with a large jeweled comb that, if it had been any bigger, could have qualified as a tiara.

After William's introduction, Alf Downes held up his glass and thanked "Lord William" for his kindness and hospitality.

Lord William? It seemed to me that we all developed a sudden interest in our feet. Anything to avoid making eye contact lest someone crack a smile and break the rest of us out in laughter. William pretended not to hear that, but then Eleanor came out with, "How long has Castle Dunlaggan been in your family, Your Lordship?"

"Eleanor, you flatter me, but I cannae lay claim to 'yer laird-ship.' I'm just plain William."

"Oh, but there you're wrong," said Alf Downes. "In Scotland, any male landowner can lay claim to the title of Lord, or, as you say, 'Laird.'"

"We dinnae pay heed to such anymore," William said.

"Are the police still here?" Amelia threw the question out to the group in general.

John answered, "They'll probably be here until after dark, and they'll be back tomorrow morning. They'll be here several days."

"Have Froggy's parents arrived yet?" I asked.

"They have," John said. "I met them in town this afternoon and brought them out to the MacBane house. They aren't emotionally ready to come to the castle yet."

"Certainly. I would imagine so."

I turned to Amelia Lipscomb. "What about you, Amelia? You said, this morning, that you know his mother."

Amelia pursed her lips and wiped the edge of her glass with her finger. "Yes, slightly."

Slightly? I had gotten the impression they were good friends.

Lettie said, "Do the police have any leads yet? Who do they think did it?"

John, Tony, and William all seemed to wait for someone else to answer. Lettie has a gift for throwing stuff like that out when a room is dead quiet and the question can't be ignored.

John said, "They can't be convinced, as I am, that it was someone local. A simple robbery gone wrong."

Tony added, "They're concentrating on the students at the dig. They're looking for a motive one or the other of them may have had."

"But that's ridiculous," I said. "They all liked Froggy."

"You've only known him four days, Dotsy," said William. "I believe the police are concentrating on that roommate of his."

I got a rush of irritation that made the back of my neck itch, but I held my tongue.

"Why?" someone asked.

"Froggy was wearing his roommate's shirt when he was found," said Tony. "Apparently he was stabbed several times in the chest with a knife, but there are no holes in the shirt."

As we pondered that in silence, William changed the subject. "Alf, is this the first trip to the U.K. for you and Eleanor?"

"No, Your…sir. This is the—what did we say, dear?—eighth time we've visited your lovely sceptered isle."

"I assume you like it here?"

"We're royal watchers," Eleanor said.

"You're what?" This, or something similar, came from all of us. I entertained a couple of fleeting images of what a royal watcher might be. A person who is a member of royalty, but watches? Watches what? Maybe it's a poker hand that beats a straight watcher.

"Royal watchers," Alf repeated. "We like to watch the royals, especially British royals. We have a Web site, www-dot-royal-blood-dot-com. It's our hobby."

Silence.

At length, Fallon Sinclair spoke up, "Balmoral Castle is not too far from here."

"Oh, indeed, and the royals are in residence there now. Eleanor and I have taken rooms in Braemar, near the castle, for four nights next week."

Taken rooms? Taken rooms? Nobody has said "taken rooms" for the last fifty years!

Christine, the kitchen helper, stuck her head out the dining-room door and shouted, "Let's eat and get it over with."

Apparently she had recovered from her traumatic morning. This was normal Christine.

LETTIE AND I SAT with John and Fallon Sinclair at dinner. Christine filled our water glasses while Maisie brought out our starters: a lovely vegetable pâté garnished with a sprig of lemon thyme, probably the herb I had seen her picking an hour ago.

Fallon held up her water glass. "Maisie, my glass isn't clean."

"I'll get you another one." Maisie left with Fallon's glass.

"Oh, John! And William, too! Guess what?" Lettie bounced in her chair and turned to find William. He sat with Tony at a table next to ours. "I was looking for information on my father's great, great—two greats, I think, but it might be three—grandmother, Flora Hynd, and her husband, Robert Hynd. So today I discovered that her maiden name was Sinclair. She was born Mary Flora Sinclair and she was born in Aviemore in 1821. Her parents were Hamish and Eliza Sinclair."

Lettie put the back of her hand up beside her mouth. This

was a unique little Lettie-gesture. It was as if she was telling a secret, but she always did it while talking in a normal voice.

"So, boys," she said, "I might be related to you!"

"You're definitely related to us," said William. "Hamish Sinclair of Aviemore was our three-or-four-greats grandfather."

Lettie's eyes widened and she clapped her hands. "How amazing! I'm your American cousin! Wait. Wasn't that the name of a play?"

Everyone in the dining room heard her exclamation, but I doubted any but the Americans among us would know that was the name of the play during which Lincoln was shot.

"Oh, but maybe you don't want to be related to me," Lettie continued. "If so, I won't tell."

John said, "I'm delighted to be a cousin of yours, Lettie, but I don't know if you should be so gleeful. William, do you think it's possible she's inherited the family curse?"

"What family curse?" Lettie went rigid, bracing herself with both hands on the table. "What family curse?"

John shook his head. "I don't know if we should tell you or not. You're so happy now…"

I glanced toward William. He was biting his lip to keep from laughing.

Maisie and Christine brought out the entrées. My salmon looked wonderful, but Lettie turned sad when she saw her rabbit. Instead of the rabbit stew she was probably expecting, this was a whole hind quarter and rather rabbit-like in appearance.

"Do you suppose this is wild rabbit?" Lettie asked.

"Probably," John said, and called across to the next table, "William, is this wild rabbit or did you buy them?"

"They're our local rabbits. Trapped or shot personally by either me or Boots," William answered. Boots, their ancient handyman cum hunter/forager, brought great volumes of plants and animals from the fields and forests nearby and stocked the castle larder with everything from fiddlehead ferns in the spring to rowan berries and deer in the fall.

I imagined Lettie was wondering if this was the bunny that had dashed across the road in front of our car the day we arrived. She sighed and shook her head, then dug in.

"You went to Oxford, didn't you, John?" I asked.

"Is there any other place? Balliol, seventy-four," John said in a loud voice. Balliol, I recalled, was one of the oldest colleges at Oxford University. He sat back and swallowed a gulp of his whisky.

Fallon rolled her eyes, "There is another place; they call it Cambridge. I went there, but in John's book that makes me an illiterate."

"What about William?" I asked. "Did he go to Oxford, too?"

John snorted. "William? At Oxford? No, no, no." He paused. "No, William got the castle, and I got the education."

I know William heard him, and it made me feel uncomfortable.

Christine interrupted us with a loud announcement. "I'm gettin' the desserts ready now and I want to know if anybody wants theirs with no cream. It's real cream, and it's full of calories, so tell me if you don't want any. I don't want to ruin a nice raspberry tart with cream if you don't want it, bein's I've got barely enough tarts to go round!"

This was an annoying habit of Christine's that Maisie apparently hadn't been able to program out of her. Rather than softly inform diners about menu items, she would stand at the kitchen door and yell like a fifth grade teacher on a field trip bus. Maisie invariably cringed, and the rest of us lowered our heads in what might be either embarrassment or amusement.

I ESCORTED THE DOWNESES to the library after dinner, explaining along the way that this is where we always had coffee in the evenings. Our path took us through the Great Hall, the ancient and gloomy square tower, and down the somber ground floor hall of the west wing, straight out of *Hound of the Bas-kervilles*. Alf and Eleanor Downes, obviously enveloped in a mutual fantasy of another century, had to be prodded along.

It was the first time I'd seen Maisie in the library after dinner. By the time she finished washing up in the kitchen, the rest of us had usually toddled off to bed. She set the tray with coffee-pot, cream, sugar, and cups on a sideboard, and then allowed herself to be persuaded to stay and relax a few minutes. She sat lightly on the arm of a chintz-covered chair. "Well, inn't this nice," she said, "sittin' here in me own house, just like I belonged here or somethin'."

We all laughed.

"You ought to do more of this and less runnin' around. I always tell her, 'Maisie, the house can wait. Relax a wee spell.'" William patted his wife on the shoulder. She held her coffee cup and saucer awkwardly in front of her, as if she were unused to such fine surroundings, but she had lived here for more than thirty years.

"Just like a man, inn't it? 'The house can wait. The house can wait.' But while you be relaxin', the house be savin' up work for ye. It don't be doin' the work for ye."

We laughed again, but all the women present knew exactly what she meant, I'm sure. I couldn't imagine taking care of a house this large and routinely feeding a dozen or more people twice a day. Deep lines of care were etched into the faces of both Maisie and William.

Fallon sank into a chair beside the hearth and drew her light-weight sweater around her. There was no fire tonight and the library was chilly. Fallon was a thin, wispy woman who looked as if she would blow away in a stiff breeze. From her husband, pouring himself another whisky, her gaze veered around the room to Tony who was scanning book spines along one shelf, then up and down Tony's well-muscled backside.

Tony turned, caught her watching him, and grinned. "I

assume we've all given the police our formal where-were-you-yesterday-afternoon statements?'"

He said it in a rhetorical way, but Lettie took it as a literal question that he intended us to answer. "I was in Inverness all day," she said, "and they can verify that at the library. I had to sign in and out."

William looked from Lettie to John. "John and I were here," he said, "in the kitchen, from about—what, John?—from about noon until maybe one-thirty, I ken. I made us our dinner. Soon as John left, I picked up my tools and went oot t' mend the fence. The fence along the road to town. One section was doon."

John said, "I came over for lunch and Maisie was gone, so William made us both an omelet and toasted some scones." I noticed that William had referred to the midday meal in the Scottish way, as "dinner," and John had used the more English "lunch."

"So you didn't actually eat a bag lunch at the dig? That's not fair, John," I chided him. Our lunches at the dig were a running joke.

John blushed as he took a gulp of Scotch. "Ah, but I did go over right after lunch, and spent the rest of the afternoon there."

Tony said, "I stayed at the dig until I saw John coming back and then I left for town. I met with the bloke at the construction company who schedules our heavy equipment rentals."

"I was at the dig all day," I said.

"I went to Urquhart Castle," said Fallon. She turned her face to the dormant fireplace.

For the first time, I noticed a strange, small door in the wall beside the hearth. It was no more than five feet tall, so one would have to stoop to enter. Its dark wood was aged to almost black and there was no knob. Only a circular hole through which, I assumed, one could stick a finger and pull the door open. What could possibly be the purpose of a door there? There were no rooms beyond it. The fireplace chimney ran up an exterior wall of the west wing, and the window a few feet to the right of the little door looked out on the central courtyard.

Everyone, including the Downeses, looked at Maisie, the only one who hadn't yet revealed her whereabouts yesterday afternoon. "I went to Aviemore," she said. "To the farm market…and they were havin' a sale on table linens, so I shopped a while."

Alf Downes said, "We didn't land at Heathrow until mid-afternoon, did we, my dear? So, I guess that lets us out."

We all agreed that the Downeses were in the clear.

"But the Merlins, noo, the police are looking for them," William said.

"Who?"

"The ladies that were here, you know, stayed in the round tower, the ones who left late last night."

"That's right," I said. "I'd forgotten all about them. They were here." I didn't recognize the name because Lettie and I had always referred to them as the weird sisters. "What were they doing yesterday afternoon?"

Apparently no one knew.

"I gave the police their home address and the license number of their car," William said. "They'll find 'em."

EIGHT

AFTER BREAKFAST THE next morning, I found John Sinclair in the parking lot dragging a corduroy jacket from his lovely black Jaguar XK convertible and walked with him to the dig site. It promised to be a warm day, and John was wearing a fresh white shirt, the sleeves rolled up, with khaki trousers. He flung the jacket over his shoulder and carried it, hooked over one finger.

"You said an expert was going to look at the coin I found," I said.

"Yes. He'll drive up in the next few days."

"He's driving here to see it?"

"From Edinburgh. Indeed, he sounded quite ebullient." John Sinclair, I had noticed, never used an ordinary word when a pretentious one would do as well.

We took the direct route to the dig, tramping diagonally across the sheep pasture to the southeastern corner of an adjacent barley field. When I walked by myself, I usually took the easier, but longer, route by the road. A paved road between the castle and the nearest two-lane road intersected with a dirt road that led past the students' camp and the dig. All the land on the castle side of the dirt road belonged to the castle, but I was unsure who owned the land on the other side. Altogether, the Sinclairs' holdings numbered in the hundreds of acres. The day Lettie and I arrived, William had pointed to a distant wooded area in the northeast and told us they had a shooting hut near a small loch in those woods. A seemingly vast expanse of rocky slopes dotted with rosy heather stretched northward. All of this was castle grounds.

I said, "What about William? Was he excited about our finding the coin?"

"William doesn't understand history, cultures, or anything, in fact, that's beyond the Highlands or before the Sinclairs got the castle. He couldn't tell you the difference between a Pict and a Viking.

"William has never been a scholar. He fishes, hunts, and farms. I doubt if he's read a book in thirty years." John trudged a few steps in silence, then squinted back toward the castle. "When our father died, I didn't think his will was fair. I admit I was resentful for a time. William got the castle, the land, and about thirty thousand pounds. I got thirty thousand pounds and nothing else. But I was able to finish my schooling on that money, and William used his money to keep the farm going. Since then he's had to 'rob Peter to pay Paul,' as they say. There's no profit in farming on this scale nowadays. At least, not the way William does it."

I spied Boots, the handyman, in the distance. Toting a floppy bag that hung like burlap, he cut across the corner of a field south of us and walked toward the woodland. A shaggy black-and-white dog, a Border collie, followed close on his heels. "How long has Boots been with your family?" I asked. I couldn't recall having heard Boots's last name; I thought he had been introduced to us as simply "Boots."

"Since I was a boy. Longer than I can remember."

"Does he live at the castle?"

"He has a wee…a small cottage at the MacBane farm."

We stopped at the fence between the sheep pasture and the barley field. John raised the metal loop off the wooden post, pulled the gate open, and bowed gallantly as I passed through. He closed the gate behind us.

"You have a lunch bag with you," John said. "Don't you like the lunches we have delivered?"

"I don't like the lunches we get on-site, but that's not the reason for this." I held up my zippered nylon bag. "I have cartons of orange juice in here. I'm diabetic and I like to have it handy in case I get a dizzy spell."

"Do you take insulin?" John tripped over a stone, but regained his balance in time.

"Yes, and I keep my blood sugar monitor in my waist pack, so I can do a test any time I'm curious."

"Doesn't the orange juice get warm in that little bag?"

"I don't mind drinking it warm. It's only for the quick sugar boost if I need it." I looked back toward the woods. Boots and the dog had vanished into its depths. I made a mental note to take a walk through those woods. Maybe Lettie would like to go with me. *Before we do that,* I thought, *I must ask William to tell me about any special dangers this woodland holds.* In my experience, every wood had at least one fearsome specter awaiting the unwary, be it poison ivy or snakes.

"Dotsy, stop by my room this afternoon when we get back. We can talk about the coin and I'll even show you where it's being kept."

"Oh, wow!" I smiled at him.

"That will make three people: you, me, and Tony, who know where it is. Have you thought about a possible connection between the coin and your friend Macbeth?"

"I have, but I don't want to get my hopes up." Changing the subject, I said, "Have you always wanted to be an archaeologist?"

"When I started at Balliol, in Oxford, I intended to become a classical historian. The Golden Age of Greece was my main area of interest. In fact, I was rather repelled by what I perceived as the coarseness of the ancient Scots, the fact that they were so wild the Romans didn't even bother to conquer them. But as time went on, I became more and more intrigued by the interplay of many cultures in Scotland, especially the Highlands."

"I see."

"I've written more than thirty papers for various journals.

My latest deals with symbolism on Pictish stones. I've also done some notable work on the spread of Ogham writing in the British Isles. But the paper on the stones, I think you'd be especially interested in. I'll let you have a copy of it."

"Thanks."

We had come to the edge of the dig. A cluster of students plodded down a rutted path that ran along the edge of the barley field, and poor, lonely, little Joyce Parsley walked several yards behind them, her head down. Behind her was the even lonelier, I thought, Hannah Dunbar. Hannah was older than the students, in her mid-thirties, I estimated, and I wasn't sure why she was here. I had the impression she was affiliated with Worcester University in some way, but was she faculty, staff, or what?

The students and a few adults, like Hannah Dunbar and Graham Jones, had pitched camp several hundred feet from the dig site and beside the dirt road. They had planted a conglomeration of little campers, bright nylon tents, olive drab tents, and pop-up trailers. There was a portable potty and a spigot, an offshoot from the waterline that ran to the camp. But no electricity, no gas, and no mother to make them clean up the place. I had walked over there with Froggy two days ago. Could it really have been only two days ago? The whole area around the spigot had become a mud hole any pig would be proud to call home.

John was still on his Oxford scholar kick as we entered the dig site. He said, "When I go back to Balliol now, for reunions and such, I'm usually asked to tea in the master's lodgings. He has a keen interest in the work I'm doing. I do love to go back there, but I have to laugh when I see my old classmates driving up in their prestige cars, working so devilishly hard to make an impression. Hah!"

And you bought a black Jaguar XK convertible because of its safety rating, I guess.

JOHN CALLED A general meeting inside the tent. There weren't nearly enough chairs to go around, so most of us sat on the ground while John took a seat on the table beside the coffee-maker. A couple of kids offered me a chair, but it was important to me that I not ask for any special consideration due to my age. I sat cross-legged on the ground, a position I can only maintain for about two minutes.

John cleared his throat and began. "I understand, that is, Tony has told me that there is some grumbling about over the fact that we have put the coin in a secure location."

Tony Marsh stood a foot or so behind me and I heard him mutter, "Sheesh! He's making me out to be the bad guy."

John went on. "Let me explain why it was necessary. We don't yet know exactly when or where the coin was minted, or have anything but guesses as to how it came to be here. As you well know, nothing like a gold coin has popped up in our years of excavation in this area. Viking hoards have been found in the north, around the Orkneys and Shetlands, and near the coast. But this is a single coin, apparently dropped, probably just lost, sometime near the start of the medieval period."

"But sir," a student piped up, "most of us didn't even get to see it before you took it away. Can't we at least see it?"

"I will try to arrange a time for all of you to see it, under supervision, of course. My worst nightmare would be for this find to be swiped and to end up melted down for the metal."

John's cell phone rang and he answered it as if he didn't care in the least that twenty-five people were watching and listening.

There was a general restless shuffling all around as students ducked under the tent skirt to get out, even though John had not dismissed them. The kid they called Ian stood up and said, loudly enough that John could probably hear, "The bloody nerve! The man just called us a bunch of thieves."

From the far side of the tent, Graham Jones shouted, "Assignments for today are posted on the board outside. Check it, and do what it says."

I waited until I could get close enough to the bulletin board to see what my assignment was. Bunching up in a solid mass, crowding around, is something an adult forgets about after they've lived in the civilized world beyond school for a few years. It felt strange to be jammed up like this, just one of the kids, getting elbowed and pushed. I found my name on the field-walking list.

There was a star on that same list beside Iain Jandeson, which meant he was the designated captain of our seven-person group. So he spelled it Iain, not Ian, did he? I had seen the name spelled that way before, but I didn't know if it was a regional spelling quirk, or what.

John Sinclair pulled me aside as I hurried to catch up with Iain. "I have to leave for a while. The Quales, Froggy's parents, are meeting with the police and they've asked me to be there. They have some issues regarding our site security, apparently. It'll probably take a couple of hours, so I'll see you back at the castle later."

"Oh dear, it's bound to be difficult for you."

"I don't look forward to it at all," he said.

JOYCE PARSLEY WAS ON the field-walking list, also. I fell in beside her and followed Iain, who announced that we were headed for the moor. Joyce was a round-faced girl who looked far too young to be in college. She always wore an old anorak and a canvas camouflage hat pulled down low so she had to tilt her head back a little to make eye contact. She didn't seem to have any friends at the dig, but I had noticed that wherever Froggy Quale had been, Joyce had tended to be also.

"You're staying at the camp, aren't you, Joyce?" I asked. "What are the students saying about Froggy? Surely they have some thoughts on what happened."

Joyce's face reddened. "Actually, I haven't heard anyone say anything, not really." She side-stepped a clump of emerging barley and glanced quickly toward me. "We've all been talking about it, of course. But nobody has said anything, like, you know, like they think they know who did it. Everyone's totally baffled."

Ahead of the group, Iain Jandeson marched purposefully toward the heather-sprinkled moor. He wore, as always, an Aussie-style bush hat, khaki shirt and pants, like a junior Indiana Jones. Two other students, a boy and a girl, caught up with him. They pushed each other off balance in what appeared to me to be more sex-play than horseplay.

"Tell me about them," I said to Joyce.

"Who?"

"Those three in front. They seem to be together a lot."

"Yeah, well. The one with the hat is Iain Jandeson. He's okay. Serious, like. He's determined to become a famous archaeologist. Discover the holy grail or whatever."

"He's a little strange, is he?"

"No, not strange. Well, maybe a bit. Determined would be a better word, I'd say." Joyce paused a minute. "He believes he was abducted by aliens."

"What?"

"He says his memory is missing a whole day, and he's pretty sure he was taken to this round sort of metal room. He says he has flashbacks."

"You are joking, of course."

"Not joking. The bloke with the bushy red hair is Proctor Galigher, and the girl is Tracee Wagg. All three of them go to Worcester, same as me and most of the people here."

I studied the young man. Like Iain, Proctor was tall. His hair shrouded his head in a roughly Hershey's Kiss—shape. His unbuttoned black shirt and low-slung jeans exposed a well-muscled torso. The girl gave him a big shove that he pretended knocked him off his feet.

"Speaking of people who might have had a reason to kill Froggy, there's one right there," Joyce said.

I grabbed her sleeve and pulled her to a halt. "What do you mean?"

"Last term at school, Proctor submitted a research paper to an ecology professor who gave it to Froggy to read. Froggy was the prof's research assistant. Froggy knew the paper was pla-giarized, so he gave it back to the prof with a copy of the article it had been copied from. Proctor got probation for a year, but he nearly got kicked out."

"He shouldn't have blamed Froggy for that," I said, "but I'm not surprised if he did. People so often blame the messenger."

We had reached the field we were supposed to walk. Iain halted us with an upraised hand. It was a flat, rock-strewn area that adjoined the woodland I had seen Boots entering earlier. It was oddly shaped, occupying a wide area south of the barley field, the sheep meadow, and the woods.

Iain said, "To field walk properly, you should maintain a uniform distance between yourself and the person beside you. Walk from one end to the other, then move over and go back the other way. Don't pick up everything you find. If you think something is good, bring it to me, and I'll decide if we should bag it or toss it." Iain had perfect teeth and a broad, square jaw which always sported two days' growth of whiskers. I wondered how he kept them from turning into a full-blown beard.

I had to ask. "What sort of stuff are we looking for?"

"Can't tell you that until you find it," Iain answered, somewhat impertinently I thought. "Flint that's been worked would be great. Anything medieval or earlier. Tile or pottery, but not stuff that's obviously modern. Animal bones would be recent, and we're not interested. Exposed bones don't last long in this climate."

One of the two kids behind me asked, "What about human bones?"

Iain ignored the question and continued, "We're not likely to find much because this area hasn't been plowed, but you never can tell. You four—" he meant Joyce, me, and the two behind me "—take the space from the barley to the fence. Tracee, Proctor, and I will take the area from here to the edge of the woods."

We four lined ourselves up at the edge of the virgin moorland, about five feet apart, and tramped slowly westward.

"Tell me about Tracee," I said to Joyce as we walked. "Do you know her?"

Joyce let out a loud snort that metamorphosed into a laugh. Her head jerked up, sending her canvas hat flying. "Tracee! I guess I oughtn't to tell you. Oh, why not? Everyone else knows. Tracee asked Froggy to the Spring Ball at school. Froggy was all flattered and everything, because he hardly ever went out. With a girl, I mean."

From the way she said it, I suspected that Joyce wished she could have gone out with Froggy, herself.

"Tracee asked him way back in February or something," Joyce continued, "and the ball was in May."

I picked up a small piece of pottery that had bits of green and orange glaze on its surface. Joyce took it from me, squinted, and flipped it over her head. "Post-medieval trash," she said.

"In the U.S., we'd put that in a display case," I said. "Sorry I interrupted. Finish your story."

"Okay, so Froggy rented a tuxedo, ordered flowers from the florist, got a haircut, the whole bit, y'know? Then the day before the ball, guess what? Tracee calls him and breaks the date. Froggy's friends asked around, and they found out that this really hot footballer, Harry Something, had asked her at the last minute.

"Froggy was embarrassed. I told him I'd go with him if he didn't want to waste the tux and flowers, but he was too upset to talk about it. So Froggy's mates, mostly blokes that worked with him in the university herbarium, made up all these signs, right? They didn't tell Froggy, because he'd have told them to back off."

"Signs that said what?"

Joyce giggled. She had to jettison her first couple of attempts to tell me because her snorts buried her words. "One sign said, 'You could have kissed a Froggy, but is this what you call a handsome prince?' Another one said, 'Get her to the ball, quick, before she picks up another date.' They went to Tracee's flat and stood on the other side of the street waving their signs, and this huge crowd was there when Tracee and Mr. Hottie came out. It was great!"

I laughed. "Were you there, too?"

"Yeah, I made a sign that said, like, 'Tracee's date for the ball.'" With her hands, Joyce pantomimed a big poster in front of her. "And it said, 'Froggy' and that was crossed out and under that it said, 'Harry,' and that was crossed out and under that it had a question mark, and that was crossed out."

A girlish squeal made me look up. Proctor, with Tracee Wagg flung over his shoulder, ran into the woods. With thumb and forefinger between his teeth, Iain whistled shrilly and waved them back. Tracee, I had decided, was here for more than the archaeological experience.

Boots and his dog emerged from the woods not far beyond them. The burlap bag now swung heavily from Boots's hand. Proctor and Tracee stepped aside to let them pass, as if the old man and his dog were lepers, the dog giving Proctor's jeans an indifferent sniff as it trotted by.

I SAW BOOTS and his dog again on my way back to the castle. The Border collie padded along beside him, head down, sneaking. Border collies don't so much trot as sneak—a sort of sniper-like creep—with their muzzles always in position to snip at a runaway hoof or heel.

Dark clouds building in the west and a freshening breeze

foretold of rain, perhaps by evening, but I wasn't returning to the castle early because of the weather. I estimated that John would have completed his visit with Froggy's parents by this time, and I wanted to see him before dinner. He had promised to show me the coin.

"C'mon, Lucy. Maisie might could gie ye some water," I heard Boots say. So the dog's name was Lucy. Lucy's fur could have done with a good combing. Burrs and thistles probably formed the nucleus of most of the fist-sized clumps in her thick black-and-white coat. As she slunk along, panting, she turned her head every few seconds and sniffed the burlap bag her master still toted.

I stayed back thirty yards, more or less, so I doubt that Boots knew I was behind them. They crossed the castle's parking area and trekked up to the side door of the kitchen. Boots rattled the screen door and called to Maisie while Lucy sat back, politely waiting. The door swung open and Boots announced, "Clear off some counter space. I got shan-ta-rellies, I got bluets, I got penny buns."

"Whoo-ee!" Maisie's voice came from inside.

A few seconds later, I heard a long, low growl followed by barks, bangs, *thunks,* and angry shouts. The screen door burst open and Lucy came flying out barely ahead of an old straw broom. "Away wi' ye! Dog's gone pure mental!" Maisie yelled as the dog landed on the asphalt and turned, fangs bared, crouched for attack. The dog slunk around, head down and growling, as Boots dashed out and swatted her with his billed cap.

"Wha's got inta ye?" Boots yelled. Lucy backed away from the door, still snarling, with Boots still slapping away at her. "Gone totally radge," he added, herding the herd dog across the parking lot and down to the road.

NINE

JOHN WAS WAITING for me in his suite of rooms on the third floor of the west wing. He volunteered the information that Fallon was out but would be back before dinner and, with a sweep of his whisky glass toward the bottles on a small cart, said, "What can I make for you?"

"Nothing," I said. "It's a bit early."

"Oh, but after a day's toil in the hot sun, you need something to slake your thirst, surely."

"It was hardly what I'd call hot today. In Virginia, we'd call this downright chilly."

John had changed shirts and added a paisley ascot to his open collar. I did hope I hadn't been invited up to "see his etchings," as they say, then I chided myself for being so vain as to even think that. He led me into a small, cozily furnished sitting room separated by a short hallway from their bedroom. Another door I saw in the hallway probably led to a bathroom, I guessed. John and Fallon didn't have to hike to the top of the tower to take a bath.

John seemed to be waiting for me to come up with something in the way of a drink order, so I said, "Plain soda, please."

He tonged ice cubes into a glass, poured in some soda, then freshened his own drink with a large splash of Scotch and a tiny blip of soda. He handed me my glass and in a faux pirate voice said, "Follow me and I will show you the hiding place of the sacred treasure trove."

He led me into the bedroom and to a closet on whose floor sat four aluminum Zero Halliburton suitcases. He pulled out the

largest of the four and plopped it on the bed. "The combina-
tion is four-four-four," he said. "Simply remember that there
are four letters in my first name."

Inside the suitcase lay a lacquered wood box with a vaulted
lid. It was about the size of a jewelry box and bound around by
four leather straps, each of which was fixed firmly to the box
wlth brass studs and buckled in the front.

"What a beautiful box," I said. "Is it very old?"

"Not very," John said. "An uncle gave me one and William
one for Christmas when I was about eight, I guess. It's one of
those things every young boy needs: a secret hiding place for
his treasures." The box tucked under his arm, John led me back
to the sitting room. He adjusted a lamp beside the sofa, placed
the box on the coffee table in front of us, and unbuckled each
of the four leather straps. He used a key on his key ring to pop
open the padlock on the lock plate.

"But wait," John said, raising one finger. "There's one more
thing you have to do." With his thumbs on the corners of the
lid, he showed me that the box still wouldn't open. "You have
to move a little pin just…over…damn."

John was apparently attempting to shift a hidden lever near
one of the back hinges, but I couldn't see clearly because he
had turned the box so as to get more light on the critical spot,
and that left me on the wrong side. He grabbed a letter opener
from the end table and worked through several more expletives
and a pinched finger, which he sucked on, then laughed.

"I've never been good with tools," he said. "I think I have a
screwdriver in the other room." He left me alone with the box.

So the coin was in a "secure location," huh? In a suitcase in
John's closet? That's secure? How hard would it be for a thief
to tuck the whole box under his jacket and walk out? The only
difficulty would be opening the suitcase, but it wouldn't be that
hard to make off with the whole suitcase. Good thing John over-
estimated the outside world's determination to possess that coin.

He called to me from the other room. "What were the years of Macbeth's reign?"

"1040 to 1057," I called back.

"Did you know he made a pilgrimage to Rome while he was king of Scotland?"

"In 1050," I said.

John reappeared in the doorway. He held up a screwdriver and smiled. "You've really done your homework."

"I told you, I got a bit obsessed when I found that so little had actually been written about the man."

"And most of what has been written is wrong," he said.

"That's the real problem," I said. "One source says he murdered King Duncan, and another says he killed him on the field of battle. One book says he was killed by Malcolm Canmore in Dunsinane, and another says he was killed in Lumphanan."

" 'Until Great Birnam wood to high Dunsinane hill shall come.' Isn't that what one of the three witches said?"

"Yes, but I don't think we should put much stock in Mr. Shakespeare's version."

"No." John jiggled the screwdriver in the little slot on the back of the box while he was talking. Then he jammed it in, and the screwdriver slipped sideways, gouging a wedge-shaped dent in the wood. "Damn!" He ran his thumb over the damaged surface.

I remembered that the eye-glass repair kit in my purse had a tiny screwdriver in it. I picked up my purse and rummaged through. "Here, try this," I said.

John went to work with the smaller screwdriver, moving the box closer to the light. "If anything happens to me, Dotsy, get this box immediately. You know where I keep it, now."

I was flabbergasted. What was he talking about? "What about Tony?"

"I want you to take charge of it. Take it to the National Museums of Scotland in Edinburgh. Take the whole box to them." John turned to me and, for an instant, I saw fear in his eyes.

"What do you mean, 'if anything happens'? What would happen?"

"I'm not saying anything will. I said 'if.'"

The screwdriver must have worked, because John casually opened the lid with a soft, "Aha." The box, lined with red felt, held three items. In addition to the coin, I saw an amethyst earring and an envelope that looked old. John lifted the little coin out almost reverently and put it in my hand.

The coin bore the face of a bearded man on both sides. Now, I could see that one was definitely Christ, with a halo and a cross behind His head. On the other side was the head of a man wearing a crown. Some primitively formed letters on both sides could be either Latin or Greek. I looked for the "REX" I thought I had read yesterday and I found it near the crown. There were some other letters I couldn't quite make out, but it was reasonable, I thought, to assume that those three letters meant that this was some king or other.

John slipped over to the cart, poured himself more Scotch, and returned to the sofa with his glass and a sheet of paper. "I got this off the Internet today. As I said earlier, I'm no coin expert, but I found a lot of pictures on the Web. This is the closest thing I could find. What do you think?"

The photos showed both sides of a coin that did look similar to ours, but the edges were shaped differently, and the relief varied enough from one to the other that I couldn't tell how close a match it was.

"This coin, the one in the pictures, was minted in Constantinople between 1042 and 1055," John said.

"That puts it at the right time for Macbeth's trip to Rome, but the wrong place. He didn't go to Constantinople," I said. "Still, coins are traded around, aren't they? This could have been picked up in France, or even in Rome."

"Exactly. If this is the correct date, we can definitely rule out any previous pilgrimages, such as the one Cnut, the English king, is thought to have made in about A.D. 1030. It's logically impossible for his entourage to have brought back a coin that wasn't produced until ten or twenty years later."

"And in those days," I went on, "people didn't go tootling off to sunny Italy for vacation. Only monarchs could afford it."

"And monks or bishops. Sometimes."

I placed the coin in his hand and reached for the earring. "Lovely," I said. The large purple stone was set in a silvery drop so that it would hang slightly below the ear. The setting was white gold or platinum, I assumed, since there was no tarnish. Little seed pearls encircled the amethyst. "Was this your mother's?"

John cleared his throat before he answered. "It was found by one of our field walkers the other day. It's not very old, of course, but, obviously, if we can find the owner, we'll give it back to him. Or her."

"A field walker? Which one?"

"Actually, I've forgotten the name. One of the girls."

"Did she find the other earring?"

"No, unfortunately not. I guess you could wear just the one earring. Queen Elizabeth the First did, and it became the fashion for a while."

"If you can't locate the owner, will the finder get to keep it?"

"No. If we don't find the owner, it'll belong to the castle."

Returning the solitary earring to the box, I picked up the envelope. "What's this?" Perhaps, I thought, I'm being too nosy.

"I've had that for probably twenty years," John said, taking the envelope from me. "The envelope is nothing. But the stamp may be worth fifty thousand pounds or more."

"Your little insurance policy against an impoverished old age?"

"Absolutely."

DINNER WAS EXCELLENT, as always. We started with a homemade mushroom soup to which, Maisie told us, she had added some of the chanterelles and penny bun mushrooms Boots had brought in that afternoon.

"I was in the parking lot when he brought them to you," I said, remembering that Boots had used those same words when he called out to Maisie. "What got into that dog?"

"Ye saw that, did ye? I have no idea. She didn't even go into the kitchen proper. She stopped at the bench in that little mud room, I guess ye'd call it, where we clean fish and such. She sniffed at the floor and went completely daft."

"Has she been there before?"

"She spends half the winter in there! She's got her favorite spot by the cooker. I don't know what got into her."

Lettie slid her soup toward me, grousing about how she didn't like mushrooms, but one cup was all I could handle if I intended to indulge in the lamb I knew was coming.

"Oh, but it's delicious," Eleanor Downes said.

Lettie and I had been tapped to do Downes duty since, as Amelia Lipscomb whispered to me before we were seated, "Brian and I had to sit with them last night. Your turn." The hardest part of Downes duty, to me, was listening to them without laughing. They lived in such a complete fantasy world, I could hardly believe they themselves were real. Eleanor slipped her reading glasses on and checked the back of the silverware. Discreetly. But it wasn't as easy for her to be subtle about checking under the china. She caught me watching her and pretended to brush something out from under her plate.

Eleanor and Alf both taught school back in Texas, they told us. She taught third grade and he, eighth grade social studies. Recollecting the behavior and stinky attitudes of my own flaw-lessly raised children when they were in eighth grade, I got a vivid mental image of what a man like Alf must have to deal with in the classroom. A room full of thirteen-year-olds is a job for The Terminator. Surely, they'd run all over Alf Downes.

"I'm rather surprised that Lady…Maisie doesn't leave the serving to the serving girl," Alf said.

He had almost said Lady Sinclair. He'd probably been calling her that, in his head, for months while anticipating this trip, I thought, and now he was hard-pressed to call her Maisie.

Maisie used a towel to serve the hot plates of roast lamb with mint and crabapple sauce. While the Downeses were distracted by the lamb's arrival, I took that opportunity to mutter under my breath to Lettie, "At least he didn't call Christine 'the serving wench'!"

Christine popped through the kitchen door and yelled, "Dotsy! Phone call!"

My heart bounced in my chest. I had given the castle phone number to each of my kids (except my daughter, Anne, whom I hadn't been able to locate, as usual) and to my next-door neighbor. This couldn't be good. My house had burned down or been burglarized; one of my boys, daughters-in-law, or grandchildren was hurt. *Oh God, please let it not be a grandchild! Take my house, steal my car, but let my kids and grandkids be okay.*

I felt almost sick as I pushed my chair back and stood up.

Christine pulled open the swinging door to the kitchen for me. "They dinnae ask for ye by yer surname. It's a woman and she said, 'May I speak to Dotsy?'"

"How strange," I said, but now it sounded more like someone from the dig. Most of them probably didn't know my last name, but I wouldn't allow myself a sigh of relief until I knew for sure who it was. I found the phone on the wall beside the fridge, its receiver clicking against the stone floor as it dangled by its cord.

"Hello, Dotsy? I'm terribly sorry but I don't know your surname, so I had to ask for Dotsy. This is Brenda Quale, Dylan's mother."

Again, my heart thumped. I had to think quickly. *Does she know he's dead? Yes, of course. John met with them and the police today.* "Oh, Mrs. Quale, I'm so very sorry. If there's anything I can do…" My words were so inadequate they sounded stupid. "I was very fond of Dylan."

"Yes, and he was fond of you."

What a surprise that was. I would not have guessed he'd even mentioned me to his parents.

"Dylan told me about you, only a day before… well, a few days ago. He told me that you were the person he liked best at the dig. He said you and he had talked about his work and that you'd shown a keen interest in what he did."

"Dylan was a brilliant young man," I said. The words tasted like bile in my mouth.

"Isn't that strange? He told me you were brilliant. That's the exact word he used. He said, 'Mother, this woman, Dotsy, she caught on to everything I told her and I could tell she understood it, too.' He said, 'She really likes hearing about spores and pollen. She's not just pretending.'"

"Of course I wasn't pretending. It was fascinating."

"I told him I was glad he'd found someone here that he could talk to. A mother hates to think of her child being lonely."

"How well I know. I have five of my own."

I expected her to make the usual noises about the number of my progeny, but she didn't. Instead, there was silence for a moment, and then she said, "Could I come to the castle and talk to you? I need to talk to someone."

Brenda didn't seem to care for the idea of being met at the door by any of the Sinclairs so we set a time when I promised I'd be waiting for her out front, and I returned to my table.

Over his plate of roast lamb, Tony Marsh called out, loudly enough for everyone to hear, "Who has that Super Bowl ticket?"

"I have it," said William.

"Have you found who it belongs to?"

"Nae, but I'm glad you mentioned it. I'm thinkin' the police might want to know about it." William caught Maisie's eye and pointed to Fallon's empty water glass. Maisie signaled to Christine, who responded with a pitcher of water.

"Oh, I should think they would," Brian Lipscomb said. "When did Dotsy find it?" He leaned sideways and peeked around Amelia at me.

"Night before last," I said, "about five o'clock." *That would have been about the time of the murder,* I thought, and I suspected everyone else was thinking the same thing. "Oh, William, I hate to mention it while we're eating, but I keep forgetting to tell you. The light in the stairwell of the round tower is burned out."

"I'll take care of it," William said.

FROM A WINDOW in the great hall, I watched Brenda Quale dash from her car to the front door, getting soaked in the process. As night descended, the storm had swept in with a vengeance, the rain now pummeling her bare head and thin jacket. I opened the door and pulled her in. "It didn't occur to me to pack rain gear," she said, shaking herself off.

Brenda was a spare little woman with short, thin hair that had gone mostly gray. The first thing I noticed about her was the deep lines between her eyebrows and running diagonally down from the corners of her mouth and nose. I wondered whether those lines had been there two days ago, or, if they had, how much deeper they had become at the news of her son's murder.

She didn't like my suggestion that we go to the library to talk. She wanted to talk to me privately so I took her to my room. On the way up the stairs, she said, "My husband would have liked to come, too. He wants to meet you, but he's not ready to face coming here, you know? I left him at our hotel."

The window in my room looked out on the pasture where Froggy's body was found. I wished I had suggested we go somewhere else, but it was too late now. And after all, it was fully dark so there was no reason either of us should look out.

Once inside my room, I hung Brenda's jacket on a doorknob, motioned her to the wing chair, and turned the little seat at my vanity table to face her.

Too late, I saw that Froggy's photo of the heart-shaped fern gametophyte lay conspicuously on the foot of my bed. Brenda must have recognized the handwriting, because she picked it up and whispered, "To Dotsy. Love, Dylan."

"Oh!" She dropped the photo and dissolved, pitifully, into the wing chair. Her hands fluttered against its upholstered arms like moths against a hot light bulb.

"I'm so sorry," I said. "I didn't realize I'd left that out, but as you can imagine, I've been mourning the loss of your son, too. I've pulled that photo out and looked at it a dozen times in the last two days."

"Dylan told me he liked you better than any of the young people at the dig." She reached down, as if for a pocket that wasn't there.

I remembered that I had taken her jacket, so I handed her a tissue from the vanity table behind me.

"He was different, you know, from most people his age," she said. "He was serious. Studious. He didn't have many close friends at college, or at home."

"Do you have any other children?"

"We have two girls; both are a good bit older than Dylan. In fact, one of them has a son who's nearly as old as Dylan." She fell silent and rubbed the back of one hand with the thumb of the other, as if there were something on it that rubbing would remove.

I waited.

"You know the people at the dig, Dotsy. Who killed him?" Her eyes pleaded for help.

"I have no idea, Brenda."

"The police aren't going to solve this murder. I know they aren't! They started out talking to us like it was some random act of violence or something ridiculous like that. Then they asked us about his roommate, Van Something."

"Van Nguyen."

"Right. This detective, Chief Inspector Coates, thinks he did it. Now, why would he think that?"

"I understand that Dylan and Van had had an argument shortly before…and that Dylan was wearing Van's shirt when he was found." It was painful for me to bring these things up and I could imagine how much more painful it was for Brenda to hear them. I was careful to call him Dylan because, so far, Brenda hadn't referred to him as Froggy, and there was a chance she didn't like that nickname.

"That was nothing more than a normal spat between roommates. You know how boys are. Dylan told me about a couple of spats they had. Nothing more than the usual pick-up-your-own-clothes type thing."

"Did Dylan ever mention a girl named Tracee Wagg?"

Brenda flinched a little. "Was she the girl he was supposed to have gone to the ball with last spring?"

"I believe so."

"He hasn't mentioned her since last spring. How do you know about her?"

"She's here at the dig."

"Dylan never mentioned it. He did tell me that a young man named Proctor—I don't know if that's his Christian name or his surname—was here. Dylan had to turn Proctor in to the department for cheating. Plagiarism, it was."

"Yes, he's here. His name is Proctor Galigher. What did Dylan tell you about him?"

"That they avoided each other. Dylan didn't know what to say to him, and Proctor is still angry."

"Angry enough to take revenge?"

"Oh, I wouldn't be able to say anything about that. I've never met the boy. But that's why I'm here, Dotsy. You're in a position to see what's going on. The police will probably end up arresting Van because they want to arrest someone and get the case off their desks. Do you think he did it?"

"No."

"I don't either, but that's what's going to happen, mark my words." Brenda Quale sat back, dug her elbows into the arms of the chair, and said, "Find out who did it, Dotsy! You're clever. You listen. You can hear things. My husband and I will not survive long, if we have to do it not knowing who killed our son!"

When she put it that way, I had no choice but to promise her I'd do my best.

BEFORE I TURNED IN, I stood at the window in my room and watched the rain. The last of the light had faded, leaving the pasture and moors in near-total darkness, but I could hear, more than see, the rain as the wind threw it against the glass panes. In this far northern latitude, evening twilight seemed to linger half the night, leaving only a few hours before morning light crept in.

One thing about Brenda Quale's visit made no sense: Why hadn't she asked to see Amelia Lipscomb? According to Amelia they were friends, and yet Brenda hadn't even mentioned her. And Amelia, as a television reporter, would know more than I would about how to investigate a murder. Perhaps Brenda didn't know Amelia was here. Oh yes, she did. Amelia told me Froggy's mother had asked her to keep an eye on him.

And why had Brenda not wanted to see anyone else? Why had she insisted that I meet her at the front door? That could have been because she simply didn't feel up to meeting a bunch of new people.

I turned at the sound of a tiny rap on the door.

"I'm returning your nail polish," Lettie said, handing me the bottle. She was already dressed for bed, green goo and all.

"Lettie, could you do me a favor tomorrow? If you're

going back to the library in Inverness, I need a copy of Shake-speare's *Macbeth*."

"I can't check books out," she said. "I'm an alien, they told me. And you have to be a citizen to get what they call a reader's ticket."

"Of course. I didn't think. Could you buy me a copy? I'll pay you back."

"Okey-doke."

I AWOKE AN HOUR OR SO later with my digestive system in crisis. It felt as if I had gremlins wringing my stomach like a wet towel. I lay in my bed through two waves of nausea and calculated that the next one would be the one that did it. I grabbed my bathrobe and dashed down the hall to the bathroom, only to find it locked.

Through the door, I heard the unmistakable sounds of mis-erable retching. My face and neck now covered in cold sweat, I flew down the stairwell to the first floor where there was a half bath with no tub or shower, but it was only the toilet I needed at the moment. I knocked frantically and twisted the knob, but this door was locked, too. From within, came a low moan and more sounds of gastric distress. And I was out of time.

I dashed through the side door and held it open with one foot while I bent over and tossed my mushroom soup, my lamb with mint and crabapple sauce, and my butterscotch pie into the grass. Then, because I didn't know whether the door would lock if I let it close and I didn't feel like checking, I slithered to the ground, my back holding the door open, and let the heaven-sent rain bathe my fevered face.

I don't know how long I sat there. More waves of nausea brought up the last bits of food, and I began to shake. This wasn't the best way for a diabetic to spend the night since an empty stomach brings with it the risk of hypoglycemia, but as I sat there, too weak to rise, I heard more noises, sounds of pain and anguish, from within the castle. Amelia Lipscomb careened down the hall and saw me, but she was in no condition to help me. She looked as sick as I felt.

"What's happening, Dotsy? Everyone's ill. Was it something we ate?"

"Don't know." I didn't feel like talking. I sat there with my back against the door and closed my eyes. When I opened them, Amelia was gone.

I crawled and stumbled back up to my room and knocked on Lettie's door. No answer. Alf Downes veered past me, his nearly hairless head swathed in a nightcap. A nightcap? Even in my pathetic state, I had to chuckle. I leaned against the wall and knocked again. At length, Lettie's door opened.

"What the hell? Dotsy! You look awful!"

Lettie dragged me inside and bathed my face with a warm, soapy cloth. She was perfectly fine, but she spent the rest of the night playing Florence Nightingale to the entire west wing.

"OBVIOUSLY IT WAS the mushroom soup," Lettie said when I dragged into her room the next morning.

"You might be right," I said. "Who was at breakfast?"

"Absolutely nobody but Tony and me and Christine," Lettie said, smearing Crest on her toothbrush. Each of our rooms had a basin so we didn't have to go down the hall for wash-ups, pill-taking, or tooth-brushing. "Even poor Maisie couldn't eat. She got things started in the kitchen and then left it to Christine." Lettie bent over her basin and commenced energetic brushing.

I unwrapped the scone Lettie had brought me from the dining room. She had also tucked in some butter and marmalade, twisted into little bits of plastic wrap. My stomach told me there was a fifty-fifty chance it would accept a scone, so I decided to give it a try. I ripped the scone in two and used a ballpoint pen to spread it with butter.

"Tony's feeling okay?" I asked.

"Yes. See, that's why it had to be the mushroom soup. Who

didn't eat it? Me. Who else didn't eat it? I noticed that Tony only had a few spoonfuls because he was talking the whole time. When Christine picked up his soup cup, it was still half full."

"You actually noticed that?" Lettie never ceases to amaze me.

"He apparently did eat a bit of it, but Tony is a very physically fit man, isn't he?"

I nodded, remembering Fallon's admiring perusal of Tony's backside in the library the other night.

"Well, if any of us could handle a bit of bad food without too much trouble, I think it would be Tony who could do it."

That made sense to me. "So you're fine, Tony's okay even though he ate a few spoonfuls, and Christine is fine. Did you ask her if she ate any of the dinner?"

"Yes, but I waited until Maisie had gone back upstairs before I asked. I didn't want Maisie to feel like we were—" Lettie put the back of her hand up to her mouth "—insulting her cooking." She tapped her toothbrush on the side of the basin and deposited it behind her soap dish. "Christine said she had pizza with some friends of hers before she came to work last evening. She admitted to having a bit of the butterscotch pie, though."

"Thanks for the scone, Lettie." I got up to return to my own room. "Are you going to Inverness?"

"I'm going around to all the rooms and see who needs help. Poor Maisie can't do much because she's taking care of William and plus, she's sick, too. She said William had a really rough night."

"You needn't worry about me anymore. I'm over the worst." I wrapped the second half of my scone in a napkin and shuffled toward the door. "If you do go to Inverness today, would you also get me a book on mushrooms? One of those field guide things?"

"Inspector Lamb is on the trail again," Lettie said.

"I believe the expression is, 'Come, Watson, the game is afoot.' "

TEN

I FIGURED THERE WAS no need to notify Tony or John that I wouldn't be at the dig for a while. John wouldn't be there, either, and Tony already knew everyone's plight. I made sure my door was unlocked lest, in a crisis, someone might need to come in and I might not be able to get to the door. I kicked off my slippers, set a wastebasket lined with a plastic bag beside my bed in case my scone decided to make another appearance, and stretched out on my unmade bed. My sheets felt clammy.

With the rain and wind of the previous night, I worried about the cordoned-off area where I had found the gold coin. I hoped someone at the dig had covered it with a tarp. I had left early, but Graham Jones normally did a walkabout at the end of the day, picking up stray trowels, ordering important spots covered, all wheelbarrows and shovels stowed. Dark clouds had been threatening before I left the site. So I told myself not to worry, that Graham would certainly have made sure that spot was covered, but I was still edgy.

The mushroom soup. I rehashed what little I could remember about it. Boots had knocked at the kitchen door, calling out, "I got chan-ta-rellies, I got penny buns, I got…" I couldn't remember what he'd said. I had never heard of penny buns, but chan-ta-rellies, I assumed, were chanterelles, supposedly a delicacy. Boots was an old hand at hunting and gathering. John had told me that Boots had worked there since he, John, was a boy, and William had mentioned that Boots lived in a cottage at the MacBane farm. So Boots should be thoroughly familiar with the types of mushrooms one found in these woods and fields.

Still, mushrooms are notoriously difficult to identify with certainty. I wouldn't trust myself to eat any mushrooms I found in the woods, but then I didn't have Boots's experience. It would be quite possible, I mused, for a new type of mushroom to pop up where it hadn't been seen before, wouldn't it? That was another reason I wanted Lettie to buy me a mushroom book.

Maisie had said, "I added some of the chanterelles and penny buns Boots brought me," which indicated that she already had the soup prepared when Boots came in. She'd probably chopped or pureed some of Boots's largesse and tossed it into the pot on top of the mushrooms and other ingredients that might have been simmering all day.

Blue something. Boots had said, "I got chan-ta-rellies, I got blue somethings, I got penny buns." Ah well, I'd have to ask him or Maisie. *Maisie and Boots must both feel absolutely awful about what's happened,* I thought.

I wondered if Boots knew about it yet. I wondered if he'd taken any mushrooms home with him. Oh dear. What an awful thought that was. If Boots had taken some home, he'd likely have made himself a simple evening meal. Single men often have one-dish dinners, but was he a single man? Somehow I couldn't see Boots with a wife. What if he'd eaten mushrooms and only mushrooms for his dinner?

Would there be any remains of those mushrooms and, if so, where would they be? Maisie might have stuck the extras in the refrigerator, or left them out on a countertop. Were you supposed to store mushrooms in the refrigerator? I did, at home, but I was no authority. The extra peelings and stem bottoms might have been tossed out or dumped into the garbage disposal. No, wait a minute. Maisie didn't use a disposal; she threw vegetable parings and such on her compost pile.

I heard cars pull up to the front of the castle. I rose, wobbled across the room to my window, and looked down on the western end of the drive that circled in front of the castle. The police had apparently decided to start parking on this side. Two panda cars had pulled off the asphalt and several men, Chief Inspector Coates among them, traipsed across the west lawn, a short walk from there to the incident room. I wished I could think of an excuse to visit them again. What were the chances they'd let me know if they'd made any progress yet? Very small, I was sure. Coates didn't like me and I didn't know why.

I thought about what Joyce Parsley had told me yesterday. She had been more than willing, I'd say eager, to talk about Froggy. But what she told me—about Tracee Wagg and her sleazy spring ball stunt, about Proctor Galigher and the plagiarized paper—were reasons for hard feelings, but not motives for murder. Kids sometimes can't put things into perspective as well as adults; sometimes they react rashly. No, that wouldn't work. I knew that wouldn't work. Young kids, twelve, thirteen, fourteen years old, could go ballistic over a verbal wound, even an imagined slight, but these kids were what the law calls adults. They might be kids to me, but there were plenty of young folks with children and full-time jobs who were the same age as these college students.

If someone from the dig murdered Froggy Quale, he or she would most assuredly be tried as an adult. That is, they would be if enough evidence came to light to have a trial at all. I intended to do everything I could to help make that happen.

Did anyone from the castle have a reason to kill Froggy? After all, his body was found here. I could think of no reason at all. Nada.

I had just dozed off when I heard a light rapping at my door. It was Amelia Lipscomb with a tentative, "Dotsy? I didn't awaken you, did I?"

Now why do people say that? How can you answer? "Yes, you woke me up," sounds rude, so I, and I suppose most people, answer, "Oh, no. I was…" followed by whatever we can invent to ease their conscience for waking us up, so I said, "Oh no, I was playing chess with my imaginary friend." That made her feel better, I'm sure.

"I can come back later." Amelia recognized the sarcasm, and I felt badly for having stooped to it, so I smiled and waved her in.

"I must say you look better than you did at two o'clock this morning, Amelia."

"How about you?"

"Now that you mention it, I think I'm better. I had a little nap. How's Brian?"

"Coming around slowly. He's doing some work on his laptop. Brian can never simply go on vacation. He has to bring work with him."

Even with no makeup and her hair pulled loosely back in a scrunchy, Amelia was pretty. She had those high cheekbones that light from any source loves. "Your friend Lettie is such a darling," Amelia said, plopping into the wing chair near the window. "She has gone around to all the rooms, running errands, fetching water, plumping pillows. She told me everyone is sick except herself and Tony."

"Yes. We discussed the possibility that it might be food poisoning," I said. "The soup."

"Why the soup, specifically?"

I explained our reasoning and said, "Is Lettie still here?"

"She was on her way to John and Fallon's room a few minutes ago. I wondered if she'd come down here." Amelia picked at the piping on the chair arm. "I don't want to bother them myself, but I want to know how they are."

I opened my wardrobe door and fingered through my clean shirts. "Amelia, you mentioned that you know Froggy Quale's mother. Do you know anything about his relationship with the others on the dig? Or about his relationship with anyone? Did he have a girlfriend?" I knew the answer to the last question had to be no, but I was fishing for anything she could give me.

"I don't know much about his personal relationships, but I understand he was already a respected authority on little…" she hesitated, as if feeling around for the right term. "Little spores and pollen grains."

"That's right."

"I know John Sinclair was paying him and some Asian kid enough to work here that they didn't have to live at the camp with the others. They had a room."

"Yes, they had a room at the MacBane farmhouse, but that was necessary because of the equipment they both used."

"The MacBane farmhouse?"

"Yes. Do you know where that is?"

"I think so," she paused a moment. "Any relation to John and William's mother?"

"I didn't know their mother was a MacBane," I said. I pulled out a green shirt and a pair of jeans.

"Haven't you seen those two big portraits downstairs in the square tower? They're on either side of the room, one of their father and one of their mother, in an eternal face-off."

I laughed. "Are you sure it's their parents?"

"They have brass plaques at the bottom. One says 'Roger-something-Sinclair' and the other one says 'Fenella MacBane Sinclair.' By the way she's dressed, I'd say the portrait was done in the fifties, so she'd have been about the right age to be John and William's mother."

"Is she dead?"

"I believe so."

"And their father?"

"He's dead, too." Amelia rose and looked out the window while I disrobed and put on my bra. "There's no doubt the woman is their mother. Take a look, next time you're down there. She has the same chin and eyes as William and John."

Amelia went silent for a minute and then said, "I hope you don't think me too nosy, but is John paying for your trip?"

What a question! I had the feeling that this was the real reason she had dropped in on me, but why did she want to know? "Heavens, no. I considered myself lucky that he invited me to come at all. John and I e-mailed back and forth all last year, after I developed a burning desire to learn more about Macbeth. But, no, this trip is coming out of my own cookie jar."

"Archaeological digs like this one normally operate on a shoestring budget. Grant money is tight as a crab's bum." Amelia pursed her lips a couple of times. Why did that little habit of hers get on my nerves? "But the reason I asked you the question is because I know he paid Dylan and his roommate enough to lure them away from their respective schools. The Asian lad, I heard—"

"His name is Van." It irritated me to realize that Amelia and I were playing the same game. Wring out of her all the information she has, but skim over the fact that you don't have much to give back. Did I dream that Amelia told me she knew Froggy's mother? She did say that, didn't she? And didn't she also say that she didn't know much about Froggy's personal relationships?

And she'd better not call Van "some Asian kid" one more time.

Happily, before I found myself getting downright rude, Lettie popped in and Amelia left.

"If you think you're okay, I'll head off to Inverness now," Lettie said. "I think everyone else is going to pull through."

I gave her a twenty-pound note for the books and wished her a safe trip. As soon as she left, I realized I had no food coming my way until dinner, and no car.

AMELIA WAS RIGHT. The woman in the picture downstairs had to be William and John's mother. It was a large oil portrait in an ornate gilt frame with a plaque that read, "Fenella MacBane Sinclair." A rather delicate-looking woman with striking brown eyes and auburn hair, she wore a blue taffeta gown with what they used to call a sweetheart neckline and a large blue taffeta flower at the waist. I couldn't put my finger on the exact nature of the resemblance, but, as Amelia had said, the eyes and the chin line were the same. William's eyes were blue but nevertheless they looked like hers. John's brown eyes were practically clones of this woman's. I studied the portrait, trying to imagine Fenella Sinclair as an animate, living soul. She would have been a kind woman, I thought. A little shy, a good mother. Now what made me think I could tell that from an oil painting? A painting showed you the person the artist saw; not necessarily the person she was.

Facing Fenella, on the opposite wall, was the portrait of Roger William Campbell Sinclair, the same size and in the same type frame as Fenella's. A burly man, similar to William and more robust than John, he wore the traditional Highland costume of kilt, beret, waistcoat, jacket, and fur sporan. My heart did a sick sort of thump against my ribs. He looked like my ex-husband, Chet, also known as the toad-sucking swamp rat, or father of my children.

An old Volkswagen minibus pulled up in front of the castle. I could see it through the window in the south wall of the tower. The minibus's dirty windows kept me from seeing in, so I waited for its doors to open. Meanwhile, William Sinclair, bent slightly forward, lumbered out to meet it.

Both doors opened at once and the weird sisters climbed out. Heeding the police summons to return for questioning, apparently, they must have driven back from their home near Newcastle, England. I had never gotten it straight, which one was Winifred and which was Wanda. Each had a haystack of long gray hair and a propensity for wearing earth tones. They were both thin, both loped rather than walked, and neither wore makeup. One, I couldn't remember if it was Wanda or Winifred, had a way of talking to you with her head tilted back, as if she needed to see you through the bottoms of her bifocals. But she didn't wear glasses. The other one looked at you with her head tilted down, as if she were viewing you over the top of her glasses, but she didn't wear them, either. I tried to remember what William had said their last name was. Something that reminded me of witches, but what? I mentally went down the alphabet until I came to M. Merlin. Aha. Funny how that works. Merlin, the magician of Arthurian legend.

One sister climbed into the back of the VW and reemerged with a ferret suited out in a red leather harness. She set the animal on the driveway and watched as it darted off in several directions, as far as its lead would allow. William bent over as if he was greeting the ferret with the respect one should show a guest's pet. I wondered what he was saying.

Coming in the front entrance meant they had to walk through the square tower to get to the interview room, which is where I assumed William was taking them. I swung one of the big wooden doors open when I heard them coming, and held it for them. The ferret came through first and skittered across my foot.

We greeted one another with smiles and handshakes appropriate for people who'd never met until five days ago and hadn't seen each other for the last two.

"We had just settled into our digs back home when the telephone rings and it's the police. 'You have to come back to answer questions,'" one sister said, making a pretend receiver of her left hand.

"There's been a muh-duh!" the other added.

"Who's been muh-duhed?" they both asked in unison.

William took one by the arm and said, "Awfully sorry, but the police told me not to let you talk to anyone aboot it before they see you. I'm to take you to the interview room straight away."

Meanwhile, I had thought of an excuse to go to the interview room myself. I wished I could turn myself into a fly and hang about on the wall in there. It had been more than two days since Froggy's murder. By now, the police should have made some progress. If not, the hope of ever naming the murderer would soon dim. The more time passes, the colder the trail grows, and two days gives a killer a lot of time to drag red herrings across the trail.

"Damn!"

I heard Chief Inspector Coates's frustrated expletive as soon as I came to the foyer that joined the stairwell, the interview room, and the door to the inner courtyard. Coates had flipped a light switch and precipitated a flash from above, around the bend in the winding stairs.

"Sir William put in a new light bulb up there not ten minutes ago. Must be some sort of a short," Coates said.

The short, or whatever it was, had blown the entire circuit. The computers, the desk lamps, the cell phone chargers, the printers, the fax machines, everything in the interview room went dark and dead. Since it occupied the bottom level of the round tower, the core of the original castle keep, this room had no windows. Having been the one who asked William to change the bulb, I felt a bit responsible, but I bit back an apology.

Instead, I said, "Chief Inspector Coates, I have something to tell you. I don't know if it's import—"

"Yes, all right. Find a chair inside."

I grabbed a folding chair and set it down beside the weird sisters, who appeared as dark lumps in the blacked-out room. I pulled my feet under the chair as breezes from stumbling police officers, muttering under their breaths, blew past me. The light from a couple of battery-powered laptops illuminated the faces of uniformed officers still tapping away at their keyboards, oblivious to the outage.

"Excuse me," one said to me as the lights came back on. "The Chief Inspector doesn't want these two ladies to speak to anyone from the castle before they've been interviewed."

"Sorry." I carried my chair to the wall and looked around for a dunce cap.

When Coates at last got around to seeing me, he sat on the edge of a nearby chair with one hand on his knee. His posture said, "Let's get this over with. I'm a busy man."

"Well," I began, "I thought you ought to know about the strange behavior of the handyman's dog, Lucy. It may be nothing, but dogs are so perceptive, aren't they? And Maisie told me the dog is quite used to their kitchen. She says she spends most of the winter there."

"Just tell me what happened."

"Yes. Well, yesterday afternoon, Boots and the dog came up to the kitchen door, Maisie let them in, and immediately the dog went berserk. Maisie had to chase the dog out with a broom."

"And?"

"Well, that's all." I felt small. "But I thought you'd want to know, because maybe the dog smelled something in the kitchen that wasn't supposed to be there. Something, you know." I also felt stupid.

"Thanks for sharing, Mrs. Lamb. I'll have a man look into it."

Ohhh! I hate "Thanks for sharing." It's right up there with "Have a nice day" in its power to crawl up my back, but my trip wasn't entirely wasted. By moseying out as slowly as possible, I checked out desktops on my way, and on one I spotted the Super Bowl ticket. Bagged and tagged as they say.

ELEVEN

I HUNG AROUND NEAR the front window in the square tower, hoping to ambush the weird sisters before they left in their Volkswagen. The little ferret preceded them through the west hall door.

"Leaving so soon?" I asked.

"Long drive back. Bloody waste of time if you ask me." The speaker was the one who tilted her head back. Either Wanda or Winifred.

"Were you able to help them at all?"

"They asked us if we'd seen anything from our window that—what was it?—Tuesday afternoon. We said no. Did we know Dylan Quale? We said no. Someone called Froggy? No. Did we hear anything unusual that afternoon? No."

The sister holding the leash stumbled and grabbed my arm, forcing the ferret to run between my legs and wrap himself up around my left foot. While she straightened out the leash, I held the ferret to keep it from making matters worse. It was wonderfully soft. "What's his name?" I asked, enjoying the sparkle in his little peppercorn eyes.

"Scarborough."

We were out of the house and in the front driveway when one sister said, "They asked us if we knew anyone going to a super bowl this year."

"We asked them what a super bowl was."

"They said it's a ball game played in America. Wanda, did they say what kind of game it was?"

Wanda ignored Winifred's question and said, "Dotsy, have you ever heard of a super bowl?"

I deduced that the ticket was not theirs, and gave them a brief explanation as we ambled toward their minibus. "So you weren't able to help them at all?"

"Winifred remembered that we saw a young man run out of the MacBane house that afternoon. Running like the devil, he was, toward the road."

"About one or two o'clock, it would have been," Winifred said.

"What did he look like?" I asked.

"Well now, there, I can't be so sure. I know it wasn't Robbie MacBane. Who could miss that flaming red hair of his?"

"Did he have long black hair? Pulled back?" I dropped Scarborough to illustrate pulled-back hair.

"No, I think he must have had shortish hair. Long hair on a lad, you'd notice, wouldn't you?"

"What was he wearing?" I asked as Wanda and I got Scarborough settled into his wire cage behind the driver's seat.

Wanda said, "I can't remember. I only vaguely remember seeing him at all, but Winifred said she thought he wasn't wearing any shirt."

Winifred jerked the passenger-side door open. "Well, I didn't really look that hard. Could have been wearing a tan T-shirt."

I RAN INTO WILLIAM in the Great Hall as soon as I had seen the weird sisters off. "Maisie says anyone who feels like eating can help themselves to whatever they can find in the kitchen," he said. "She's still busy tendin' to folks upstairs."

Poor Maisie. She had been sick, too, and yet she had to wait on the others. *What about Fallon Sinclair?* I wondered. Fallon was, after all, Maisie's sister-in-law. She and John kept a suite of rooms in the west wing that weren't rented out to guests, but Maisie waited on them as if they were guests. Didn't that ever rankle?

William and I headed for the kitchen where I made Swiss cheese sandwiches for both of us, and we ate at the big wooden work table in the center of the room.

"Maisie and I are so sorry about the…whatever it is that hit us," William said. "We don't know what to say."

"But you got sick, didn't you?"

"Aye, and Maisie, too. Let me tell you, we dinnae get a wink o' sleep. Neither o' us." He took a large swig of his Diet Coke. "I dinnae ken but it was somethin' we had for supper. Must ha' been."

"Lettie and I discussed the possibility that it was the mushroom soup. Maisie said Boots brought her some wild mushrooms from the woods."

"Aye, and she put some in the soup. The police ha' already scrabbled through the compost and collected what they could find. Coates said they'll do some tests."

I smelled chicken roasting. When had Maisie had time to put dinner in the oven? While William cleaned up our plates and glasses, I told him I wanted to take a walk over to the woodland east of the castle and I asked if it was okay.

"Aye, but I'm headin' that way myself. We can go together and I'll show you the shootin' hut."

We shinnied across the drystone wall that defined the limit of the parking area and tramped east across a cow pasture. "William, I noticed the two wonderful portraits in the square tower. Are they your parents?"

"Aye."

"Your mother was beautiful."

William turned to me as if he was checking my face for sincerity. "She was a lovely woman."

"And she died?"

"Aye. Breast cancer. I was seven and John was five."

He plodded on a few yards more, then looked up and pointed eastward, past the woodland and across the paved road. "Castle lands used to go way over there, past the road and into the hills. Can you see there? Those hills?"

I nodded.

"The Sinclairs used to farm all of that."

I wondered where this was going.

"Then, when our father married our mother—she was a MacBane—our grandfather leased that whole plot, from the road to the hills, to the MacBanes for a hundred pounds a month. Twelve hundred pounds a year." William stopped and looked straight at me. "They signed a one-hundred-year lease with a clause that states the rent will never go up."

"It's still in effect?"

"You got it. Our mother, Fenella, her father died and her brother took the farm and then his son and now his great-nephew, Robbie, has it. For one hundred friggin' pounds a month! Do you know what we could get for that land noo? And they've still got forty years to go."

I laughed. We had reached a wire fence at the edge of the woods. Beyond the fence, tall bracken ferns carpeted the forest floor between trunks of tall pines.

William bent the top of the fence down with his foot so I could climb over.

"Your father never remarried after your mother died?"

William didn't reply at once. "Aye, he did. He married a woman named Becky, but she died, too, when John and I were still lads. And then, a few years later, our father died."

"I'm sorry," I said. "I couldn't help staring at your father's portrait this morning. He looks as if he would have been a robust, dynamic sort of man."

"Radge Roger, they used to call him." William led the way into the pine-scented woods. "Radge means slightly crazy. Not necessarily an insult, but in my father's case, it wasn't always meant as a compliment, I fear."

In a clearing ahead of us nestled a small lake fed by a stream on its eastern side and drained by another on the north. A solitary wooden cabin on our side of the lake, unpainted and covered with a rusty tin roof, stood silent, its chimney and windows showing no sign of life. It gave me the creeps.

William must have read my mind. "We rent it oot to fishermen and hunters, mostly businessmen from Glasgow lookin' for a place to get drunk. Away from their wives."

"Is anyone here now?"

"Nae, not for the last week or so." He led me toward the cabin. Under my feet, a thick blanket of dead leaves, pine needles, and cones crunched as I walked, so that each footstep sank an unpredictable distance into a hidden layer of twigs and rotten wood. I picked my way to the corner of the cabin.

Here, against the side of the cabin, was a plain wooden bench and on it lay a large black-handled knife. "That's our fish-cleaning table," William said as he walked over, picked up the knife, and swiped its blade a couple of times against his trouser leg.

"You want to see inside?"

He plucked a key from over the door frame. The door opened with a creak and a scrape. The one-room cabin was bare inside, except for a stove, a small refrigerator, four single beds covered with navy rib cord spreads, and of course, a wet bar. Three grimy windows let in barely enough light to see by, one wall having no windows at all due to its being dominated by a large fireplace.

"Do people have to bring their own towels and bed linens?" I asked, not really interested in the answer. I had to say something.

"Some do. Most don't want to bother, so we bring sheets and towels over from the house for a small extra fee." William took the knife to the sink and laid it on the drain board.

I led the way back out of the woods, forging through the bracken along what I thought was the same way we had come in, but it turned out to be a more northerly path. My unintended detour still took us out of the woods, but by a longer route. I kept expecting to step out into the pasture after the next line of trees. Then the next. Had I gotten us lost? Surely William wouldn't let that happen. But as I turned to ask him for help, swallowing all my Girl Scout pride, I slipped.

"Watch oot!" William dived toward me and grabbed my upper arm. He dug his feet into the loose leaves and leaned back the other way, pulling me with him. Beneath my right foot, a cascade of rocks, twigs and soil fell—where? They made no further sound, as if they had fallen but not landed. My heart raced, and I lay beside William for a few seconds. He had landed on his tush, in a sitting position.

"This is a verra dangerous spot. I've been meanin' ta put up a fence here. Noo, I'm definitely goin' ta do it."

Fortunately, the dangerous spot was at the extreme edge of the woods. The wire fence surrounding the pasture was only a few feet from where we had fallen. William helped me over the fence and I, now feeling quite safe, crept over to the fence corner and looked down.

We were on a cliff. The fence ran along the edge of the woods, turned west, skirted the crest of a precipice for about a dozen yards, then sloped down to a wide valley. In the valley floor, a stream, probably the same one that drained the lake in the woods, flowed over cobbles and around boulders and disappeared in the distance. The cliff, with its exposed, lichen-covered granite, ran only about twenty or thirty feet horizontally, but stood at least fifty feet above the valley floor. That's how far I would have fallen if William hadn't caught me.

I estimated that we were now as close to the dig site as we were to the castle. "I think I'll go put in an appearance at the dig," I said. "Tony might be there even if John isn't, and Graham will have everybody working on something, I'm sure."

William walked with me as far as the castle drive. He still seemed shaken. Was it from my close call?

"Will there be an inquest into Froggy's death, William? I've read enough British murder mysteries to know they always have an inquest. We don't have that in America. We have a grand jury, I think."

"There is a post-mortem, of course. I'm sure that's already been done. But in Scotland, the inquiry is handled by what we call a Procurator Fiscal who takes over the investigation and kind of directs the police."

"I see. So Chief Inspector Coates is a Procurator Fiscal?"

"Nae, he's a policeman, but the Procurator Fiscal's office will be directing the investigation. They'll be advising the police."

I couldn't imagine Chief Inspector Coates taking advice from anybody.

Tony, Graham, and several others stood by, arms folded, and watched Van Nguyen go crazy with the mattock. Van had shed his shirt and by the time I joined them his torso glistened with sweat, and his face was flushed a dark red.

"Look at it this way. He's doing the mattock work for all of us for the whole of next week," Graham said.

"I'm concerned, though," Tony said. "I think we ought to make him stop."

"Why?"

"He'll knock himself out."

"He's healthy."

"He's insane." Tony stepped forward but didn't get close enough to the flying mattock to lose a body part. "Van. Van!" He clapped his hands. "Van, stop!"

Van paid no attention.

I tried. I inched up as close to Van as I could afford to go and said, "Stop, Van. I want to talk to you."

Van paid no attention. The rubber band on his hair had slipped down his back and his long, straight hair draped around his shoulders like tie-back curtains. I considered touching him to see if that might get his attention then thought better of it, so I dashed up to the toolshed, got my own mattock, ran back, and fell to work beside him. Mattocking is strenuous, but I felt confident I could keep this up for maybe ten or fifteen seconds.

"What are you doing?" Van said.

"Helplng you."

"Stop it."

"I'll stop when you stop." My gamble, that Van was too much a gentleman to let me kill myself, paid off. Together, we took our mattocks back to the toolshed. I fetched a bucket of water from a tap beside the shed and Van poured it over his head. While he wrung out his hair, I turned over a couple of dry buckets for us to sit on.

"Are the police giving you a rough time?" I asked.

He nodded, resting his elbows on his knees, and extended his lower lip to blow the water off the tip of his nose. "Froggy's parents came by the room again yesterday. The first time they came, they were like, well, they'd just lost their son, you know, and the police told them they couldn't take any of his stuff out of the room yet."

"And when they came back again yesterday?"

"They looked daggers through me the whole time. I could tell they'd been talking to the police, and the police had let them know I was their prime suspect. They knew all about Froggy and me arguing. They made it obvious. They think I killed him because the police think I killed him."

"That's ridiculous. They have no reason at all to think it except for a silly little fight between roommates."

"And the fact that he was wearing my shirt."

"But he could have simply taken your shirt if he didn't have any clean ones."

"Froggy always had clean shirts."

"That's still not evidence." I could tell there was more. I waited.

Van swiped his hand across his face. "Do you know that girl, Tracee Wagg?" he said, squinting toward the open toolshed door.

"I know who she is."

"She's making trouble. She's been coming on to me for weeks. One night last week she came up to my room when Froggy wasn't there. He came in later and…caught us." Van cleared his throat and squinted. He seemed embarrassed.

"And after she left, Froggy told you she was bad news, right?"

"Now, how did you know that?"

"I heard about an incident involving Froggy, Tracee, and a certain footballer whose name I don't remember. She apparently stood Froggy up and went to the ball with a better-looking guy."

"Is that all? I thought, from the way Froggy talked, that she had some kind of disease or something!" Van rose from his bucket. "I wouldn't have anything to do with her after that, so I figured we could avoid each other the rest of the time we're here. But when the police interviewed her, she apparently tried to get even with me by telling them… I don't know what she told them."

"Did she know that you and Froggy sometimes argued?"

"I don't know how she'd know that. I hadn't told her, and she and Froggy weren't even on speaking terms."

"Van, it'll all work out. I don't know how, right now, but you are not a murderer."

"How do you know I'm not?"

"Because I've seen how you deal with anger. You take it out on the ground."

Van pulled me up from my bucket seat and grinned. "Thanks."

TWELVE

EVERYONE BUT JOHN came to dinner that evening. Fallon said he was still a bit "wobbly" and asked Maisie to take him some broth and tea. "Why doesn't she take it to him herself?" Lettie muttered. "Are her legs broken?" Maisie had prepared an easy-on-the-stomach roast chicken with "neeps and tatties," a purée of potatoes and turnips.

Eleanor and Alf Downes came to dinner in eleventh-century attire. Now I understood why they had brought so much luggage. He wore a thigh-length linen tunic over close-fitting pants, a leather belt, and pouch; she, an embroidered linen dress with what she called a sprang-woven belt.

"Eleanor and I are celebrating the discovery of that eleventh-century coin. We thought we might enhance the ambience by wearing these outfits we made ourselves," Alf said with a courtly bow. The silliness of the whole thing really did lighten us all up. I was starting to like the Downeses.

"What if Dotsy had found a sixteenth-century coin?" Tony asked.

"Then we would be wearing Tudor attire," Alf answered without blinking an eye.

Only Lettie, Brian Lipscomb, and I took our coffee in the library that evening. I told Maisie she might as well pour three cups and take the tray back to the kitchen. I wanted to save her the extra trip because the events of the last twenty-four hours were showing on her face and in her pace. Maisie needed to flop into bed as soon as possible.

"Did you get any work done today, Brian?" I asked. He looked confused, so I added, "Amelia came to my room this morning. She said you were working on your laptop. Can't you even take time off to be sick? You were sick, like the rest of us, weren't you?"

"Oh, indeed, and Amelia was as well. I'm rather inclined to think it was the mushrooms in our soup. What do you think?"

"Lettie and I both think it was the mushrooms. In fact, I asked her to look for a book on mushrooms for me. Did you have a chance to do that, Lettie?"

Lettie slipped into a chair by the fireplace and took an exploratory sip of her coffee. "I did, and I got the Macbeth book you wanted, but the bookstore had to order the mushroom guide from somewhere else. They were out of stock. I went ahead and paid for it today, and they said they should have it in a day or two."

"How much do I owe you?"

"Nothing. You gave me twenty pounds. The mushroom book was thirteen, I believe, but the Macbeth was only five."

Brian set his cup and saucer on a side table and turned to us, nodding slightly as he did so. "And speaking of Macbeth, if you'll excuse me, I think I shall go and get a bit of the 'sleep that knits up the raveled sleeve of care,'" he said and then left us.

I looked around the wonderful old library, wishing I could have a room like it at home. Could I do something similar but on a smaller scale? I'd have to get bookshelves and the fireplace surround custom-made. My gaze fell again on that very odd door beside the hearth.

Lettie interrupted my thoughts. "Do you remember the night before last when we were all in here talking about where everyone was when that poor kid was killed?"

I said I did.

"Didn't Fallon say she was at some castle or other that day?"

"Urquhart Castle. Right. It's on the shore of Loch Ness."

"I think she was lying. Today I remembered, as I was driving through Aviemore, I happened to look at a parking lot as I drove by and I said to myself, 'Hey, that little convertible that John and Fallon drive; it was there on Tuesday afternoon!'"

"Hold on, Lettie. If you didn't know that before, how come you remember it now?"

"I didn't think it was important at the time. I simply drove by on Tuesday afternoon, and said to myself 'That's the Sinclairs' car,' but I thought no more about it because I didn't know there'd been a murder here at the castle. Then today, when I drove by again and thought about it, I remembered that Fallon had said she was at some castle and John had said he was here. He had lunch with William and then he went to the dig."

"You're right. John was definitely at the dig. I saw him."

"And if Fallon was at a castle on the shores of Loch Ness, what was their car doing in Aviemore?" Lettie tilted her head to the side and raised one eyebrow.

"Are you sure it was Tuesday?"

"Absolutely. As I drove by, I remember brushing cracker crumbs off my green sweater, and I wore my green sweater on Tuesday."

That settled that.

The little door beside the fireplace called to me. What possible reason could there be for a door to nowhere? Beyond it would be nothing but the stone of the castle's thick wall and then the courtyard, which had no doors from this wing leading into it. The little door couldn't lead into a hall; to its left stood the fireplace and to the right, a window. I peeked into the fireplace and assured myself that its sides looked solid, then slipped over, stuck my forefinger through the hole in the little door on the side opposite the hinges, and pulled. After a second, firmer yank, it opened with a pop.

Inside, a tiny stone staircase ran up to the left. I could find no light, no switch, no cord, and it took a minute for my eyes to adjust to the gloom within. The steps were no more than eighteen inches wide, but they were extremely steep. The air was stale and musty. It smelled of damp stone. At a height of about nine feet, a landing, hardly big enough to be worthy of the name, seemed to lead to another flight of steps or something on the right side, because to the left was nothing but a solid stone wall.

"Lettie, wait here while I dash up to my room for a flashlight."

"Oh, no."

When I returned with my minilight, Lettie agreed to stay right there with the door open while I explored. If I got into trouble, she could quickly run out for help. The bottom flight of stairs was pretty easy because I had some light from the library below, but each step was high and there was no handrail. At the landing, my beam found another flight of stairs like the first, but ascending to the right.

This flight was scary. No light made it around the corner so now I had only my flashlight to go by. A spider's web of magnificent proportions partially blocked my way, forcing me sit on a step, remove a shoe, and swipe away enough of it to get by. I resumed climbing, as much with my hands as with my feet, past a scattering of tiny bones, past more sticky cobwebs, and finally to another landing. Which led to another flight of stairs. And another landing.

At that point I would have quit and turned back, but my light now showed me the end of the climb; the fourth flight was the last. I leaned against the stone wall and flicked off my light. *There isn't enough oxygen in here,* I thought. *Or maybe I'm just breathing hard because I'm frightened.* A thin vertical sliver of light peeped out at the very top. I switched my light back on and finished the climb.

The top step was barely wide enough for me to sit on if I rested my feet on the next step down. I turned my light off again. I heard voices.

I heard Fallon Sinclair say, "Is this close enough? Can you reach it?"

Someone else said something I didn't catch.

I put my left eye in the crack through which the light poured. I was apparently sitting behind a door similar to the one in the library, except this one didn't seem to have a finger hole for opening it. By shifting my head left and right, I could scan a part of the room beyond, a foot or two at a time. It was John and Fallon's bedroom. I recognized the closet door behind which John kept the suitcase with my coin in it. I saw a red brocade counterpane and one post of their four-poster bed. Fallon stood on the right side of the bed.

"You must try, John. At least take a little of the tea. You're in danger of becoming dehydrated."

More undecipherable mumbles and grumbles. I figured John was in the bed, facing away from me, and that was why I couldn't make out what he said.

"I'll make a bed for myself on the settee in the next room, John. That way I can hear you when you need me."

Yet more murmurs from the bed.

"No, I will not bring you a Scotch and soda."

At that point John turned over in the bed and I could hear him clearly. "We drink a toast to Tony, and to Hannah… and to you, ha-ha. We drink a toast to those we love the best, our noble selves, God love us! There's none better and many a damn sight worse!"

John Sinclair was delirious.

I fumbled for the switch on my flashlight but it slipped out of my hand. I heard it clatter down steps, and that left me with the frightening prospect of descending those stairs in pitch darkness. I sat for a minute, felt around the step below me to get my bearings as well as I could, took a deep breath, and began lowering myself on my butt, one step at a time.

From beyond the door, I heard John's voice one more time.

"Here's to Becky's eyes and Becky's ears and Becky's…whatever. Vengeance is mine!"

I touched the barrel of my flashlight on the last step before the landing, just in time to avoid going mad myself. In the dark, the cold mustiness of these ancient stones seemed multiplied a hundred times. I continued scooting on my butt down the last three flights because I felt too shaky to risk standing.

With her fists jammed together in front of her face, Lettie was waiting for me. "Well?" was all she said.

"It leads up two floors to John and Fallon's bedroom. I didn't go in."

"Did they know you were there?"

"I doubt it. Lettie, John Sinclair has gone stark raving mad."

Go bid thy mistress, when my drink is ready,
She strike upon the bell. Get thee to bed.
(Exit Servant)
Is this a dagger which I see before me,
The handle toward my hand? Come, let me clutch thee.
I have thee not, and yet I see thee still.
Art thou not, fatal vision, sensible
To feeling as to sight? Or art thou but
A dagger of the mind, a false creation,
Proceeding from the heat-oppressed brain?
Macbeth, act 2, scene 1

Reading myself to sleep with Shakespeare is not my normal thing, but on this night, curled up in bed with my new copy of the play, I sped through Act One. Throughout the past year as I researched King Macbeth, I had consciously not allowed myself to consult the Bard's version for fear that it would influence my concept of the man, but now I saw no need to continue the abstinence. These lines reminded me of poor John Sinclair. How could John, unable to keep down weak tea, possibly ask his wife for a Scotch and soda? The very thought turned my stomach.

Proceeding from the heat-oppressed brain? Maybe it was as simple as that. John had a high fever. He was babbling nonsense. Why else would he link Tony, Hannah and Fallon in an imaginary toast? Hannah who? The only Hannah I could think of was Hannah Dunbar from the dig, and other than a common interest in archaeology, I knew of no connection.

I must have fallen asleep at that point, because I woke up later with the little paperback booklet on my face, my nose marking the first page of Act Two. Nature called, so I got up, ran my feet under the bed for my pink slippers, and shuffled off down the hall. In contrast to its popularity of the previous night, the bathroom was empty.

As I clutched the doorknob, Fallon Sinclair slipped out from the stairwell at the south end of the hall. She wore a soft yellow robe and matching slippers. Her hair and makeup showed no hint of having touched a pillow.

"Dotsy, are you okay?" she asked as she passed.

"I'm fine. How's John?"

"He can't sleep, so he's sent me down to get this season's diary from Tony. I guess he figures he might as well put his insomnia to good use."

Alone in the bathroom, I took a moment to figure out what was wrong with that picture. Hair not messy, makeup in place. If John's rantings had kept her up until now, those things might make sense. My watch said it was 2:30 a.m.

Got it. In Fallon's wake, I had sniffed freshly applied cologne. That's what was wrong with that picture.

THIRTEEN

"It's a laird's lug," Maisie told me.

Maisie and I lingered over our tea that morning after everyone else went on their way. Everyone, that is, except John Sinclair, who, according to Fallon, was no better. Maisie gave Fallon the home number of her own doctor and suggested she call soon because, it being a Saturday, the doctor would likely be "off fishing before long."

"What's a laird's lug?" I had told Maisie about opening the little door and finding the staircase, but I stopped short of admitting that I had actually climbed them to the top.

"Lug. That's a Scots word for ear, so a laird's lug would be a laird's, that is, a lord's ear. It's for eavesdropping, dinnae ye ken? But it'd be good if ye dinnae mention it to the other guests, because William likes to make a sort of game of it. When we have a houseful he'll offer a prize to the first one who can find the laird's lug. It's fun. Ye'll see folks snoopin' around lookin' for God knows what."

I chuckled. "William loves this house, doesn't he?"

"Oh, aye. Well, it's where he belongs, inn't it?" Maisie went to the kitchen door and gave Christine some clean-up instructions. When she returned to our table, she said, "It's hard to keep a place like this going, nowadays, what with taxes and everythin' bein' so high. But I knew that when I married him, din't I? I knew it'd be farmin' and cleanin' and work, work, work.

"It's been close a few times. Times I was sure we'd be losin' the place, but William's always managed to come up with enough to get us by. His family, ye ken, they've lived here nearly two centuries."

"Did you know William's parents?"

"I recall his father. William and I began seein' each other when we were mere bairns. In our teens. But old Roger, he scared me. Reminded me of a great bear. Always grumblin'. I wonder sometimes if he'd approve of me and William marryin'. Even noo, when I walk by that big portrait of him, ye ken, I give him a wide berth."

"You feel like he's going to reach out and slap you?" I asked, grinning.

"Somethin' like that."

"What were William and John like when they were young?"

"Aah." Maisie looked toward the ceiling. "As different as ye see them today! William was the athlete, the outdoorsman, a Highlander through and through. Never much of a scholar, but he made a real name for himself in the Highland games. The hammer throw, tossing the caber.

"But noo John, he was aye the bookish one. Thought the Highland folk were backward, ye ken? He's softened up a good bit as he's gotten older, but when he was a lad, most folk around here thought he was a snob."

"How old were they when their father died?" I tried to remember if William had told me.

"When William was aboot twenty-one, I guess. John was away for his first year at Oxford."

"What did he die of?"

"Oh, he killed himself, I fear." Maisie lowered her gaze to the table, and I felt sorry I had asked so bluntly.

"Roger married another woman after William and John's mother died, didn't he? They had a stepmother for a while."

"Becky. Aye. Becky was a high-class woman from London. A society dame, dinnae ye ken?" Maisie slapped her hand behind her head in imitation of a high-class woman. "She tried to turn this old castle into Buckingham Palace, North. Cars in and oot all the time, parties that went on for days, but at least there was no unemployment aboot because all the locals were on staff here!"

"Did she and Roger get along?"

"Like oil and water!"

"What about the boys? Did they get along with their step-mother?"

Maisie didn't actually answer, but she shrugged in a sort of so-so way.

"And what did she die of?"

"Ohh, she killed herself, din't she?"

ROBBIE MACBANE WAS hand-feeding his coos as I tramped up to his house. Coo is the Scottish pronunciation of cow, and the adorable shaggy-haired Highland cows are locally referred to as "Heelan coos." If there is anything cuter than a Heelan coo, it's a Heelan calf. I ripped up a clump of grass and strolled over to join them at the fence.

"May I feed them, too?" I asked.

Robbie's head jerked around at the sound of my voice, but he merely grunted.

"Can the little one eat grass yet?" I betrayed my ignorance of cows with that question.

"He can eat whatever he likes."

Robbie wore denim overalls and heavy work boots this morning; quite a change from his tuxedo. The adult cow, the calf's mother, I assumed, nuzzled Robbie's hand with her big, soft nose. Through the mop of hair cascading over her horns, brown eyes twinkled. Robbie grabbed another fistful of grass from our side of the fence.

"Are Highland cows hard to raise?" I asked.

"Nae."

"They look hardy. I guess they're well-adapted to your harsh winters."

No answer.

"How old is this little one?"

"Four months."

I ran my hand through the mother's mop of hair. I hadn't realized before, how short the Highland cows are. Short legs, stocky body. The mother cow was only as high as my shoulder.

"Is Van in his room this morning, or has he gone to the dig?"

"He's in his room," Robbie said and bent over for more grass. "I'm sorry, Mrs...."

"Lamb. Dotsy Lamb."

"Right. Sorry I'm bein' rude. I'm in a bad mood today." Robbie rolled his words out as if he had a mouthful of marbles.

"It's perfectly okay. I'm sorry I intruded."

"Here's why." Robbie jerked a single sheet of paper, tri-folded like a letter, from his back pocket and handed it to me.

It was on nice letterhead stationery, headed "Bobble, Bangle and Bede, Solicitors."

Dear Mr. MacBane,
Our office has looked at the contract concerning rental of the property (here followed a technical description of a plot which I assumed was the same as the MacBane farmland) and, in light of the time that has passed since the original signing of the contract, we recommend that it be reviewed. A number of laws and ordinances which may or may not affect the validity of this contract have been enacted since the original was drawn up.

Please contact us for an appointment at your earliest convenience.

"Oh dear," I said. "I'm afraid I don't understand more than a few words of this. I flunked business law in college." Which was a cop-out. I didn't want to admit that William had already told me about the MacBane/Sinclair hundred-year-hundred-pound-per-month contract. I handed the letter back to Robbie.

"It means I may lose my let."

"Do you think it would be all right if I went up and spoke to Van?"

"Aye, but give him a shout first. When a lady calls, he likes to put on clothes before he opens his door."

I stepped around to Van's window and called up to him, then climbed the stairs to his room. The room looked much as it had on my last visit, except, I soon noticed, the mushrooms under inverted drinking glasses, which had been beside the binocular microscope on Froggy's desk, were now gone.

"What happened to the mushrooms?" I asked.

"Police took them."

"Have you talked to them since yesterday?"

"No, but I'm sure they'll be in touch," Van said with a note of heavy sarcasm.

"Van, if I'm being too nosy, tell me so, but there's this woman staying at the castle who keeps asking me about the finances of the dig. Of course, I know absolutely nothing about how the dig is financed, but she seems awfully curious about how much Dr. Sinclair is paying you and how much he was paying Froggy."

"What woman?"

"Amelia Lipscomb."

"Never heard of her," Van said, flopping back on his bed, his hands behind his neck.

"She's a TV reporter," I explained. "You might have seen her on the news. She works for a Brighton station, I think."

"I've never been to Brighton."

"I forgot. You're from Cambridge, aren't you? Well, anyway, she questions how John Sinclair manages to pay you two enough for all this equipment." I waved my hand around Van's side of the room where electronics were stacked nearly to the ceiling. "All this and a room just to keep a record of the season's work?"

"Much more than that, Dotsy. Dr. Sinclair is giving me five thousand pounds plus this room and this equipment. The equipment is his, not mine. But he's hired me to do more than a video record of the season. I'm putting together a very sophisticated presentation that includes topographic maps of the area, demographics, local tourist facilities, roads, and the dig site. He wants the history of the area so that it ties in with the Neolithic, the medieval, and the fifteenth-century stuff they're finding. I'm putting in 3-D graphics, music, voice-over, the works. This is a big deal."

"Whatever for?"

"I get the idea he wants something to present to, I don't know, businessmen or something."

As I LEFT THE MacBane house, Tony Marsh stopped his car and picked me up. The dig site lay ahead no more than a hundred yards, but I accepted the ride anyway. He pitched a stack of papers into the back so I could hollow out a nest to sit in amid the jackets, socks and CD cases remaining on the seat.

"Have you seen John this morning?" I asked.

"I dropped by his room to give him some papers, but Fallon said he didn't feel like talking."

"He's having a much worse time of it than the rest of us had."

"I'm not surprised. Food poisoning has to be fought off by one's liver, and John's liver is bound to be in terrible shape."

"He does drink a bit," I said.

"He's an alcoholic. At least, he's what I would call an alcoholic."

"So he wouldn't be able to get rid of the poison as readily as the rest of us did." Tony's reasoning made sense to me.

Tony turned off the road and stopped, his wheels straddling a mud puddle beside the big tent. He yanked the hand brake up. "Fallon told me that John…"

At that moment, Hannah Dunbar and Graham Jones emerged from the tent. Hannah glanced toward the hood of our car, and then quickly turned, following Graham toward the toolshed.

I looked at Tony. His expression had changed to one of—what was it? Pain? Regret? Yes, both of those, I thought. Neither Hannah nor Graham had looked straight at us, but it was as if Tony had been briefly transfixed.

"Fallon told you what?" I prompted him.

Tony snatched his keys from the ignition. "I lost my train of thought. Let's check the bulletin board and see what brave deeds Graham has assigned you today."

The bulletin board said I was to work on the Neolithic campfire area. Tony and I walked toward the toolshed together, but he stopped short of going in. I wondered if it was because Graham and Hannah were in there. I, however, needed to go in and grab a trowel and bucket.

Before Tony left me, I said, "You know where John keeps the coin, don't you?"

"Yes, he showed me."

"He showed me, too. But do you have a key to the box, Tony? I don't. What if something, well, happens to John, and the coin expert does pay us that visit John mentioned? Don't you think you should get the key from John? Just in case?"

"I think not. I'd hate to suggest to him that I think anything might happen to him. But don't worry. I was a locksmith-slant-safe-cracker in the S.A.S. I can get into that little box if need be."

I SETTLED DOWN TO troweling the charcoal-blackened area of the Neolithic camp site. I sat on my foam kneeling pad, leaned on the heel of my left hand while troweling with my right, and, after a few minutes, traded hands and turned my legs to the other side. It's amazing how knapped flint retains its razor-sharp edge, even after five thousand years in the ground. I raked my trowel over one spot, catching the tip of a flint flake as I did so. The flake shot up and cut my forefinger.

I dashed to the first aid box we kept in the tent. Graham Jones smiled, not bothering to remind me that he'd already warned us about the dangers of buried flint. "A little alcohol first, on cotton wool," he said.

"Cotton wool? In America we just call it cotton. Wool is what comes from a sheep; cotton comes from a plant. Two different things."

"What do you Americans know?" He grinned and handed me a Band-Aid.

I went back to my post and did it again. Another flake, another cut on the other forefinger.

"You're a slow learner, aren't you, Dotsy?" Graham said when I plodded back to the first aid box.

"Shut up and hand me the cotton wool."

"And another plaster, right?"

"In America we call them Band-Aids."

"What do you Americans know?"

Both forefingers now shielded with "plasters," as Graham called them, I went to work in earnest. It made sense to me that we'd find many more flakes than actual arrowheads. So far we'd found only one flint arrowhead at this site, but dozens of flint flakes. The flakes, naturally, were concentrated in the area around the charcoal where early people would have sat in the evenings. They would have knapped flint, sewn hides with bone needles, and what? Sung songs? Did they have songs?

The arrowheads, now. The people would have reused them when they retrieved them from their quarry. The quarry that got away, wounded perhaps, might have carried arrowheads far away across the fields and through the woods, to be deposited wherever the animal did die, so you wouldn't expect to find arrowheads near a campfire. Were there Heelan coos in Scotland back then? There was a coo-like animal called an aurochs.

Maybe aurochses were ancestors of Heelan coos. I'd try and remember to ask John or Tony.

I troweled away, thinking about John. He was awfully sick, I thought. I hoped Fallon had called the doctor this morning as she had indicated she would. If I hadn't been where I wasn't supposed to be, I could have told Maisie and William what I had heard last night. John had been raving, out of his head.

What the hell was wrong with me? I should have told them!

Thoroughly ashamed of myself, I scrambled to my feet and dashed across the barley field. Talk about maturity! If I found a snake in the cookie jar, I'd let somebody get bit before I'd admit I'd been sneaking cookies.

I had gotten no farther than the gate at the edge of the barley field when I heard the siren scream out from the castle and saw the ambulance streak past, down the castle drive.

The black Jaguar sped by, close on the tailpipes of the ambulance, and followed by William's Volvo. At the end of the castle drive, all three vehicles made a left turn, taking the road toward town.

I found Maisie and Christine standing like stalagmites in the parking area outside the kitchen door. Maisie shielded her eyes from the sun with her right arm but neither of them moved until I was right up on them.

"They've taken Dr. John to hospital," Christine said.

Maisie pushed her frizzy hair back with both hands. "The doctor came oot and checked on him, and straight away he called for an ambulance. They brought John downstairs on a stretcher. Wouldn't even let him walk down by himself. They took off, flyin'."

"I know. I saw. What did the doctor say was wrong?"

"I dinnae have a chance to ask him before they dashed off. Fallon ran to her car, and William shouted for me to help him find his car keys. All William said was, 'John's delirious. Doctor said it might be liver failure or kidney failure.'"

"Crikey, what next?" Christine shook her head.

"What hospital are they taking him to?"

"I dinnae ken. The closest one is in Fort William but the largest is in Inverness." Maisie threw an arm around Christine's shoulders. "William took his mobile phone with him, so he may call when he sees which way they're headin'."

Maisie turned with a deep sigh toward the side door. "I'd better get back to the kitchen in case the phone rings."

"And check the eggs on the stove," Christine added.

"Oh, Lord, the eggs! Pot'll be boiled dry by noo."

FOURTEEN

THE LUNCH VAN BLASTED me out of the way with its horn. I was lost in thought as I crossed the muddy parking area beside the tent. On my walk back to the dig site, I had decided to find Tony before I did anything else, and tell him about John. I'd let him decide whether or not the others should be told. I found him in the tent, bent over a stack of site grid plans, tapping his cheek lightly with a metal ruler. He dragged out a folding chair for me and shifted it to a couple of different spots on the down-trodden grass before he found one that let all four chair legs touch ground.

"Did you know John's been taken to the hospital?" I asked.

Tony's eyes widened. "Why?"

I related all I knew about it. Tony listened, absently squeezing his lower lip into a V between his thumb and fore-finger.

"I haven't mentioned it to anyone else yet, Tony. Do you think we should tell everybody?"

"Not yet. You can tell Graham, of course, and Hannah, if she asks, but before we tell the kids, I want to find out more." Tony plunged through the tent flap, pulling a cell phone from his pocket as he went. The grid plans he'd left on the table rolled up around his ruler as if they had a life of their own. Tony stuck his head back in and said, "Dotsy, the lunch wagon's here. Would you take care of it for me?"

In case I should fantasize I'm Lara Croft, Tomb Raider, there's always someone to remind me I look more like Betty Crocker.

Since the police were now gone, most of the kids brought their lunch bags inside the tent because it eliminated the chasing of napkins caught by the wind and the spilling of drinks on the bumpy ground. I took a seat at a table occupied, so far, by Hannah Dunbar. Hannah, I noticed, had eyed Graham Jones when he came in with his lunch, but Graham had gone to the table Tony had recently vacated. Graham unrolled the grid plans, setting his canned soda on one side of the paper and a rock on the other.

"Aren't you getting a little tired of camp food, Hannah?" I asked.

"A bit, yes. I do have a car here, you know, so if I get desperate, I can drive into the village for a proper meal."

"With the wonderful breakfasts and dinners at the castle, I need this inedible junk at noon. It keeps me from gaining too much weight."

We chatted a few more minutes before I told her about John being taken to the hospital. "The night before last," I said, "almost everyone who ate dinner at the castle got sick. Several of us think it might have been the mushroom soup because there were wild mushrooms in it, but the soup tasted fine, you know? In fact, the only people who didn't get sick were my friend Lettie Osgood, who doesn't like mushrooms, and Tony Marsh, who Lettie says didn't eat much of his soup."

"But everyone got better, apparently," Hannah said. "I mean, you're here now."

"Right. All of us recovered within a few hours. All of us, that is, except John. He's been in his room ever since, and today, when the ambulance came for him—"

"An ambulance? They took him in an ambulance?"

"He's so sick, he's delirious. They took him out on a stretcher."

"Liver failure," Hannah declared. "John's been showing signs of jaundice, edema, especially around his ankles, spider veins all over his face; all signs of cirrhosis. John drinks way too much."

"You sound like a doctor," I said.

"I'm an endocrinologist."

I'm sure my mouth fell open, not because I don't realize that a pretty woman can also be a doctor, but because, let's face it, an archaeological dig is hardly where you'd expect to find an endocrinologist. "I'm looking for a connection, Hannah, and I'm drawlng a blank. Okay, I glve up. Why are you here?"

She balled up her sandwich wrap and tossed it into her lunch bag. "This is my hobby. One does need a change of pace sometimes, doesn't one?"

I agreed with her wholeheartedly while making note of the facts that she had shrugged her shoulders, rubbed her nose, and her voice had climbed upward a full octave as she said it. She was lying.

"Dotsy, you knew Froggy rather well, didn't you?" Hannah said, changing the subject. "And I know you talked to Van yesterday, at some length. What do you think has happened? The police are leaning on Van pretty hard, I've heard."

"Hey, I only got here last week. You and everybody else have known both of them longer than I have."

"But you have a way about you. People confide in you, don't they?"

"Yes, I suppose they do. I'm interested in people, and I guess it shows."

"Your eyes sparkle when you're listening to someone. It's quite flattering to the person who's talking, you know."

"You're embarrassing me," I said. "But to get back to your question, I have no idea who killed Froggy. No one here has a motive, and the police's alternate theory about some random thief wandering across the moors, looking for someone to rob and kill. It's ridiculous." I studied Hannah's face. "Have you heard anything? You stay at the camp so you've heard the kids talk."

"I've heard nothing. They all thought Froggy was a bit odd,

but nice. There is that kid, Proctor Galigher, though. He didn't like Froggy, but I don't know why."

I didn't mention what Joyce Parsley had told me about Proctor, Froggy, and the plagiarism charge. Hannah, I thought, was probably "out of the loop," as they say, around the camp.

I had an idea. "I'd like it if you'd come to the castle some evening for dinner, as my guest."

Hannah didn't answer at once. She ran her finger around the wet circle her soda can had left on the table and made a swirly pattern with the water. "I do fine in the evenings with my tin pot and my Sterno."

"A change of pace would do you good." I smiled, pushed my chair back, and stretched my legs. I didn't want to pressure her.

"Perhaps," she said.

At another table, Proctor Galigher was flipping grapes into the mouths of his tablemates, while Tracee Wagg ate a banana in a manner that would get a film an X-rating. Another kid had crammed all the leftover sandwich crusts from the entire table into his mouth until his cheeks ballooned out like a chipmunk's, and yet another stepped on the chipmunk's foot, as if the foot was a step-on trash can. What a group! It reminded me of the banquet scene in the movie *Tom Jones.*

"That girl, Tracee. Do you know her?" I asked Hannah.

"She stays at the camp, of course. She could, I think, benefit by a serious talk about high-risk behavior…from someone."

"But not from you, right?"

"Not from me," Hannah said. "It's not my job. I'm on vacation." She smiled a little; it was the first time I'd seen her smile. "Tracee needs to stay out of the bushes, if you know what I mean."

"Stay out in the open," I added, and that reminded me. "Hannah, someone, a girl, John said, found a pretty amethyst earring and gave it to him for safe keeping. Do you know who that was?"

"Me. I found it."

"Where?"

"Do you know that patch of woods over there?" Hannah pointed roughly northward. "Where the Sinclairs have what they call a shooting hut?"

"I was there yesterday."

"There's a pasture between that woods and the castle. We were field walking that pasture about a week or so ago, and the earring was simply lying there, between a couple of clumps of grass."

"As if it had been dropped recently?"

"I couldn't say. It was sort of embedded, as if it had been rained on. Settled into the soil. But with rain and wind and erosion and whatever, I suppose it could have been there quite a long time."

"Buried and then re-exposed?"

"Yes, or dropped there two days ago. How could you tell?"

"I'm sure I couldn't," I said. "Was it near that fence between the woods and the pasture?"

"No, it was in the middle of the pasture, about the same distance from the woods and the castle and that cliff. Did you notice that horrible cliff on the other side of the fence?"

"I nearly saw more of it than would have been good for me," I said. "If it hadn't been for William Sinclair, I would have gone over the edge."

"How? There's a fence."

"Not on the woods side, there isn't. Someone needs to put one up."

SEVERAL TIMES IN THE COURSE of the afternoon's labor, I heard "Shroooom!" from one or another of the kids as they tramped over my feet or yelled across the top of me as if I were part of the subsoil. In one instance, when Joyce Parsley had squatted beside me in a painful-looking position and was prattling on about Froggy, Proctor Galigher lurched by and "Shroomed" at Joyce.

She shot him the old watch-your-mouth-there's-a-mother-type-person-listening glare.

I could have asked her to explain, but I didn't want to get her off the subject of Froggy. "Have you heard anything about Van Nguyen being questioned by the police, Joyce?"

"They suspect him, I've heard."

"Do you think there's any basis for their suspicion?"

A sliver of flying flint hit me on the cheek. I twisted around and found that the source was Iain Jandeson in full Indiana Jones regalia, Aussie bush hat and all, sitting cross-legged on the grass and knapping a chunk of flint with another rock. "Watch out, Iain," I said. I swiped my hand across my face and checked my fingers for blood. "If you let those flint flakes fly in here, someone might think they're Neolithic."

"I'm not a complete idiot," Iain said. His attitude sometimes crossed over the boundary from pomposity into pure arrogance. I elected to drop the subject and turn my attention back to Joyce, who still sat in that folded-up squat.

"Van doesn't seem like the type, does he?" Joyce said. "Still, I know that he and Froggy had a few fights. Not…" Joyce pummeled the air with her fists. "Just arguments. But since Froggy was wearing Van's shirt when they found his body, and since no one can remember seeing Froggy after he went back to their room, I guess it does look suspicious."

"What do you mean, after he went back to their room? When did he do that?"

Joyce jammed her camouflage hat over her face. "I don't remember. Somebody said they saw him, but I can't remember who."

LETTIE BOUNCED INTO my room, waving the mushroom book. She handed it to me with a big, "Ta da! Fast work, eh? The book store had it waiting for me when I stopped in on my way to the car."

I thumbed through the book. It had pages and pages of glossy photos with common as well as scientific names and detailed descriptions. It was exactly what I wanted, but I couldn't read it yet. I still had to shower before dinner, so I laid the book on my nightstand and turned back to Lettie.

"John has been taken to the hospital," I said.

"I'm not surprised. You said he was raving mad last night. He probably should have gone yesterday. Do you think it's because of the mushroom soup?"

"If so, why did the rest of us get over it so quickly?" I picked up my new book again and looked at the table of contents to see if it had a chapter on poisonous mushrooms. It didn't; the species were arranged according to their shapes. "Two people have suggested to me that it might be cirrhosis of the liver."

"What two people?"

"Tony Marsh and Hannah Dunbar, this woman at the dig. You haven't met her, but she's an endocrinologist, so she should know."

"John does drink too much, doesn't he?" Lettie said as she backed out the door. With her hand still on my doorknob, she tilted her head and said, "What's an endocrinologist doing at an archaeological dig?"

WILLIAM CAME BACK from the hospital in time for dinner and told us that Fallon planned to stay the night there. "They're doing tests, and they've put him in the intensive care unit. There's no point in any of you going to see him, because they won't let you in," he told all of us as we took our seats for dinner. There was an extra party of six with us that evening. Locals, they told me, celebrating an anniversary.

"Have you talked to his doctors?" I asked.

"I tried to, but they were in a rush. Dr. Ashton, me own regular doctor and the one Fallon called this morning, noo I did talk to him. He fears John's kidneys and maybe his liver, too, are failin'. If that's the case…" William's voice trailed off. He shook his head and pulled out chairs to seat Lettie and me.

Amelia and Brian grabbed the other two chairs at our table as Christine barged through the swinging door from the kitchen to make her nightly spectacle of herself. Her commando-waitress image was enhanced this evening by the large combat boots and argyle socks she had chosen to wear with a soft blue dress and little white apron.

"Listen up! I don't want to have to say this but once! We have two starters tonight: Caesar salad or clam chowder. The clam chowder is made with broth; not milk and not tomato. Broth. Got it? If ye don't like it made with broth, have the salad!"

The four of us looked at each other and sighed.

"Do you know what hospital they've taken John to?" Amelia asked.

I shook my head and relayed the question to William's table.

"He's at Fort William, but I heard some talk that they might move him to the hospital in Inverness."

A low humming sound, like a bumble bee on the other side of the room, barely audible, started up. At first it was so faint I thought I was imagining it, and then it got a little louder. Lettie stopped what she was saying and turned her head left, then right.

"Do you hear something?" she asked.

Alf Downes, at the next table, guffawed over something, drowning out any other noise for a second or two. The four of us sat silently, forks poised in midair, waiting for the other table to get quiet. There was a noise coming through the window. It grew louder, more insistent.

Someone in the party of six, the anniversary celebrants, proposed a toast, followed by loud hear-hears and clinking crystal. Then a persistent drone, definitely coming from outside the window, became too loud to ignore. Another toast at the anniversary table was cut short by a blare that sent William Sinclair scurrying to the window. He threw up the sash, opening the way for a blast so loud it vibrated the curtains.

"What the hell are ye doin, ye damn fool? Pipe doon!" William yelled.

The noise became a tune that sounded like a funeral dirge.

We all dropped our napkins and rushed to one or another of the windows on that side of the room. A lone bagpiper stood in the parking lot. In kilt and work boots, he advanced one step closer to the windows every eight bars or so. Over the top of the air-filled bag was a red face surrounded by an even redder mass of curly hair. It was Robbie MacBane, and the dirge he was playing sped up and morphed into "The Campbells are Coming," a call to arms if I ever heard one.

William, still clasping his dinner napkin, dashed out through the kitchen door and stood about six inches from Robbie's ear. He yelled, but I couldn't hear what he yelled because Robbie's pipes had by now reached the decibel level of a Concorde jet.

Several people retreated to the anteroom adjoining the dining hall, but the Downeses returned to their chowder, smiling gaily and waving their spoons in time to the music. I dashed through the kitchen and out the side door, mere inches behind Christine and Maisie.

"Haud yer whisht!" William yelled into Robbie's ear.

The cacophony died only when Robbie was good and ready. He bellowed through another chorus and squeezed out the last of the air with a sort of squawk. He threw the pipes on the ground and squared off against William, beet-red face to beet-red face. Having divested himself of his bulky instrument, he stood chest out, chin forward, and I saw the cartoon character on the front of his T-shirt: Spongebob Squarepants.

"Yer mither's turnin' in her grave!" Robbie shouted.

"What are ye talkin' aboot?" William's face showed total baf-flement. I felt sure he didn't know what Robbie was talking about.

"Ye know damn well what I'm talkin' aboot!"

Within a few feet of the two men were a number of items that might serve as lethal weapons if the men lost control, and it looked to me as if they might. The bagpipes could become a bludgeon, William's dinner napkin, a garrote. There was a lug wrench on the hood of William's Volvo. Weapons everywhere.

"Robbie, I don't think he does know!" I shouted.

"Know what?" William asked.

"Dinnae tell me ye dinnae get a copy of the letter ye made yer solicitors send me."

"I know nothin' aboot a letter."

I saw a chance to intervene. As the mother of four sons, I've learned a few things about boys and fights: Number one, boys don't usually want to fight, and if you can give them a way to get out of it with their dignity intact, they'll take it. Number two, boys almost always push before they hit. There'd be a shove to the shoulder followed by a reciprocal shove from the opponent. Number three, if the would-be combatants are seated, preferably facing each other (not side-by-side on a sofa; I made that mistake once), it's less likely they will come to blows, because doing so requires that they stand up, shove, and get shoved back, all before the first blow is thrown.

Where could we sit? My first idea was the hay bales outside the barn which was immediately behind the parking lot, but one quick glance in that direction showed me a pitchfork stuck into one of the bales. A lethal weapon.

"Men," I announced in my most authoritative voice, "I think I can help you both understand if you will follow me around to the front, please." With outstretched arms, I herded them off as if they were little boys getting taken to the principal's office. The steps to the big front entrance were flanked by low walls on either side. Obediently, the two men sat where I indicated they should, on opposite walls, facing each other.

"Robbie, did you bring the letter with you?" I asked.

"Nae, why should I? He knows what it says."

"I have no idea what he's talkin' aboot."

"I think he's telling the truth, Robbie." I turned to William and described the contents of the letter Robbie had showed me that morning. "If I recall correctly, William, the MacBanes have forty years left on a one-hundred-year lease on the farm."

"Forty-one," Robbie said.

"The rent is one hundred pounds a month and the contract states that it will never rise above that amount."

"And a contract's a contract, William." Robbie jabbed a pointed forefinger at his landlord.

"It's a license to steal, if ye ask me!" William planted both hands on his knees and leaned forward. I caught my breath.

"William, did you ask your solicitors to write that letter?" I asked.

"Nae. I know nothing aboot it."

"Then the solicitors must have done it of their own accord. Perhaps they're simply reviewing old contracts, cleaning out their files, you know?"

"Why would they do that?" Robbie fired back at me. "The contract's nothin' to do with them. They're just the ones that drew it up to begin with. They don't care if it's still in effect or not. We could make paper doilies oot o' it for a' they care!"

"Good point. What we need to do, then, is call and ask them."

"It's eight o'clock," Robbie said. "They won't be there."

"We'll call in the morning."

"Tomorrow's Sunday," William said.

"Okay, Monday." At least I had them both arguing with me, now. "If I may make one more comment, it occurs to me that your contract might, indeed, need to be reviewed."

"If the rent goes up, I'll go broke! D'ye ken what it costs to raise a Heelan coo? D'ye ken what I get for a ton o' barley?" Robbie waved an arm at me. Spongebob grinned goofily at me.

"Same as it costs me to raise a Heelan coo. Dinnae forget, I've got twenty head meself, and I get the same price for my barley as you do." William crossed his arms in front of his chest. "And I've got a castle to run! D'ye ken hoo much that takes?"

"Maybe you two could work out something that wouldn't involve money," I suggested.

"Like what?"

"I don't know," I said, searching my brain desperately for an idea, even a bad one. "Robbie plays the bagpipes beautifully and I know also he plays the violin."

"Fiddle," both men said.

"Didn't you say you play with a group, for dances and such?" I asked Robbie.

"Aye."

"Well, how about entertainment here at the castle? William's guests would love it, and if you did it for free…"

"Then we wouldnae have to involve the tax man!" they both said, practically in unison.

Give a Scotsman a way to beat the tax man and you've made a friend for life. My idea needed some work, but, at least for now, they had forgotten about the fight.

FIFTEEN

I GOT PENNY BUNS, I got chantarellies, I got blue...blue some-things. That had to be my starting point. It was, as nearly as I could remember what Boots had said when he took Maisie that burlap sack that I now knew had contained wild mush-rooms, some of which had ended up in our soup that evening. The soup had other mushrooms in it, since Maisie had indi-cated she added Boot's contribution to what was already in the pot, but I had to assume that those were mushrooms she had bought at a reputable market. Maisie had told us she drove to a market in Aviemore two days earlier. The day Froggy was killed.

I sat by the fire in the library this evening with my new mushroom book. Lettie and the Downeses were my only com-panions. Alf Downes walked around the room, his hands clasped behind his back, and studied the paneling in minute detail. I would have bet that he was making mental notes for a room of his own back in Texas. Eleanor had tucked herself up in an overstuffed chair with a copy of Robert Burns's poetry. She yanked off her glasses and looked up.

"Did Lord William and that bagpiper get their differences settled?"

"I think that's what they're doing now. I saw them leave, walking down the road together, right after dinner," I said.

"Where's Tony?" This came from Lettie, who was simply sitting, tapping her fingers on the arm of her chair and swinging her legs to a tune only she could hear. Lettie is short, 5 foot 1, so her feet often don't touch the floor when she's seated. She has the habit of crossing her legs at the ankles and letting them swing.

"Tony's gone to some hotel or other to talk to the parents of that young man who was murdered," Eleanor said. "At dinner he told us the parents are leaving tomorrow because the coroner hasn't released the body yet, and there's nothing much they can do here."

"The poor couple," I said.

"Tony said they would have a memorial service for him here, so all the students from the dig can attend. Most of them wouldn't be able to travel back to southern England, where he was from, and where, I assume, a funeral will eventually be held.

"That's why he had to go see the Quales tonight; to make plans for a memorial service here," Eleanor said. "Dr. John would have done it himself, but of course he can't."

"When you say here," Lettie asked Eleanor, "do you mean here at the castle?"

"I don't know."

I went back to my mushrooms, starting with the chanterelles because at least I'd heard of them before. The book had photos of chanterelles in cinnabar-red, bright yellow, bright orange, white, tan, even black. Their distinguishing feature seemed to be a frilly, trumpet shape, but not all were frilly and not all were trumpet-shaped. I had always heard that it was hard to identify wild mushrooms. Now I could see why. Chanterelles are edible and some are highly prized by gourmets, but another type, the Jack O'Lantern mushroom, sometimes called the False Chanterelle, is poisonous, causing gastric distress from a few hours to a couple of days. That sounded like a good candidate. Reading on, it got even better because the book said that, when freshly picked, the Jack O'Lantern glows an eerie green in the dark.

Penny buns, I discovered, were the same thing as porcini mushrooms which I had seen in stores back home, members of the boletus family. Pretty little chubby things, they are easier to identify than most, but not all are choice or even edible and some are poisonous. How was one supposed to tell? I decided that the penny bun must be a common name for the species that this book called the King Bolete, considered by many to be the best of all boletes. In the pictures it didn't look much like its cousin, the poisonous Red-mouth Bolete. I decided I could tell the difference if I found them in the wild.

Blewits. That had to be what Boots had said. None of the other names started with anything that sounded like blue. Latin name: *Clitocybe nuda,* aka, *Lepista nuda.* A fragrant blue or violet-tinged mushroom with white spores. A strongly flavored mushroom and one of the most highly prized of all. (That's what it said on one page.) A mildly flavored mushroom, not very tasty but quite pretty. (That's what it said on another page.) It can be confused with the Silvery-violet Cort, which was declared poisonous on one page in my book, edible on another. Then there is the Deadly Cort which has rust-colored spores and is…I turned the page…deadly. At last, something that made sense.

I thought about the mushroom caps I had seen under inverted drinking glasses on Froggy's desk. The police had taken them, but I wondered what color spore prints they made.

I shut my book. "Lettie, what are your plans for tomorrow?"

"I have no plans. It's Sunday, and the library is closed."

"Let's go to the hospital in Fort William. They might let us in to see John, if he's any better. And let's go for a walk in the woods."

SIXTEEN

IT WAS SATURDAY NIGHT and by eleven o'clock the camp was under the spell of magic mushrooms. In the center, around a dying fire, several kids sprawled or lolled, making sporadic observations about the color, essence, and true meaning of fire. Three large orange juice bottles sat on the tow bar of a small trailer nearby. They had been purchased specifically for this evening because one of the participants declared the taste of orange juice to be "effing awesome" if drunk while tripping on magic mushrooms.

Proctor Galigher sat on an upturned plastic milk crate with Tracee Wagg between his legs. She had both hands on one of Proctor's knees, her head on her hands, and her bare feet stretched toward the fire. Both of them stared into the flame, their unblinking eyes reflecting its light.

"Is my right arm up in the air?" Tracee asked no one in particular.

"No," said another girl. "Is mine?"

"What arms?" asked a third, with a small giggle. "You have no arms."

Proctor stood up. Tracee, her hands now deprived of support, toppled sideways to the ground. "I gotta move!" he said. "I can't sit still." He bounced like a boxer, ducking and weaving, out of the circle of campers and tents and into the darkness beyond. He did jumping jacks, he shook his arms, and he ran in a little circle until he staggered from dizziness. Then he looked up at the revolving stars, and tears ran down his cheeks.

Not everyone was participating in the magic mushroom party. Hannah Dunbar lay on her bunk in her little tent, reading by lantern light. Graham Jones merely watched the kids, circling the camp site occasionally, on the theory that, since he hadn't managed to prevent this from happening, at least maybe he could catch any who might wander off before they got hopelessly lost on the moors.

Someone called out, "Ready for the dry-cleaner bag light show? Come on in."

They all abandoned the dying fire in favor of the camper from which the call had come. Inside, a thin, plastic dry-cleaner bag, knotted at six-inch intervals, hung suspended from a coat hanger taped to the roof. Directly below it sat a skillet full of water.

"You're not gonna believe this." The young host indicated places to sit, until every conceivable spot was occupied. "We light this thing on the bottom, turn out the lights, and then watch."

"Wait! Let me get my black light. That'll make it even cooler," said Joyce Parsley.

"No! That'll ruin it. This makes its own light."

A lengthy but disjointed discussion as to the desirability of a black light followed.

Beyond the camp, all was quiet on the moor and along the dark road from the camp to the MacBane farmhouse. Other than a few little rectangles of yellow light from the farmhouse and the distant castle, the only lights were those of the stars and a faint glow from a village beyond a ridge to the north. The only sounds were the hoot of an owl, a soft burble from the stream trickling through the glen to the north, and the crunch of Van Nguyen's Nikes as he tramped along the road, head bowed.

A dozen yards back and, like Van, walking southward toward the camp, were Boots and his dog. Boots called out to Van, "What they got goin' on over here tonight? Sounds like a party."

Van turned, stopped, and waited for Boots to catch up. They left the road and entered the camp together, first stopping at the abandoned fire with milk crates and canvas chairs scattered around it. The door of the little overcrowded camper stood open to the cool night air, but Van and Boots stood back a fair distance from it. Pixelated ribbons of flame were falling from the camper ceiling in an orderly procession, each flame making a strange little *zooop* sound, followed by a *psst* when it hit the water in the skillet. Every flash illuminated the faces of a dozen hypnotized kids.

"What the hell?" said Van, pushing a long strand of hair out of his eyes.

Lucy, the dog, snarled and crouched down on her haunches, ready for combat. Boots grabbed her by the scruff of her neck.

From within the camper, Joyce Parsley jumped up, pointed out the door, and screamed, "You killed Froggy! You killed Froggy!"

SEVENTEEN

"YOU DRIVE, DOTSY." Lettie bounced out the door on Sunday morning, waving her keys at me.

"I haven't driven a stick shift in years and besides, you're used to these roads." I climbed in on the passenger side of the little Nissan Micra, making it clear that I was not going to drive.

"Maisie gave me some things to take to Fallon. Toothbrush, undies, stuff like that. Fallon's been at the hospital all night, you know." Lettie tossed a plastic bag into the back seat and took her rightful place on the right hand side behind the steering wheel. "Maisie's very thoughtful, isn't she?"

I agreed and looked down at the gear shift, which was on the floor between my seat and hers. As Lettie lurched backward out of the parking space and jammed the car into first gear, I noticed that it had to be done left-handed; extremely clumsy, I would imagine, for an American. Lettie, however, needed both hands to force the stick over and up from reverse into first.

"How many gears does this thing have?" I looked at the shift diagram incised into the knob. I'd never seen one quite like it before.

"Five, I think, but I only use a few of them."

"Five forward gears, plus reverse?"

"Yes, but I only use reverse when I need to back up."

We wound down a few miles of back roads and turned left onto Highway A86. From rolling hills, we passed into high hills and then mountains. This was the first time since our plane trip over that Lettie and I had really talked.

She told me that her son and his new wife were too busy career-building to start a family, so she had prepared herself for a few years' wait before grandmotherhood. Her daughter, Lindsay, had finished med school and was looking forward to her first year of residency. "And with any luck, Ollie will be able to retire in three more years," she said.

"I don't want Ollie to retire," I said. "If he retires, you may not want to travel with me anymore. What would I do without my traveling buddy?"

"Fear not. When Ollie retires, he won't want to go any farther than the nearest river. He'll spend all his time fishing."

"And you? Will you go fishing with him?"

"Occasionally, but fishing goes on for hours, you know," Lettie said, yanking the steering wheel to the right, to avoid hitting the left ditch. "I get antsy sitting around all day, waiting for a bite."

Of all the people I knew, Ollie and Lettie Osgood had the most stable marriage. They never questioned their total devotion to each other, and neither seemed to have anything to prove, so there was room in their marriage for both of them to be completely themselves. I was envious; not because my marriage had ended while hers endured, but because, even at my age, I still had no idea how to achieve such a relationship. Chet and I had never accepted each other as we were. At least, he never accepted me; I had always felt I had to prove myself worthy of him.

Lettie must have known in what direction my mind had wandered, because when I next tuned in to her, she was saying, "Are you going out with anyone, Dotsy? I mean, are you having any fun? You work so hard at your teaching."

"I'm having fun. My teaching is hard work, but it's fun, too."

"What about that sexy policeman you had in Italy last summer?"

"Marco?" I felt the blood rush to my face. "I didn't have him in Italy last summer. When you say it that way, it sounds like I had him for dinner."

Lettie giggled and reached for her map, which had fallen under the seat. I leaned over and retrieved it for her. A gradual increase in the density of road signs hinted that we were approaching something. On our left loomed a cloud-shrouded Ben Nevis, tallest mountain in Scotland, and ahead of us, the town of Fort William, on the banks of Loch Linnhe.

Lettie asked me to figure out how far we were from the junction with A82 and added, "You still haven't told me if you've heard from Marco since we were in Italy."

"He called me…and we exchanged Christmas cards." I didn't tell her how many times he'd called me.

I shook out the map and refolded it, centered on the Fort William area.

"Lettie, I have a horrible feeling about John Sinclair. Did I tell you what he said about 'If anything happens to me' the last time I talked to him? That was no more than an hour before the dinner where we all got sick. I felt strongly that he was saying 'Something will happen to me,' not 'if something happens.'"

"Are you saying the mushroom soup was deliberately poisoned?"

"I'm not saying that at all. I don't know what I'm saying." It made no sense; that someone would poison a whole houseful of people just to kill one of them. Too cruel to even consider. How could the poisoner know who would die and who would recover?

"Did you know that John and Fallon had a child?" Lettie asked.

"No, where did you hear that?"

"From Maisie. She told me that they had a little boy who died when he was eighteen months old. It was horrible. John, according to Maisie, gets so tied up in his work, he forgets about everything else.

"They'd been trying for a long time to have a baby, so when this little boy was born, Fallon was over the moon. They'd been married almost ten years. Anyway, John took the baby with him to a dig somewhere and left him in the car while he talked to some reporters. They even filmed an interview. It was on a local news show in Brighton that evening." Lettie shivered. "It was a hot summer day, and, while John was talking to the camera, the little boy was in the car, dying from the heat. It was so awful, Maisie said, because the TV crew left with their tape and took it back to the station before the child's body was found. So they showed it on TV that evening, like everything was all roses, but by the time it hit the air, everyone who knew John and Fallon knew the baby was dead."

I felt a knot forming in my chest. How many times have I, myself, come close to doing something that could have proven fatal to one of my children? How many nightmares have I awoken from, bathed in cold sweat? How fragile life is, especially babies' lives; it seems way too reckless of God to let us have them.

"Does Fallon blame John?" I asked.

"Maisie says Fallon doesn't act like she blames him. Fallon never talks about it, but you can't tell, can you?"

"Slow down, Lettie. That sign said 'A82, one mile.'"

Lettie pulled her purse from under her seat and scratched through it. "I have to find those directions to the hospital. I wrote them in my notepad." A pencil flipped out of the purse. Lettie stuck it in her mouth and continued her search with one hand while the other clutched the wheel. "Oh, dear, we've got a roundabout coming up. I hate these things," she said, the pencil bobbing between her teeth. "We have some back home, but you go around them to the right. Here, it's the opposite way. In fact, everything here is opposite. So I try to think of what seems like the right thing to do and then reverse it."

To push the clutch pedal down, Lettie had to straighten her leg and point her toes. She slowed for the roundabout, down-shifted, and turned right. A truck grill ballooned ahead, filling our whole windshield with the glint of metal. I heard a horn, saw a radiator cap, felt a tremendous bump. My head hit the roof as I heard a thud-crunch. The horn faded. Tires squealed behind us.

I caught my breath and looked around. We had hit a metal signpost. Lettie, apparently, had swerved to the left in time to miss the truck, driven across the curb, and onto the grass in the center of the roundabout. Our rear wheels were still on the pavement. I tested my neck and found it still turned both ways. Then I looked at Lettie.

"Ohmigod!" I said.

"Sorry abou tha," Lettie said. The pencil she had stuck in her mouth dangled out of it now, flopping against her lower lip. Blood was oozing out around it. "Wha are you ooking a'?"

"The pencil, Lettie! You've impaled yourself!"

Lettie leaned over far enough to see herself in the rear view mirror. "Aaaaghh!" she yelled. She started to grab the pencil and pull it out, but I remembered reading somewhere that you should leave any impaling object where it is and get a doctor. I grabbed her hand and pulled it away from her mouth.

"We need to get you to a hospital, right away."

"Ucky us, ass where we're headed, anyhow."

Cars in the roundabout were slowing to veer around us, but at any moment, one could hit us. *Should I drive us to the hospital or could Lettie do it? If she isn't in shock, Lettie could do it better, because she's used to this car and she wrote the instructions for finding the hospital.*

The decision was taken out of my hands by a policeman. He tapped on Lettie's window, took a look at her, and winced. By now, blood covered her chin and dripped onto her blouse. Lettie rolled her window down, but I did the talking. "We're awfully sorry, officer. We're visitors here, but I think my friend needs to get to a doctor."

The policeman shuttled Lettie into his squad car quickly and called back over his shoulder, "You follow us. Your car will still run; you've only damaged the bonnet. Do you have the keys?"

I nodded, but I didn't have a chance to tell him that I probably couldn't drive this car. He had already backed his squad car off the grass and pulled out, turning right, into the clockwise-circling traffic. To the right. To the right. To the right, I repeated over and over to myself as I started the motor, lest I make the same mistake Lettie had made.

The policeman drove slowly and kept his blue light blinking, making it easy for me to follow him. The hospital was close by, but a maze of one-way streets kept us from going straight to it. I made the whole trip in first gear.

EIGHTEEN

THEY TOOK LETTIE straight into an examination room within minutes of our arrival at the hospital's emergency room. I suspect they shifted her to the head of the waiting list because she made such a ghoulish sight, what with the blood and the pencil, and several youngsters were sitting there, getting traumatized. One buried his face in his mother's sweater.

I tried to deal with the insurance difficulties while Lettie was being treated. She had left me her purse, and I found the relevant cards in her wallet, but navigating the arcane world of health insurance proved too much for me. The ER would give us a bunch of paperwork that Lettie could take to her company back home for reimbursement. The intake nurse sighed and looked pointedly at the wall clock. I had to leave several questions unanswered for Lettie to deal with later. Meanwhile, I located the intensive care station and asked about Dr. John Sinclair. A nurse told me that only his wife was being allowed in to see him.

"Can you tell me how he's doing? I'm a friend and...co-worker of his." Co-worker didn't sound quite right, but it would do.

"He had dialysis treatment last evening." The nurse clicked through a couple of screens on her computer monitor and glanced at another nurse, as if for confirmation. "You can talk to his wife when she comes out."

At a loss for what to do next, I found a ladies' room and scrubbed a few blood spots off my shirt. I didn't want to leave the bag of toiletries with the nurses but if I couldn't find Fallon or get into the room to see them, I might have to. Perhaps, if I took the bag to the nurses and gave them a long, complicated message to deliver to Fallon, they might call her out to talk to me. I tucked my shirt into my waistband and checked in the mirror to see how obvious the wet spots were.

A row of plastic seats ran right in front of the door to the ladies' room. As I came out, my hand still on the door, I saw Fallon Sinclair and Tony Marsh sitting there side by side. They were facing away from me, Fallon's hand on the back of Tony's neck. I stepped backward and let the door close half way.

From my hiding spot behind the bathroom door, I heard Fallon say, "We have to decide. There's no sense putting it off."

"This is neither the time nor the place, Fallon. John needs you. When he comes round, he'll need you."

"He won't come round. He won't!"

"Then we have other decisions to make. What do I do with the dig for the rest of the season? We have twenty-five kids who've paid tuition. Most of them have sub-let their rooms at college, they have to get the credits they've applied for, and I don't know if we'll lose our funding."

"Bugger the funding!" Fallon spat out the words. "Bugger the dig!"

I opened the ladies' room door and walked out with what I hoped looked like surprise to see them plastered across my face.

"Fallon, there you are. How is John?" I gave her the bag of toiletries sent by Maisie and quickly explained why Lettie wasn't with me.

"John's kidneys and liver have both failed. They did a lot of tests yesterday and a doctor came in a few minutes ago with the lab results. It doesn't look promising." Fallon's face was a sickly gray and her eyes sagged.

"Is he in pain?"

"No, thank God. He's been unconscious since last evening."

"Do they know what's caused this?" I asked.

"No. Of course, he had that stomachache, but we all got that."

Tony walked around the row of chairs and joined us. "I asked the doctor about kidney or liver transplants. I thought that if those functions don't return, maybe transplants would be the answer, but he said John is too sick to even think of a transplant. First, he would have to get better."

"And a transplant is probably out of the question anyway. They'd have to do a tissue match," Fallon said.

"William is his closest kin," I said. "He'd be the one most likely to be a good match."

"William, like most of us, is Rh positive," Fallon said. "John is Rh negative. He can't get an organ or even a transfusion from an Rh positive donor." She stepped over to the nurses' station while Tony and I waited.

"John's not going to make it, Dotsy. I saw him," Tony whispered.

When Fallon returned, she took me by the arm. "Nurse says it's all right if I take you in to see him for a little minute. Will you wait here for us, Tony?"

I HAD TO TAKE their word for it that the man in the bed was alive. His eyes had sunken into a jaundiced face. The skin was stretched over his bloated arms, and his feet, protruding from the bottom of a sheet, looked like those of a water-logged corpse. They had him plugged into a maze of tubes and wires.

Fallon must have read the shock on my face. "Shall we rejoin Tony?" was all she said.

Tony was standing with a white-coated doctor when we came out. "No change?" Tony asked.

The question required no answer.

"As I was telling..." The doctor paused. Apparently he didn't know Tony's name. "I was saying that we would like to move Dr. Sinclair to the hospital in Inverness. It's a larger facility. We're primarily an acute care hospital here. Most of our business comes from skiers and hikers who take the short way down from Ben Nevis."

It was inappropriate, but a laugh slipped out of me when I pictured the "short way down from Ben Nevis."

"But we can't move him in his current condition," the doctor added.

"Do you have any idea what caused this?" Tony asked.

"None. The lab tests are clear that the liver and kidneys are not functioning, but why they've ceased to function at this particular time, we don't know." The doctor turned to Fallon. "Is he a heavy drinker, Mrs. Sinclair?"

"Yes. I've been telling him for years to cut down."

"The liver was probably in a weakened state already, and then perhaps a virus, something he ate, something happened, and it started a chain reaction. A snowball effect."

Lettie pushed through a stairwell door and waved to me. As she approached, the doctor took his leave of us and retreated down the corridor. I needed to talk to him. I tossed a quick "back in a minute" in Lettie's direction and scurried off, chasing the white coat.

"Excuse me, doctor." I tugged at his sleeve. "Is it possible that Dr. Sinclair is suffering from mushroom poisoning?"

The doctor stopped dead in his tracks and stared at me. He had sparkly brown eyes and a lively face. "Why? Do you suspect mushrooms?"

"We all had mushroom soup for dinner on Thursday evening." I explained who "we all" was. "The rest of us were sick that night and part of the next day, but Dr. Sinclair never did seem to come out of it. Of course, we can't be sure it was the mushrooms that made us sick, but I know some of them had been picked in the wild by the castle's handyman, and the illness seems to have affected only those who ate the soup."

"What were your symptoms?"

"Stomach cramps, vomiting, nausea."

"I know very little about mushroom poisoning, Mrs…"

"Lamb. Dotsy Lamb." I smiled and he smiled back. He had the most charming dimple on one side of his mouth.

"Aye. Do you have a minute? Come to my office. It's down the hall." He ushered me into a cluttered office and ran his hand along a row of hefty medical books. He pulled out one with a title that included the word "Toxicology," laid it on his desk, and turned to the index. I stood behind him awkwardly while he read. He hadn't offered me a seat, and I thought it might be presumptuous of me to take one.

"This is going to take me a while," he said, "but I can see that, with mushrooms, you could be talking about several different toxins as well as some psychoactive chemicals."

"You mean hallucinogens?"

"Aye. Magic mushrooms, they call them." He looked up from the book and winked at me. "The problem is that, within a few hours or a day, the liver will have altered most of these chemicals into various metabolites, that is, various break-down products. But the lab may be able to find these break-down products for us. I'll put them to work on it."

"Will it make any difference in the outcome for Dr. Sinclair?"

He led me to the door. "I fear it won't, at this stage. After two and a half days, what's done is done."

I went back to Lettie, Tony, and Fallon. I still didn't know the doctor's name.

"YOU HAVE TO DRIVE HOME, Dotsy," Lettie told me on our way out. "They gave me a pain killer and made me sign a paper saying I wouldn't drive for eight hours."

"How do you feel?"

"Fine. They had to stitch me up, and they said I was lucky I hadn't driven the pencil completely through the roof of my mouth. It could have gone right into my brain!"

"That beats damaging something you use."

Lettie gave me a playful jab. "What happened to that nice policeman?"

We were in the parking lot by this time, and I hadn't the vaguest recollection of where I had left the car. I sniffed the air for the smell of burning clutch, and spotted the little car under a tree, straddling two parking spaces. "Oh, right. What did happen to him? He should have at least written us a ticket. Shouldn't we pay for the sign we trashed?"

"Let's call them tomorrow and insist on paying."

By the time I got us jerked and lurched back to the A86, I was able to shift into high gear and relax. It was smooth driving for the next twenty miles. I pulled into a grocery before we had to turn off the main road and said,, "We need to get some waxed paper if we're going mushroom hunting."

"Let's get some bug spray, too," Lettie added.

Back in our rooms, we changed into jeans and sprayed ourselves with insect repellent. I put the roll of waxed paper, a carton of orange juice, and my mushroom book in a woven wood basket I'd bought at the grocery. The book said that if you gather mushrooms, you mustn't put them in plastic bags or they'll sweat and become slimy. It recommended wrapping them loosely in waxed paper and putting them in a flat-bottomed basket.

There must be some law or other that says if you look for any sort of thing, you find it all over the place. It's like programming your eyes to find all the orange shirts in a stadium full of people; orange dots pop out by the hundreds. If you think blue, you see blue. Seek and ye shall find, everywhere you look.

And so it was with mushrooms. I'd have sworn, before Lettie and I started out, that we'd be lucky if we found two or three, but we found some nice ones before we even left the parking lot. I spotted them growing out the side of the wire mesh around Maisie's compost heap beside the herb garden. My first specimens. I snapped two off and wrapped them in waxed paper.

While we tramped through the pasture, the sheep turned

their backsides to us as usual. Lettie laughed when I told her that was the sheep's way of making people disappear. At the edge of the woods we found a fairy ring of mushrooms—they looked a lot like the ones we had collected from the compost—and a strange yellowish growth on some sheep droppings which I did not collect.

"The mycelium is the main part of the fungus's body," I told Lettie. "It grows underground in a circle and every so often it sends up fruiting bodies around its edges. That's what mushrooms are."

"Are you trying to destroy my belief in fairies?" Lettie asked, her fists planted on her hips.

A vigorous mass of blooming heather lined a path into the woods. Beyond the heather, mossy groundcover gave way to bracken ferns and rocks encrusted with lichens. We followed a clear, apparently well-trod path, but it soon branched and intersected other paths. "Should we be dropping bread crumbs?" I asked.

Lettie looked all around. The trees were branchless up much higher than our heads, letting daylight in. "I don't see how we could possibly get lost, Dotsy. Not unless we stay here 'til after dark."

We found more mushrooms and more mushrooms; within twenty minutes we had a dozen samples in our basket. Most of them had an umbrella-shaped cap with rows of gills underneath, but some had cute little conical tops that looked like coolie hats, some had gills on the top, and some had caps like umbrellas blown inside out.

I had never seen chanterelles in the wild before, but beside our path we found some yellow ones and another type of mushroom that looked so totally phallic that Lettie blushed and hesitated to touch it.

"Go ahead, Lettie. I won't tell Ollie," I said, thumbing through the book for a picture of something similar. I found a photo of its twin. "It's a *Phallus impudicus*."

"I could have told you that," said Lettie. "Is it edible?"

I was forced to find a rock to sit on until I could stop laughing and get control of myself. Through my tears, though, I saw another mushroom that looked a lot like the chanterelle. It was frilly, yellow-orange, and it was growing out of a decayed stump. "A Jack O'Lantern!" I gathered one quickly, ripped off my jacket, and threw it over my head.

"What are you doing, Dotsy?"

"Looking for an eerie greenish glow."

"Of course. I knew that. And are you seeing a greenish glow?"

I closed my eyes for a few seconds to let my pupils adjust to the dark, then turned the mushroom over and over. No glow. Nothing. "Maybe it's not a Jack O'Lantern after all," I said, tossing the jacket off and grabbing a piece of waxed paper to wrap the mushroom in.

On the opposite side of the same old stump, there grew a cluster of a different type mushroom. Tan with thin stems and flat caps. Lettie knelt beside me and picked a couple of them as I wrapped and stashed the possible Jack O'Lantern.

"Drop 'em!" a voice from above growled.

I froze. Lettie and I both turned toward the sound and found ourselves staring at the barrel of a rifle.

Slowly, my gaze traveled up a pair of denim overalls to a plaid jacket, and I breathed again. It was only Boots, and he wasn't pointing the rifle at us. In fact, he had it broken and draped across his arm, the way you're supposed to carry a rifle.

"They be poison. Drop 'em."

I explained what we were doing and unwrapped one specimen to show him.

."Ye think I gave Maisie bad mushrooms for the soup, dinnae ye?"

"No!" My instinct cautioned against suggesting any doubt whatsoever in the competence of a man with a gun.

Boots put his rifle down and examined every sample in the

basket. "Then why the sudden interest? Maisie said ye went all peelie-wally 'til morn."

"I did wonder about what caused us to get sick, but mainly, we're exploring around to try out my new book." I showed him the book, wondering if he found my explanation plausible.

"Ye dinnae need a book! Ye need ta ken these woods. Like me. I've lived here since I was a bairn and ye cannae find a mushroom in these woods that I have'na seen before. But that book—" Boots made a derisive hiss with his mouth, and flipped my book with the back of his hand "—that book'll make ye think ye ken more than ye do."

"So how about helping us with these?"

Boots peered into the basket and pointed to the first mushrooms we'd collected. "Blewits. Good. More blewits. Chan-ta-rellie, verra good! This be stinkhorn." He held the *Phallus impudicus* under my nose.

"I think we can toss that," I said, dumping the foul-smelling thing on the ground.

He took a long time examining the yellow-orange specimen from the stump.

"That looks like what the book calls a Jack O'Lantern," I said. I showed Boots the photo in the book. He studied it a while longer and squatted down beside the stump, examining the ones that were still attached. He took the book from me and held the specimen beside the picture.

"Nae, this one—" he tapped the photo "—has different gills, ye see?" He ran a rough, cracked finger along the underside of the specimen. It took a minute, but at length I did see that, unlike the Jack O'Lantern, our specimen had branched gills. Other than that, they looked almost identical.

"The Jack O'Lantern is poisonous," I said. "Is this one, too?"

"Nae, but it has no flavor. I don't pick these. Noo, the one your friend here was aboot to collect; that'll give ye a stom-achache ye willnae soon forget!"

When Lettie got to her feet, Boots slapped his thigh as a signal for Lucy to hop to it and guided us around the woods with a running commentary on mushroom identification. If nothing else, I learned that Boots either poisoned us all deliberately or he didn't poison us at all. He knew the woods and its fungi so well, there was no way he could have picked bad ones by accident. Several times I checked my book's description of a particular species, only to find that Boots and the book were in agreement.

I started feeling woozy. My signal that hypoglycemia loomed. "I need to sit down and have some OJ," I announced, pulling my little juice box from the basket. Boots used his billed cap to dust off a couple of rocks for Lettie and me. Gallantry in the rough. Lucy watched Boots, not committing herself to a spot until she saw where her master was going to sit. My fingers itched to get into Lucy's matted fur with a good brush. She had some clumps that would have to be cut out, I was sure.

With a groan, Boots lowered himself onto a rock. He ran his hand across the stubble on his lantern jaw and sniffled. Boots's face had the texture of a dried apple and his ears had lengthened with age until they grazed the collar of his plaid jacket. He squinted at me as I tipped up my juice carton, but he made no comment.

"Has this place changed much since you were a kid?" Lettie asked him.

I waited for the wonderful surge of energy the orange juice always brought me.

"Nae, not the castle itself, or the grounds. From the outside, it looks the same as it did fifty, sixty years ago. Inside, they got electricity in every room, noo. Dishwashers, TV, computers." He turned and nodded toward the east. "The dig didn't used to be there, o'course. Used to be all barley."

"Did you know William and John's parents?" I asked. "Their father was named Roger, I heard."

"Oh aye." Boots tapped his temple with a gnarled finger. "Radge Roger, they used to call him. Nothin' much he wouldnae do. Now Fenella, their mother, was a beautiful woman. Not like a film star, ye ken, she was plain, but beautiful. Sweet natured. Pretty brown eyes. Reddish hair. She was a MacBane. She'd be Robbie's great-aunt. Nae, she'd be a cousin. I dinnae ken how ye figure it. Maybe third cousin."

"And after she died, Roger remarried?" I asked.

"Becky, they called her. Lady Rebecca. She had money. She was an actress in London before they married. Hung around with a fast crowd. Always gettin' her name in the paper. She was a beauty, too, but not like Fenella. Becky was the sort that made your eyeballs pop. She was film star pretty. She had these eyes, these…not blue, not purple…violet."

Boots tilted his head as if he could still see Becky's eyes. "She and Roger got along like cats and dogs. Whew! She'd always got her own way, ye ken? And Roger had always got his way, too. Neither one o' them had any practice with things not going to suit them. Roger had his way of doin' things. Same as they'd always been done, right? Men go fishin' in summer, huntin' in autumn, coos eat grass, women do whatever it is they do around the castle. Meals be there when ye be hungry, bairns be clean.

"Becky, she had parties. Big parties. Fancy folk from London come roarin' up here on weekends, sometimes stayed 'til Wednesday! Becky'd tell Roger what to wear, who to take grouse huntin' and how long to stay. Her friends talked about plays, art, books, things Roger had no interest in."

"One wonders how two people so different from each other would get hooked up to begin with," I said.

Boots shifted his rifle out from under Lucy's front paws. "After Fenella died, Roger was at sixes and sevens, so to speak. He had two little lads to raise, all this land to see to, and a castle to run. Plus, Roger never was too reliable, and bairns need washed and fed on a regular basis. Need somebody to make sure the nanny is doin' her job. Roger was the sort to go off for days at a time. I guess there weren't any lasses, hereaboot, for him to marry. He knew everyone from here to Inverness and they knew him. There were those as Roger thought too plain, or plain ugly, and those as wouldnae go out wi' him because their folks wouldnae let them!"

Boots grinned and looked at me, his watery blue eyes twinkling. "So he started to hang aboot in Edinburgh and London wi' a fast crowd. Folks wi' more money than sense. That's where he met Becky. Lady Rebecca."

"Where did she get her money?" I asked.

At the same time, Lettie said, "Did she really have a title?"

"She'd been married several times before Roger. Came oot o' more than one divorce smellin' like a rose, they said. Plus, she was a successful actress; came by some of her money honestly."

"And she killed herself?" I asked. "She sounds as if she had the world by the tail on a downhill pull. Why did she kill herself?"

Boots didn't answer immediately. He stroked Lucy's head. "She left a note. Said she couldnae stand it here, and couldnae go through another divorce."

"How did she—"

"Jumped." Boots pointed northward through the trees. "Over near the shootin' hut there's a cliff that goes straight from the woods down to the glen. She jumped off. They dinnae find her body for almost a week because she landed in a spot where the autumn leaves were fallin' and blowin' aboot. She was covered up. It took search dogs to find her."

"And Roger?" Lettie asked. "I guess he was devastated."

"Aye. I wouldnae ha' thought it, because they never had gotten along that well, in my opinion, but Roger was never the same after that. Crawled in his shell—"

"And finally killed himself." Remembering what William had told me, I finished Boot's sentence for him. "Did he jump, too?"

"Nae. He shot himself."

NINETEEN

LETTIE TOOK THE BASKET of mushrooms to the castle, and I walked with Boots to his little cottage at the MacBane farm because I wanted to check on Van, if he was around. Lucy trotted along beside us, her thick, matted coat flopping from one side to the other with each step. Boots still carried his rifle draped across his arm as he led me off the road and up the gravel drive, taking one long stride for every two of mine.

"If ye do find that lad, Van, make him tell ye aboot the party they had last night," Boots said.

"What do you mean? Where?"

"At the camp. Ask him to tell ye." Boots's tone of voice told me that he had no intention of telling me himself. He directed me off the driveway and toward a little stone cottage a few yards away. "Ye'll come in for tea, will ye?"

Boots sounded as if he was issuing a sincere invitation, not an obligatory one for the sake of politeness, so I said okay. He stamped his boots on the stoop and pushed the front door open. It wasn't locked. We entered a small hallway, so crammed with junk I had to walk sideways through the narrow gap between old magazines, odd bits of furniture, newspapers, and a stack of neatly folded clean towels that looked quite out of place.

In his kitchen, I sat at a wobbly wooden table covered with a red-and-white checked oilskin cloth while Boots put the kettle on the stove and a cellophane pack of Bourbon Creams on the table. He filled Lucy's bowl with fresh water and set it on the linoleum floor. Lucy lapped it up sloppily.

A large wicker basket on the table in front of me brimmed over with picture postcards. Hundreds of them. I turned over one of Hadrian's Wall and saw that it was from Wanda and Winifred Merlin, the weird sisters. I glanced toward Boots; he was searching an open cabinet for something, probably the sugar.

I slipped another card out from the bottom of the basket. It was a glossy photo of azure tropical water and a white sand beach, from someone I didn't know, but it bore a 1987 postmark. From the smudges in its lower corners, I deduced that this, and probably all the cards in the basket, had been thoroughly enjoyed. In this basket was a quarter-century's accumulation of "wish-you-were-here."

I doubted if Boots kept fresh lemons about, so when he asked what I took in my tea, I said, "Nothing, thanks," for the sake of simplicity. He brought out two mugs, dropped a tea bag into each, and poured in the steaming water.

"Would ye like toast and butter wi' yer tea?" Boots pulled a saucer of fresh creamery butter from his fridge, buttered two split scones, and popped them into a toaster oven. They were excellent.

"Back to the Sinclairs," I said. "What were William and John like when they were little?"

"Verra different. Hard to believe they had the same parents. William was athletic. He played football. He made a name for himself in the Highland games, tossing the caber, the hammer throw. Had a room full of trophies, did William. He set a record for the stone throw at the games in Braemar."

I knew he was referring to the annual Highland games held each fall in Braemar, near Balmoral Castle. The royal family often attended, I had heard.

"Noo, John, he was the bookish one. Dinnae ha' any interest in sports. John was his mama's lad, ye ken? William was his daddy's. If Fenella had lived, I've wondered if she would ha' always looked oot for John like she did. She tried to protect him from William and from Roger. Roger dinnae think John was going to turn oot to be all man, ye ken?" Boots glanced at me through his lowered eyebrows.

"Fenella's death must have been really hard on John," I said.

"He was never the same after she died. He was a wee lad, five years old, when she died, but it took away..."

When it became apparent that Boots didn't intend to finish that sentence, I said, "How did the boys respond to their father's remarriage?"

"William seemed to accept it. By that time he was aboot ten or so, and John, eight. It was John who never even pretended to like Becky. She was not his mother, and he made it plain she'd better not try to be. O'course, Becky had no interest in bein' anyone's mother, so that was fine with her.

"I don't think I ever heard John even speak to Becky. I recall him leavin' the room most times when she came in."

I thanked Boots for the tea and the lesson in mushroomology, and left by his kitchen door. From the general direction of the barn, Robbie MacBane tramped toward me. He had a chainsaw in one hand and a large metal tool box in the other. Having shed his kilt in favor of jeans, he was apparently back in farmer mode today.

"I want to apologize for my behavior las' nicht," he said, blushing.

"No apology necessary," I said. "It's understandable that you were upset."

"But I shouldnae ha' ruined your dinner."

"You didn't ruin it. Most of the guests thought your bagpipes were the evening's entertainment."

"I nearly blasted the napkins off the tables!"

I laughed and slapped him on the shoulder.

"I'm half convinced that William dinnae ken anythin' aboot that letter from his solicitors."

"I agree. I don't think he did," I said.

"Well then, who did tell them to write it?"

"No idea. Maybe John?"

"It's not John Sinclair's land. It's none o' his business."

"Are you still going to call them? The solicitors?"

"Aye, first thing the morn."

Robbie promised he'd let me know what he found out when he talked to the solicitors, and pointed me up the stairs when I asked if I could see Van. "Knock before ye open his door, unless ye want to get an eyeful," he cautioned me.

I PAUSED OUTSIDE Van's door until I decided that the strange sound filtering through from the other side was merely a human voice speaking a language in soft undulating tones. Short sentences followed by long pauses. Van must be on the phone to his mother, I decided, because mothers do eighty percent of the talking when on the phone with their children. I knocked.

Van, a little cell phone held to his ear, opened the door. With a toss of his head, he invited me in but continued his phone conversation. I recalled that Van had told me his family had immigrated to the United States at the end of the war. Had his mother never learned English? Van seemed to be at ease speaking Vietnamese, but then how could I tell if he was speaking it correctly or not?

His whole bank of electronic gizmos danced with blinking lights and flashing screens. On the other side of the room, Froggy's side, a microscope and a laptop sat idle and dark.

"Sorry about that. That was my mom," Van said, punching a button on his phone with his thumb.

"You always speak Vietnamese with your mom?"

"She speaks English, but when she's on a rampage, she flips over to her native language. She came to America with my grandparents when she was about eighteen. I learned to speak Vietnamese at home when I was little."

"What's she on a rampage about?"

"She thinks I'm waffling about coming home for Christmas."

Van was wearing jeans but no shirt, shoes, or socks. His long hair was wet, so I concluded that he'd recently showered.

"Put something on your feet," I said. "This floor is chilly."

Van put his phone to his ear. "Mom?" He scowled at it and thunked it against the palm of his hand. "That's funny. I thought I heard someone tell me what to put on my feet."

I lowered my head in mock humility. "Forgive me. It's a habit I'll never break." I glanced at Froggy's abandoned desk again. "Have the police talked to you since yesterday?"

Van sort of grunted and stretched out on his bed. "Nope. Maybe they've decided to get off my case and start looking for the real killer."

I relaxed a bit at this news. "Boots said something about a party at the camp last night. He wouldn't tell me about it."

"I ran into him last night when I was walking over there. We went in together but we didn't stay long. At least I didn't. Boots might have."

"What was it like?"

"Very strange. They were all in this one camper. Proctor's, I think. There was this fire coming down and making this weird noise and they were all just sitting there, staring at the flame with their mouths hanging open."

"You mean the camper was on fire and they weren't doing anything to put it out?"

"No, it wasn't on fire. I don't know what it was. It was more like some kind of bogus light show."

"Do you think they were on some sort of mind-altering substance?"

"Yep. I think that's a safe assumption." Van cupped his hands behind his head. "Then all of a sudden, this girl, Joyce. You know Joyce?"

I nodded. "Joyce Parsley."

"Well, Joyce stands up and points out the door, toward me, and yells, 'You killed Froggy!' and I 'bout freaked."

Horrified, I said, "Then what?"

"Then nothing. They're all sitting there like zombies and I said something like, 'Me? You're crazy!' and she didn't answer me. I definitely didn't want to go in there with her calling me a murderer and fire coming down and a dozen kids in lalaland. I'm not that nuts." Van looked at me and quickly averted his gaze. "So I split."

"And that's it?"

"That's it."

I filled him in on my trip to the hospital and told him that John was in a coma. "I don't know what's going to happen to him, Van. His liver and kidneys have both shut down, and his wife says he's Rh negative so the odds of a tissue match are slim. The doctor told us he's too weak to survive a transplant anyway."

Van rose up on one elbow. "What if he…no, that's selfish, I shouldn't say that."

"Say it."

"What if he dies? Would I be stuck here with no rent money and no tuition for next term? I'm counting on the money he promised me for putting this presentation together."

"Do you have anything in writing, or was this an oral agreement?"

"Oral. I mean, his wife, Fallon, she's a Cambridge graduate, and he's a college professor. I didn't think I'd need a written agreement."

"Perhaps you don't," I said, looking at the stack of open documents on Van's computer monitors. "What is this presentation for, after all? How far have you gotten with it?"

Van popped up from his bed and dashed to the wheeled chair in front of his keyboard. He slid the mouse around, clicking windows shut. "You want to see what I've got so far? Have a seat."

I pulled out the chair at Froggy's desk and turned it around to face Van's wall of electronic boxes. What he had so far amounted to fifteen minutes of photos with voiceover in places, music in others, and a couple of short segments with John Sinclair and with Tony Marsh talking about the dig and about Scottish history. There was a scene in which ghosts from the past—taped, I assumed, by some sort of double exposure process—walked through the current dig site. Neolithic ghosts in hides and furs, medieval ghosts in tunics and leggings, fifteenth century ghosts in their Sunday finery. A chill ran up my arms because this was so very close to the vision I had had the other day as I worked at the old wall. It was as if Van, or whoever had thought of this, had crawled into my head.

"Here's where he wants me to put in a picture of the coin you found," Van whispered.

This was followed by several segments in which the camera panned around the area of the MacBane farm, the road past the dig, the meadow, and the castle. It lingered longer on the castle than the other spots. The next snippet showed a hand-drawn map on which I could make out the castle and the dig site, but everything else looked unfamiliar. There was no narration in this part.

"This is about as far as I've gotten. I'm going to have to cut some stuff because Dr. Sinclair wants the finished product to run no more than twenty minutes," Van said, reaching toward the mouse beside his keyboard.

"No, wait! Don't click it off yet. I want to see this."

There was a hotel drawn on the map, as large as the castle in area, and located east of it so that the castle, the hotel, and the dig site formed a roughly equilateral triangle. The MacBane house was gone. The roads between the three places had obviously been widened. They had median strips!

The moors between the dig and the woods where Lettie, Boots, and I had walked an hour ago, had been renamed the Grimpen Mire. Shades of Sherlock Holmes! I was aghast.

"Whose idea is this?"

"Dr. Sinclair's. He drew the map. He said we'd put in a professionally drawn map later."

"He's planning to make this place into Disney World, Highland Branch. Oh my God! How awful!"

"Bogus. Yeah. I thought so, too."

"Do William and Maisie know about this? Is Tony Marsh in on it, too? What about Robbie? Has he seen this?" I waited for an answer but someone was knocking at the door downstairs.

Van called out, "Robbie! Get the door."

The knocking got louder; more insistent.

"Oh, crap. I better go down," Van said. He still had no shoes on. "I guess Robbie's gone somewhere."

I heard him pad down the squeaky stairs and I heard the front door open with a pop.

"Nguyen Van Duc? We're here to arrest you for the murder of Dylan Quale."

TWENTY

I DASHED DOWN THE STAIRS to see who was there and how many of them there were, but Van's tall frame blocked most of the doorway. Past his right shoulder, I glimpsed Chief Inspector Coates and a uniformed man I thought I had seen in the incident room back at the castle. "Now wait a minute," I said. "You can't come barging in here like this!"

"Don't, Dotsy," Van said, turning his head slightly toward me. "Let me handle this."

"What evidence do you have?" I spat out the words. "A Hawaiian shirt?"

"Be quiet, Dotsy."

Van said that in a tone of voice that sent me back up the stairs. I stood in his room and trembled with rage. Almost immediately, Van came in and fell to his knees. I knelt to help him up, but then realized he had not collapsed; he was merely looking under his bed for his shoes.

Dragging out a pair of huge Nikes, he rose and turned, the scent of coconut shampoo swirling around his head. He pulled on a sock while standing on one leg, fell to the bed, and tried unsuccessfully to twist the heel of the sock around to the back of his foot. He got it as far as his instep and gave up on it. Ripped it off and flung it against the wall. His trembling fingers broke off two shoelaces when he tried to make a bow. "Shit!" He swiped his cheek across his shoulder and said, "Hell with it. In jail, they take your shoelaces, anyhow."

I felt so helpless. I could see that it was taking a Herculean effort for Van to hold back the flood of tears behind his eyes. I wanted to help him tie his shoes, but that would have really made his humiliation complete. "What's your home phone number?" I asked. "I'll call your parents for you."

"No! They can't find out! No way! Dotsy, if you tell my parents about this, I'll—"

"They have to know, Van. You'll need a lawyer." I thought of how I would feel if one of my children was in this situation and going through it alone. "They need to know!"

"Pleeasse. Don't tell them." The look in his eyes forced me to promise that I wouldn't. For now, at least. His hair, falling like a shroud around his shoulders and bowed head, would need to be combed and tied back when it dried. But they'd probably take combs and rubber bands away from him, too. I pulled a shirt off the peg on the back of his door and handed it to him. Van looked confused, as if he was unaware that he didn't have a shirt on.

Outside the bedroom door, a uniformed man in a navy sweater and a hat with a checkered band stood silently. I hadn't noticed him before, but he might have been there the whole time. He followed close behind Van as they descended the stairs.

I watched from Van's window as they led him off, in handcuffs, to one of the two cars they had arrived in. Two uniformed officers and two men in suits. Who was the other suited man? He might be the Procurator Fiscal that William had told me about, I decided.

I pressed my forehead against the cold window glass and willed my tears to hold back a little longer. They drove off with no sirens or flashing lights, thankfully, because I hoped this wasn't being watched by the kids at the camp. They would've been able to see this far down the road, if they were looking.

I didn't trust myself to shut down all of Van's electronics, and, in fact, I didn't know how to, so I clicked off the open programs on his computer, turned off the two power strips into which everything seemed to be plugged, and drew his curtains.

"I'LL TAKE YOU in my car," William offered when I ran into him at the entrance to the castle parking area. He backed down the stepladder he was using to reach the top of a tall shrub with his gas-powered hedge trimmer.

"I can drive myself," I said, "if you'll tell me where they've taken him. I'd get Lettie to take me, but she's on pain killers. Did you hear about our accident?"

"Oh, aye. Maisie told me. You lassies need to take care; this is a different sort of driving for you." He folded his ladder and carried it along as we walked across the parking area. "They'll have taken him to the police station in Aviemore, I ken. Let me call them before we head that way. I'll make sure, so we'll not be wastin' a trip."

William stowed his hedge trimmer and ladder inside the kitchen door and stepped in to make the phone call. I waited at the door until he reemerged. "The lad on the desk said ye probably won't be allowed to see your young friend. Do ye still want to go?"

I definitely did, but I hated to take up William's time. He led me to his greenish Volvo and moved an armload of boots, jumper cables, and boxes of ammunition to the backseat to make room for me to sit. The car smelled of diesel fuel and hay. "Have you been to the hospital today?" I asked as I fastened my seat belt.

"Maisie and I are going there as soon as I get back. She's tellin' Christine how to handle dinner, but she hates to leave all of ye to yerselves. Can't be helped, though. We need to spell Fallon for a bit. She's been there since yesterday, and she needs sleep."

"Will you spend the night there?"

"Aye, so ye'll be at Christine's mercy for breakfast, too."

"Don't worry about us. We can take care of ourselves."

William drove past the woods where the shooting hut stood and beyond it to the low-lying glen. I looked back over my shoulder and saw the cliff off of which I had nearly tumbled to my death. From this side, it didn't look as high as it actually was because the trees and gorse bushes below camouflaged its base. William stopped when our narrow road intersected a paved two-lane one and turned right onto it.

"If John comes to, that is, if he regains consciousness tonight, I willnae tell him aboot this lad of his gettin' arrested. He doesnae need anythin' more to worry aboot."

"Oh, of course not," I said. "Do you have the same system as we have in the U.S.? You're entitled to have a lawyer, I mean a solicitor, present when you're being questioned?"

"Aye, and if ye cannae afford one, they'll give ye one."

"That's just it. Van can't afford one, and if it works like it does back home, the court-appointed lawyer doesn't always knock himself out to help you."

"They appoint a duty solicitor from a list of regular practicing solicitors. They're competent, I'm sure."

Competent wasn't good enough. I didn't want Van to be at the mercy of the merely competent. I wanted him to be represented by someone who would fight for him as if his own life depended on it. As I watched meadows and grazing sheep roll past my window, I realized that I was going to have to hire that solicitor myself. Could I afford it? No. Was I going to do it anyway? Yes. Maybe they'd let me put it on a credit card. I could take out a loan when I got home.

William pulled up to a boxy granite building on the main street in Aviemore. A big sign in front read "Police," and it seemed to me that Aviemore consisted of not much more than one main street with smaller ones leading off it. I really could have found the station myself, assuming that I could have driven this far without destroying the Micra's transmission.

A man I'd never seen before was on duty. When I asked about Van, he said, "Van Nguyen? We have a Nguyen Van Duc (which he pronounced Nooyen von Duck) we brought in this afternoon."

I was confused about which of those names was his first and

which was his family name, but this was no time to worry about it. "May I see him?" I asked.

"Are you a relative?"

"A friend."

"Sorry, but we cannae let him see anyone before he's been questioned."

Slowly, I dragged out of him the information that Van would be interviewed tomorrow morning and that he would be allowed to see a solicitor first. After that, he would, if appropriate, be formally charged.

William stood silently behind me until, through an open office door off the reception area, he spotted a man he apparently knew. The man beckoned to William with a subtle jerk of his head, an invitation into his office that obviously didn't include me. I noticed he took William's elbow in a familiar way while William, I assumed, explained to him why we were here. My common sense told me William would get a whole lot more information from that man than I ever could from Mr. Formality at the front desk. It was a matter of friend-to-friend versus junior officer-to-total stranger.

I scooted around the desk until I was as close to William and his friend as I could get without an invitation to join them, and tried to keep the duty officer engaged in a discussion about solicitors.

"I want to retain the best solicitor I can find to represent my friend," I said. "How might I go about doing that?"

"People usually ask around. Ask other people they know."

At length, he was persuaded to pull out a printed list of local solicitors and let me look at it. Perfect. I could kill a lot of time standing there, writing down names. Unfortunately, William stood with his back to me, about five feet beyond the office door, so I couldn't make out what he said, but the other man's voice, although conspiratorially low, was somewhat audible. By straining my ears, I could hear about half of what he said.

I fished a little notepad from my handbag and started copying names.

I heard: "The lad was wearing this Van kid's shirt when his body was found…know they had an argument…students at the dig told us…some girl he was shaggin'…stood young Quale up, they said…might have been still sweet on her…ticket for an American football game…"

At this point, I was pretty certain William's response was something like, "I'm the one who turned in the ticket." He may have also told him that I, the lady standing at the counter, was the one who found it because, without actually looking up, I got the feeling they had both looked my way.

I heard: "Aye, fingerprints all over…but I told Duncan Coates, I said… Right…I said, nobody buys one ticket… searched his desk, and what do you think we found? Another ticket. For the stadium seat right next to the other one."

I felt sick. Even with half the conversation missing, I had heard enough to know that they'd searched Van's room and found another ticket, obviously half of a pair. I needed to talk to Van, to hear his explanation, but at the moment I couldn't think of any possible one. I swallowed hard and forced myself to keep writing, or rather, pretending to write. I wanted the policeman to tell William about the fingerprints on the second ticket. That would tell the whole story, wouldn't it?

"He denied knowing anything aboot it," William's friend said as he walked around William and closed the door.

ON THE DRIVE HOME, I determined to find out how much William knew about John's plans for the future of the castle lands and whether or not William himself was involved, but I figured I'd better do it without revealing what I'd seen in Van's video presentation. I didn't want to be accused of starting a war between brothers if, in fact, William knew nothing, as I suspected he didn't.

So I broached the subject by saying, "How do you see the Castle Dunlaggan, say, fifty years from now, William?"

"Ach! An American question if I ever heard one. Americans assume a place will be different fifty years from now, but we Scots think more in terms of centuries. Fifty years is nothing."

"You don't see much changing during your lifetime?"

"Are ye assumin' I'll be dead in fifty years? In fifty years I'll be a hundred and…aye, you're probably right. But, no, I don't see much changin' as long as I'm there. It's my heritage, ye ken? It's my responsibility to keep it and to keep it up right."

William turned his head to the side window and was quiet. I imagined that he was composing himself lest he get too sentimental about the "auld hoose." I waited.

"I see the coos disappearin', though," he finally said. "I cannae afford to keep 'em, I fear."

"Oh, but they're so adorable! You can't get rid of the coos." William glanced toward me and chuckled.

AT DINNER THAT EVENING I had to kick Lettie under the table because the pain killers she had brought back from the hospital had loosened her lips to the point that she monopolized the conversation. It was only the Downeses, the Lipscombs, Lettie and me. Christine, with responsibility for the whole meal, was uncharacteristically subdued; she didn't yell at us once. But perhaps that was because we were all at one table, and yelling was unnecessary.

We exchanged all we knew about John's precarious condition, about Van's arrest, and about the car accident that sent Lettie to the emergency room. Amelia Lipscomb had gone to the hospital in mid-afternoon, and she reported that there was no change in John's state. I voiced the opinion that the police had arrested the wrong person for Froggy's murder, and the other five at the table reminded me that they had never met Van, and therefore had no opinion.

Brian Lipscomb raised his wineglass as if to propose a toast and said, "At least the police will have no further reason to keep their incident room in the round tower open. Perhaps now we'll be able to go for a shower without parading past the constabulary in our bathrobes."

"And perhaps now," Lettie said, "you won't have to 'assume the position' anymore." She threw her arms up and out in imitation of Brian's pat-down against his car on the morning the police searched our vehicles.

I kicked her under the table.

"What was that all about, Brian?" Lettie ignored the kick. Given the numbing effect of her pain pill, she may not have even felt it. She prattled on, making it worse. "They had you up against your car good and proper, didn't they? Did you say something that set them off? The rest of us didn't get felt up."

This time, I kicked her hard.

"Ow! Whaja kick me for, Dotsy?"

Brian rescued us before I had to haul Lettie out by the collar. "It was poor judgment on my part," he said. "That's all it was. I had brought some rather confidential papers from my office to work on while we were here. I'm responsible for protecting them, and when the police said they were going to search cars, I panicked. If I had stopped and thought first, I would have realized they'd have no interest in those papers. As long as they didn't confiscate them, no problem."

Amelia scraped the frosting from her strawberry cake and made a mound of it on the side of her dessert plate. "Dotsy, did you take a look at those portraits of Roger and Fenella Sinclair? Did you notice the resemblance between William and John and their mother?"

"Yes," I said, "but I wonder why there are no portraits of Roger's second wife around. Did you know he remarried after Fenella died?"

Eleanor Downes jumped into the conversation. "Of course.

Everybody knows he married Lady Rebecca Seton, of the London stage. A spectacular mismatch if there ever was one, wouldn't you say?" She turned to her husband for reinforcement.

"Terrible," Alf said, and a blob of frosting flew off his bottom lip as he said it. "Terrible."

"Sounds as if you know the whole story," I said, "Tell us."

"You know already that we're royal watchers, and that includes the people who surround the royals as well," Alf said. "The people who flatter them, party with them, dilly-dally with them…"

"Are you saying that William and John's stepmother had an affair with one of the royal family?" Lettie asked.

"No one knows what goes on behind closed doors, do they?" Eleanor said, taking center stage. "Or on the royal yacht, *Britannia,* either. But Lady Rebecca was a renowned beauty in her day. In the fifties. She was the toast of the town as they used to say. She had a string of husbands, each wealthier than the last, and she was certainly a guest on the royal yacht, usually when the wives of the royals and their guests were elsewhere. There was talk."

"Well, of course. You know the London tabloids," Brian said. "They always infer fire whether there's any smoke or not."

"In this case, there was plenty of smoke, wouldn't you agree, dear?"

Alf nodded and harrumphed. "Lady Rebecca, they said, had the most striking eyes, not really blue, but a brilliant—"

"Violet," I said.

"How did you know that?" both Downeses asked in unison.

"Boots, the handyman, told Lettie and me about her. He said her eyes were violet."

"Yes. Well, she and Roger Sinclair had the stormiest of marriages. Roger was the wild Scotsman, barely tamed. Lady Rebecca was the prima donna. Oh, there were stories! The servants had hiding places around the castle and they knew when to take cover. It all ended, of course, with Lady Rebecca's violent death."

"Boots told us she committed suicide. Jumped off that cliff on the other side of the pasture," Lettie said, nodding roughly eastward and out the dining-room window.

"Right. Her body was found, days later, at the foot of the cliff. But although they found a suicide note, there were those who didn't think it was suicide."

"Aren't there always?" Amelia said. "Whenever there's a sudden death, someone always cries 'murder.'"

Lettie volunteered to take the coffee tray to the library so Christine could get on with her kitchen clean-up. That didn't seem like a good idea to me, given the fact that Lettie was too woozy to walk straight, but she insisted she could do it. I caught Christine by the elbow and suggested she load the tray with something other than the Royal Doulton bone china.

As the six of us ambled through the Great Hall on our way to the library, I managed to pull Amelia Lipscomb aside. I wanted to clear up the discrepancy between what she and Mrs. Quale had told me. Froggy's mother had come to the castle specifically to see me, a person she'd never met before, and had not attempted to see Amelia, although Amelia had told me that Mrs. Quale had asked her to keep an eye on Froggy while she was here. That made no sense. Obviously, Mrs. Quale knew that Amelia was staying here at the castle. Why hadn't she asked to see her?

With anyone in the news media, I think the quick and dirty approach works best. "Amelia," I said, steering her away from the group, "Brenda Quale was here Thursday night. Did you talk to her?"

"Who?" Amelia said, then caught herself. "Oh, yes, Dylan's mother. I mean, no. I didn't know she was here." Amelia led me to a front window while the others walked on. A floodlight shone through the window, highlighting her sculpted cheekbones with silver. She stared out the window for several seconds before she said, "Okay, truth time. The fact is, I'm not here on holiday, as I said I was, and I've never met Dylan Quale's mother. I told you she'd asked me to keep an eye on him because I was pumping you for information. I was trying to find out what you knew about the financing of John Sinclair's archaeological dig."

"Why?"

"You're aware that I'm a news reporter, aren't you? Well, I convinced the station I work for to let me come here and see what I could uncover. John Sinclair is a professor at our local University, Worcester. He has too much money for an archaeologist. Digs are normally financed on a shoestring budget, with everyone involved paying his or her own way. Bring your own trowel, you know. But John has brought his own media man, a pollen expert, and at least fifty thousand pounds' worth of video and computer equipment. Where is that money coming from?"

"Grants?"

"Grant money is so tight, you're lucky if you can get enough to rent a tent."

"Do you suspect John is involved in something illegal?"

"If he is, I haven't uncovered any evidence of it." Amelia's pursed lips glistened in the floodlight. "Brian, my husband, is here because he didn't want me to come alone. The only way he could leave his office was to bring work with him and do it here. He has a laptop and a phone, so he's in touch with his company every day. That's why he had that flap with the police over those papers. He sneaked some very sensitive papers, dealing with radioactive wastes, I think, out of his company. He knew they wouldn't be missed since he's the only one working with them right now, but those papers are never supposed to be taken off the premises. He'd get in big trouble if his company found out he took them to Scotland."

"He was worried about you coming here by yourself?"

"Yes, but he should know by now that I can take care of myself. Perhaps, if we had children, he'd have someone other than me to worry about." She sighed. "Brian and I have been trying for years to get pregnant, but so far, no luck."

"I never had that problem, myself. I was like the old woman who lived in a shoe." That sounded a bit flippant, I thought, so I added, "Children always change a marriage. Sometimes for the better; sometimes not."

Amelia stared out the window as if she was debating whether or not to tell me something important. At length, she cleared her throat and said, "When I was a new journalist, barely twenty years old and recently hired by the Brighton TV station, one of my first assignments was to go to a dig out in West Sussex and interview John Sinclair. It was a hot day." Amelia paused, and my heart did a flop.

I knew what was coming next.

"I saw that he had a little boy in his car. A beautiful little boy. I did the interview. John Sinclair preened. Basked in the limelight. Boasted." She choked a little on that last word. "Such arrogance! It didn't even occur to me to wonder where the little boy was. I suppose I assumed Sinclair had left the child with someone. But the child was in the car the whole time. With the windows rolled up." Great tears ran freely down Amelia's face.

"You don't have to go on," I said. I took her hand in mine. "I know what happened."

"I didn't find out until we went on the air that evening with the taped interview."

"I know."

"That bastard."

LETTIE HAD POURED the coffee and Eleanor Downes was cozily tucked into her favorite chair with her Robert Burns poetry when Amelia and I entered the library. Alf Downes bent over a large world atlas, and Brian Lipscomb held Lettie captive with a lecture on the purity of the waters in Loch Ness.

I tasted my coffee, found it too cool, and poured myself a

wee dram of Drambuie instead. As the warming amber liquid slid down my throat, the doors swung open and William and Maisie slipped in, both their faces drained of color. It was Maisie who first found her voice, but it came out in a croak. "John died tonight. He's gone," was all she said.

TWENTY-ONE

I PLUMPED MY PILLOWS against the headboard and settled my back against the downy fluff while Lettie perched on the chair at my vanity table. Our basket of mushrooms sat on the floor by her feet. "Lettie, do you know the difference between cause of death and manner of death?" I asked.

"No, but I bet you're about to tell me."

"It's important. The cause of death on John's death certificate will probably say cardiac arrest, or renal failure, or something like that. I know this stuff because I saw the death certificate when my father died.

"That would be the immediate cause of death, but they have another space on a death certificate for underlying cause of death. In my father's case it was diabetes, but what would it be in John's case? Mushroom poisoning? Alcoholism? I don't know. I hope they do an autopsy. If it was the mushrooms, would any of the poison still be in his system? Would they find it in an autopsy?"

Lettie shrugged.

"Now, manner of death. Here we have five choices: natural, accidental, suicide, homicide, and don't know. What should John's death certificate say?"

"Accidental?" Lettie guessed.

"I think homicide, Lettie."

Lettie gasped. "You don't know that!"

"I don't know it for sure, but I can't forget what John said to me the evening of the dinner when we had the mushroom soup. 'If anything happens to me,' he said, and something did, didn't it?" I crammed a pillow under my armpit and rested on one elbow, facing Lettie. I wanted her to see how serious I was.

"But, Dotsy, he could have been speaking generally. He didn't say, 'If someone murders me.'"

"But you should have seen his face, Lettie. It wasn't a general statement. He expected something to happen to him."

Lettie and I unwrapped the mushrooms one by one and arranged them in a row on my vanity table. I asked her to recall where we had found each one because, according to my book, knowing the habitat helps in identification. Lettie is blessed with an almost photographic memory for details, so she slipped a piece of paper under each one, with "beside the path," "on a rotten log," or "in the middle of a patch of moss" identifying it.

"William called one of his lawyer friends for me this afternoon," I said, easing into what I knew would elicit a sharp response from Lettie. "I'm going to hire one for Van. I don't want him to be represented by a generic solicitor, so I made an appointment to meet with this guy in Aviemore tomorrow morning. Can you drop me off on your way to Inverness?"

"You're going to what?"

Stupid of me to think I could slip in "hire a lawyer" in the midst of "I need a lift" and Lettie wouldn't notice it. "This is something I want to do."

She took a step back and yelled, "How much is that going to cost? You're crazy, Dotsy! You don't owe that kid anything. If he can't afford a lawyer, let his parents get him one!"

"He doesn't want his parents to know. It's odd, but I think I understand how he feels. His parents have immigrated to the United States, worked hard to make a decent life for their children and they have high expectations for them. Van doesn't want to shatter their dream. Can you imagine calling home and saying, 'Hi, Mom, this is your son doing graduate work at Cambridge. Guess what? I've been arrested for murdering my roommate.'"

"If it was one of your own kids, wouldn't you want to know?" Lettie's voice was softer now.

I thought about that. Sure, I'd want to know. I'd hate for a child of mine to go through something like this alone. I'd want to be there. But I could also imagine my daughter Anne not telling me. Anne was the only one of my offspring I could possibly imagine getting arrested for anything, and for her, my breath was perpetually held. My four sons were pillars of their communities, but Anne...

"Well, wouldn't you?" Lettie repeated.

"Yes, but the decision is Van's, not mine."

Lettie fiddled with the mushrooms and their labels for a minute, then snapped her fingers. "Hey! Why don't you take the car tomorrow? I want to spend a day in Edinburgh. That's where the General Registry House is, where they keep the birth, marriage and death records. And I'd rather go by train than try to drive."

"Sounds sensible to me, given our experience at the roundabout."

"The train station is in Aviemore. I've already picked up a train schedule." In a flash, Lettie was out the door and back again with a small printed folder. "There's a train that leaves Aviemore for Edinburgh at eight twenty-nine. Could you get me there that early?"

"That'll work. I can be at the lawyer's office by nine."

"Oh, how exciting! I've never ridden on a train." She studied the schedule and decided she could take the return train that would get her back to Aviemore at seven-thirty. "Could you pick me up then?"

"Sure." I thought about driving to Aviemore at seven-thirty p.m. and realized that it wouldn't even be dark at that time. Assuming I hadn't worn the gears down smooth by that time, it would be no problem. "Would you look some stuff up for me while you're at the registry? Find out what they've got on the marriage of Roger Sinclair and Rebecca Seton. No, wait. Seton may not have been her last name at that time. Look for Roger William Campbell Sinclair. And find out all you can about the deaths of both Rebecca and Roger."

Lettie worked part-time at her library back home and was the best I knew at ferreting out information. With her memory, she didn't even have to bother writing down the names. "Will do. A man in Inverness told me they call this place the 'hatch-match-dispatch' building," Lettie said, and laughed longer than that joke deserved.

After Lettie left for her own room, I sorted out my thoughts by writing the day's events in my trip journal. Were John's death and Froggy's murder related? I couldn't see how, but the odds that they weren't, given the fact that I was convinced John's death was also murder, were long. Two unrelated murders right here, in less than a week? But I was at a loss to find a connection.

The connection, I decided, must have something to do with the dig. That was the only link between John and Froggy. Might Froggy have discovered something that John found inconvenient? Maybe Froggy's pollen study had thrown doubt on the ages of the three spots we were excavating, thus ruining John's plans for building the place into a tourist attraction. If John killed Froggy, who killed John? Maybe Tony, because he wants to take over the dig? Maybe he wants to take over Fallon. It didn't take a behavioral psychologist to see that something was going on there.

As for the people at the dig, there was Proctor Galigher, whom Froggy had turned in for plagiarizing. There was Tracee Wagg, who might resent Froggy for warning Van away from her, or for embarrassing her before the spring dance, although, in that instance, it was Froggy's friends who did it; not Froggy himself. There was Iain Jandeson. Ambitious. Very strange. That's all I knew about him.

And then there was Van. I had to find out about those Super Bowl tickets. If they were Van's, why was one lying in the stairwell here, shortly after Froggy's murder? If they weren't Van's, what was the second one doing in his desk?

What was going on at the camp last night? It hit me. Mushrooms! Psychedelic mushrooms. That would explain why the kids had been saying "shroom" to each other all that afternoon. There was to be a magic mushroom party that evening and they all knew about it. Who would have been their supplier? Were psychedelic mushrooms to be found in the woods around here? Did I have one before me right now?

I opened my mushroom book to the labeled diagrams and spent the next hour learning the parts of a mushroom and the terminology that mycologists use to describe them. As is always the case with any branch of biology, the specialists have to make up a five-syllable word for every little thread and do-hickey one might find on any sort of mushroom. I learned about asci and basidia and rhizomorphs. I learned about veiled mushrooms and cobwebby rings; about polyphores and slime molds and jellies and stinkhorns. Just reading about some of them made me sick, but I also learned that it was important to make a spore print of each specimen, and the book explained how to do it.

It suggested inverting a drinking glass over each cap to minimize air currents and it suggested setting the cap down on paper that was half white, half black so whatever color the spores were, they would contrast with one side or the other. I recalled the mushroom caps under glasses on Froggy's desk, and my eyes welled up with tears.

I had only one glass in my room and I didn't want to contaminate it by contact with something that might have killed John or made us all sick, but I recalled seeing a shoe box in the bottom of my wardrobe. I had to get down on my knees and scramble through the pile of laundry I'd been collecting since I got here. Towels, shirts, underwear, jeans. I really needed to find the castle's laundry room. I knew they had one some-where. I pulled out a brown paper bag that smelled musty and contained some sort of dark, mushy stuff. What the hell was it? Oh, yes. It was the stuff I had found in the cellar the other day. I tossed the whole bag into the wastebasket beneath the basin.

When I dragged out the shoe box and opened it, I found it contained a couple of sheets of black tissue paper of the sort they wrap new shoes in. I cut several strips of it using the scissors in my travel sewing kit and laid them on sheets of white paper that I ripped from my notepad. Voila! Half-black-half-white paper for making spore prints. I placed several of the mushroom caps, gill sides down, over the papers and set the empty shoe box over all of them.

I crawled into bed with my book and read until my eyes crossed, then got up and splashed my face with cold water. It wasn't simple. There are thousands of species of mushrooms and hundreds of them are known to be poisonous. But only a few of the poisonous species are really deadly and death by mushroom poisoning is a fairly rare occurrence. Many are hal-lucinogenic or psychoactive but there seemed to be more anec-dotal evidence than hard facts in this area.

The worst poisons, the book said, are heat-resistant chemi-cals known as amatoxins and phallotoxins. That answered my question about whether or not cooking would have rendered them harmless. It wouldn't have. The *Amanita* mushrooms included the species *phalloides* (Death Cap) and *virosa* (De-stroying Angel), both of which could kill you. But there were also Amanitas like the *muscaria* (Fly Agaric) and the *pan-therina,* which could fly you to the Land of Oz. So confusing. There was the Deadly Lepiota, the Poison Pie, the Jack O'Lantern (which looked and sounded harmless but wasn't) and the Deadly Cort.

When I found the section on the symptoms of Amanita poi-soning, I read it over several times.

There is a long latent period of approximately ten hours before the first symptoms appear. Then a period, lasting about one day, of nausea, abdominal cramps, and vomiting. Followed by yet another period of apparent remission. It is during this symptom-free period that severe damage is done to the liver and kidneys. In the last stage, the patient may lapse into a coma and death may follow. Patients who survive this last stage will often require a liver and/or kidney transplant.

Pharmacological treatment with large dosages of penicillin and/or milk thistle extract may be effective if started soon after ingestion.

TWENTY-TWO

I DELIVERED LETTIE to the Aviemore train station at eight twenty-nine to catch the eight twenty-nine train. I parked the car and walked out on the platform in time to see the train's automatic door close on Lettie's purse then slide open again when she yanked from the inside. As the door slid shut for the second time, a uniformed conductor appeared behind her, and Lettie threw her hand over her mouth in an exaggerated "Oops" gesture.

The Aviemore station was amazing. Over the platform, a white frame canopy trimmed in red looked as if it had been painted that morning. The whole place, preserved in the style of the early 1900s, was spotless. I allowed myself a five-minute rest on a varnished wood bench before heading on to my appointment with the lawyer I hoped to hire for Van.

His name was Edward Cross and he was an associate in the firm of Bobble, Bangle and Bede, Solicitors. Where had I heard that name before? The reception room appeared to have been recently renovated, the smell of new carpet mingling with that of morning coffee. Computer cables neatly encased in plastic ran along the baseboards.

I had been there only a minute when Robbie MacBane loped out of one office, his jumble of red curls slicked down today in a rough approximation of neatness, and I remembered where I had seen the name Bobble, Bangle, and Bede. This was the same firm that had sent Robbie the letter that he had interpreted as threatening his lease of the farm. It made sense in light of the fact that William had recommended Mr. Cross to me. These folks had probably been the Sinclairs' solicitors for generations, and, given the sparse population hereabouts, it might be the only multi-partner law firm between Fort William and Inverness.

Robbie crooked his finger at me as he walked past, so I followed him outside. "You were right," he said, closing the big oak door behind us. "This was all John's doing. Bangle says he cannae guess why John is so interested, but he says John came in a week or so ago and told him to go over my lease with a fine-tooth comb."

I caught Robbie's arm and stopped his progress toward the parking lot. "I have to stay close by. I'm waiting to see someone myself."

"So, the bottom line is, John and William Sinclair can do any damn thing they want. They can offer me some sort of incentive to give up the farm if they want, but if I refuse to leave, they can make up any bleedin' reason in the world why I'm an unsatisfactory tenant, and the lease is null and void. I cannae believe it. I'm their own flesh and blood! Sort of."

"You haven't heard yet, have you?" I looked deeply into his blue eyes. "John died last night."

Robbie turned more colors than a schizophrenic octopus in the next few seconds. Embarrassment, regret, relief, confusion—all flashed across his ruddy Scottish face. "I dinnae ken! I'm sorry. What did he die of?"

"That's still to be determined, but the short answer is, his liver and kidneys failed."

Robbie ran his fingers through his hair, returning the sides to their normal jumble of red curls. "Is there anything I can do? Anything I can do to help?"

"Do you know about Van's arrest?"

"What?"

I explained why his tenant wasn't in his room anymore. Robbie had assumed that Van was simply gone for the night, perhaps hanging out at the camp. He fell back against the granite front of the building, his gaze darting left and right. "They think he murdered Froggy? But why?"

I asked Robbie if he knew anything about some Super Bowl tickets and if he had heard quarreling between the two roommates. He could offer no help on either. "Also, have you seen the presentation Van has been putting together for John? It might have some bearing on why John had that letter sent to you."

"Nae. I dinnae go into their room often. I like to let boarders have a bit of privacy." Robbie said he wouldn't know how to turn on Van's computers or run the presentation even if he did. "But you say they've got him at the police station, noo? I'll drap by and talk to him."

"They won't let you see him. I already tried that. They'll be questioning him this morning and, after that, maybe they'll let him see visitors. In fact, that's why I'm here now. I want to get him a good lawyer."

"You? Why you?"

I tried to explain, but felt Robbie still didn't understand why I would put myself out for someone I knew so casually. Not that it mattered if he understood or not. I told him I would probably go to the police station later today and asked if it would be all right for me to stop by his house beforehand and pick up a few things from Van's room.

"I'm sorry, but I willnae be home until late this evening. I'm drivin' to Inverness to see me wife."

"Your wife?" I had no idea Robbie was married. Were he and his wife separated? Fortunately, he explained before I had to ask.

"Me wife and I are expectin' a bairn in aboot three months." His chest puffed out as he told me. "She's had two miscarriages before, so this time we decided she should stay with her folks in Inverness so she'll be close to the big hospital if there's any... if she needs to get there quick, ye ken."

"Oh, of course. Quite sensible."

"If ye need to get into the hoose today, Boots can let ye in, if ye can find him."

The front door opened, and the receptionist stuck her head out. "There you are, Mrs. Lamb. Mr. Cross is ready to see you."

Ed Cross was a soft, little man with gray, thinning hair, and his office smelled of old smoke. "I'm curious, Mrs. Lamb, as to exactly what your interest is, in this young man."

I was growing tired of explaining. "I have gotten to know both him and the murdered boy, Dylan Quale, through our work at John Sinclair's dig. Have you seen it? The dig?"

"The tent and such out by the castle? Aye."

"I'm convinced that Van Nguyen didn't do it, and I very much want the person who did do it to pay and pay dearly. I know that Van can't afford to hire his own solicitor, but I want someone who will protect his interests to represent him. William Sinclair recommended you." Flattery, flattery. William hadn't exactly recommended him. He'd merely made this appointment for me.

"I see. Can you tell me anything more concrete than that you're convinced he didn't do it?"

I was at a loss to offer anything more concrete than Van's lack of a sufficient motive to kill his roommate and ruin his own bright future. I filled Cross in on the Super Bowl tickets, the shirt, the nature of Van's work and Froggy's work, and the discovery of the body.

He scribbled notes on a yellow legal pad as I talked. At one point he interrupted me with, "You say Duncan Coates is in charge of the investigation?"

"Yes."

Cross's face didn't betray what he thought of Chief Inspector Coates. He scribbled some more, then placed his pen precisely alongside the yellow pad. After several seconds of silence, the only sounds soft taps from the receptionist's keyboard outside our door, Cross said, "Let me explain my fee."

It was almost obscene how easily the death of John Sinclair, leader and prime mover of the Dunlaggan dig, was accepted and overcome. By the time I walked into the tent, about ten o'clock, Tony Marsh had taken control, promoted Graham Jones to assistant director (Tony's own job until yesterday), and Iain Jandeson to site supervisor. Tony had already held a general meeting and told everybody about John's death.

As I entered the big tent, Iain Jandeson strutted across to the coffee urn, waved a finger at me and said, "You're on the church wall today, Dotsy. Grab a trowel."

The nerve! I'm almost old enough to be his grandmother and he's bossing me around like I'm some kind of quarry slave. Yesterday Iain and I were equals; today he's my boss. I considered the possibility that I might have to remind him that I was a volunteer and I could leave any time I wanted to.

Instead, I grabbed a trowel and proceeded to the site of the fifteenth-century church. Joyce Parsley sat, Indian style, on the ground at one corner of the wall, her trowel scraping along the bottom of a stone. As usual, she had her camouflage hat pulled down so low that I couldn't see her face. I dropped my kneeling pad a few feet farther along the wall and plopped down on it with an audible "Oof."

"I heard you had a magic mushroom party at the camp Saturday night," I said, deliberately giving her no time to make up a story.

"Who told you that?" Joyce dropped her head a bit closer to the ground, until her shoulders touched her knees.

"Van," I said. "Who got the mushrooms, Joyce, and where did they get them?"

"Why do you care?"

"Did Iain Jandeson get them?"

"No, Proctor did."

"Where did he get them?"

"How should I know? Maybe he picked them in the woods.

Maybe he got them from somebody else. It's not illegal, you know. It's not against the law to pick mushrooms and eat them."

Was that right? Were the picking, buying, selling and consumption of hallucinogenic mushrooms illegal, or not? It seemed as if it ought to be illegal, but I didn't know for sure. "Look, Joyce, be careful with that kind of stuff. You never know what effect it's going to have. It can be dangerous."

"Yeah, okay," she said, like a scolded child.

"And what was that light show all about?"

Joyce sat up quickly and turned to me, her eyes sparkling. "It was so cool! I wished Froggy could have been there to see it. You get this plastic bag, you know, a thin one like they use at the dry cleaners, and you tie knots in it every few inches, and you hang it from the ceiling or something and put a pan of water under it, you know, so you won't burn the place down, and then you light the bottom end of it, and it makes these amazing streaks of light and every time a blob of it falls, it makes this sort of 'zweeep' sound." She was fairly bouncing with excitement as she explained it to me.

"Why did you yell out, 'You killed Froggy,' when you saw Van, Joyce?"

Her face went blank and she turned back to her troweling. "I don't remember that. I don't remember seeing Van at all."

Iain Jandeson tromped by us. He pulled off his Aussie hat, smoothed his hair back and replaced the hat, squinting into the sun as he did so, as if he was deciding whether the sun should be moved to another part of the sky. "Back to work, girls. This isn't a social hour," he said.

I just stared at him.

Joyce, her back to Iain, flipped him a one-finger salute that only I could see.

"Iain, I need to get my good trowel," I said. "Is the finds shack open? I left it in there." This was not true, but I felt certain there would be at least one trowel in the finds shack and

I could say it was mine. Actually, I wanted to have a good look at the computer that Froggy used.

Iain walked me to the door and popped the brass padlock open with one of his keys. I looked around, spotted a trowel on the floor, and said, "Here it is." I bent over to pick it up and fell to my knees. "Uh-oh," I said, placing both hands flat on the floor, "I'm having one of my spells, I fear."

I stuck my hand into my jacket pocket and pulled out a little carton of orange juice. "I'm diabetic, Iain. When I forget to eat properly, my blood sugar goes down too far. I need to drink this and sit here a few minutes." Matching the deed to the words, I sat on the floor looking as spacey as I could.

"Are you going to be all right? Should I go and get someone to help you?" he asked.

"No, no. I'll be fine in a few minutes." I sat there staring at the wall until Iain got bored and left.

"When you come out, don't forget to get Tony, Graham, or me to lock up the finds shack," he said.

As soon as he was gone, I hopped up and ran to the computer. Someone was already logged on, so I clicked out of their document and considered how to log on as Froggy. The user name they had given me was dlamb, so I tried dquale. It worked. I got the screen that asked for a password. Now I was stuck. What password would Froggy use? Probably something clever, I thought. This could take forever, and I knew the computer only gave you a certain number of tries before it cut you off. Would he have been so obvious as to use "froggy" as his password? I tried it and stared incredulously at the screen. It worked. I was in.

With as many errors as one would expect of a woman not born in the computer age, I checked Froggy's recently used documents and files and then went online and checked the recently visited Web sites. I couldn't get into his e-mail because that required another password, and "froggy" didn't work.

Froggy had accessed a spreadsheet program, several word

processing documents, a large file of photos, a pinball game, and some sort of combat game. On the Internet, he had looked at several scholarly papers, all related to spores or pollen, a half dozen microscope and laboratory equipment suppliers' sites, and some more games. I was happy to see that Froggy had been a typical young man in that respect.

Then I found what I had hoped, or perhaps feared, I'd find. Froggy had accessed sites that dealt with *Psilocybe, Paneolus,* and *Conocybe* mushrooms. These were all hallucinogenic mushrooms whose names I recalled from my reading last night. He had read about the physiological effects of ibotenic acid, serotonin, and muscimol—all chemicals found in hallucinogenic mushrooms—and he'd visited one site that dealt with laws on the selling, harvesting and buying of magic mushrooms.

Joyce had told me that Proctor had supplied the mushrooms for the party, and I believed she was telling me the truth. Not the whole truth, though. Joyce was hiding something. I felt certain she did remember yelling at Van, but didn't want to discuss it now, in the sober light of day.

Froggy could have actually been the mushroom procurer. He could have obtained them and given them to someone who simply saved them until party time on Saturday night. Froggy would have been better qualified than anyone else to identify mushrooms from the woods, and I knew he had been out somewhere, collecting. There was a woven basket beside the desk in his room much like the one I had bought myself.

If Joyce was telling the truth when she said that Proctor was the mushroom man, Froggy might have found out what he was doing, researched it online, and threatened to tell John Sinclair. That might have gotten Proctor thrown out. That, plus the fact that Froggy had already turned Proctor in for plagiarism, might be a motive for murder.

From the finds shack, I walked the few feet to the main tent to locate someone who could relock the door for me. Tony and

Graham were seated at a table with a site map between them, unrolled and held flat with a couple of rocks. Tony was on his cell phone. He flipped it closed, looked toward me, and waved me over.

"That was Maisie on the phone. You need to run over to the castle, straightaway. The coin expert from Edinburgh is on his way."

"Oh, no! I don't know what to tell him."

"Apparently, when John talked to him last week, he gave him your name and told him to see you if he wasn't available. His name is Kenneth Owen. Dr. Kenneth Owen."

I dashed to the grass on the side of the tent where we all kept our backpacks and found my car keys.

"You have a car, Dotsy?" Tony asked. "May I ride over with you? I've left my own car at the castle."

Pulling out of the dig site parking lot added one more challenge to my already overtaxed driving skills, and I thought the crumpled hood was quite enough damage for Lettie to have to explain when she returned the car. Mud holes big enough to swallow the little Micra, at least up to its axles, peppered the lot like Swiss cheese. I had to steer around them while shifting gears with my left hand and remembering which pedal was the clutch. Tony, ever the gentleman, maintained a straight face and said, "Maisie has called a couple of local women in to do the cooking and see to the guests for the next few days."

"Very sensible. I was thinking about volunteering to help her, myself. Obviously, Christine can't handle it all."

"Maisie and William will have all they can manage with funeral arrangements and such. There'll be friends and family coming in, and people dropping by. Fallon has been on the phone all morning, passing the word along to the college and to their friends back home."

"It would be nice if we guests would leave until the funeral is over. We're just one more problem William and Maisie don't need. She should kick us out, or at least tell us to get our meals somewhere else."

"Maisie would never do that," Tony said as I swung into the castle's parking area. A woman I didn't know met us at the front door and told me I could find Fallon in the library. Tony asked if Maisie was around and was directed to go to the kitchen.

Fallon was on the phone. Pacing back and forth in front of the fireplace, she pushed her limp hair out of her eyes and kneaded the back of her neck.

I could tell she was exhausted. I waited until her caller hung up and said, "Fallon, I'm so very sorry." Such an inadequate, stupid thing to say, but it was the best I could do.

"I'm glad you're here, Dotsy. I can't deal with that museum man on top of everything else."

Fallon and I talked for a few minutes. She told me that she'd given permission for an autopsy and that the doctor had ruled John's death to be natural and the result of massive organ failure.

"I'm glad of one thing, Dotsy. He never regained consciousness after he went into that coma. If he had, he'd have been in horrible pain, so at least he was spared that."

"What happened to him, Fallon? Why did his liver fail like that?"

"Well, we all got sick that evening, didn't we? I think it's obvious. The rest of us fought it off and got better. John couldn't because he drank too much, and his liver was already half-shot."

I followed Fallon to their suite on the third floor. Four days' worth of clothes and towels hung off the unmade bed, the chairs, the dressing table, the lamp stand. Two or three trays of petrified food still sat on the floor and the top of John's dresser. I went to the closet and pulled out the big metal suitcase.

"Oh, that's where it is," Fallon said. "John told me he was keeping the coin in that old box of his, but he didn't tell me where he had put the box. Oh, dear, I'm supposed to know the combinations to the luggage locks, but I never use that big one. I've forgotten what numbers he used."

"Four-four-four," I told her, spinning the number wheels myself. "Four letters in the name John." The little treasure chest was inside, exactly as John had left it. "Do you have the key?"

"It's in the sitting room, I think."

Not exactly high security, I thought, keeping the box and the key to the box within thirty feet of each other. I followed Fallon into the sitting room. The sofa where John and I had sat on the only other occasion I had been in this room, caught my eye and made a lump in my throat. I could still hear him saying, "If anything happens to me, Dotsy, get this box immediately and take it to the Museums of Scotland in Edinburgh."

Well, that was okay. The museum was coming to us, today. Fallon scrambled through a couple of drawers but couldn't find the keys. "I know they're here," she said, pulling up the sofa cushions. She ran her hands around the inside and down in the grooves. I checked under the chair cushions, beneath the slip-cover skirts and then spotted a pretty lacquered box on a demilune table against the wall. I opened it and said, "Ta da! Are these the right keys, Fallon?"

"Wonderful! I don't know why I'd have put them in there, but I obviously did."

Fallon and I hurried back to the bedroom.

The box was still on the bed where I had left it, but it was open. And empty.

TWENTY-THREE

I COULD HAVE BEEN sick right there, but I didn't have the time. The door to the hallway stood slightly open, as Fallon and I had left it when we came in. To the best of my recollection, we hadn't completely shut it before I fetched the box from the closet. I dashed down the hall and into the square tower from which the only egress, at this level, was the one stairwell that extended all the way down to the cellar. Thanking the Lord for my rubber-soled shoes, I flew down to the second floor and peeked down that hallway. Deserted. All the doors along the hall, including the ones to Lettie's room and my own, were closed. Down again, to the first floor and into the room in which Fenella and Roger Sinclair's pictures still stared at each other. That hallway was also empty, but the library door on the right-hand side was open, I surmised, from the fact that a rectangle of yellow light poured across the stone floor and onto the opposite wall.

The only other doors in the portrait room were the two large ones leading into the great hall. I opened one of those wide enough to peek through and saw a gray-haired gentleman perched rigidly on one of the two huge Jacobean chairs that flanked the stone fireplace opposite the front door. Uh-oh. The coin expert; the man I least wanted to see right now. How had he gotten here so quickly?

I backtracked to the other door and into the west hall. There was an exit door on my left, the one out of which I had tossed my cookies the other night. I stuck my head out and looked up and down the west lawn of the castle, along the stone wall where Froggy's tarp-wrapped body had lain, and to the pasture beyond. Boots stood, doing something with a garden hose, at almost that very spot.

I called out, "Boots, have you seen anyone out here in the last few minutes?"

"Nae," he called back. "But a car pulled up in front aboot ten minutes ago."

That had probably been Dr. Owen, the coin expert. Hurrying down the hall to the library, I found William and a woman I'd never seen before. William motioned me in to meet her. She was one of the local women Maisie had called in to help. As soon as I made the mandatory comments about how glad we were to have her, I asked them both if they'd seen anyone else in the last few minutes. They hadn't.

Back up the stairs, this time via the stairwell in the round tower, and down to Fallon and John's suite again. The door was still open, and I found Fallon lying on the unmade bed, the open treasure box at her side. A tear had left a trail across her right temple and into her hairline.

"I've let John down. Of all things to get stolen, why does it have to be the coin?" She seemed too defeated to even lift her head. "Did you find anyone, Dotsy? Surely, someone… I mean, how did it happen so fast? There were four leather bands to unbuckle and the lock to open. And we had the key! It would take a Houdini to pull that off."

"Fallon, do you know what else was in that box?"

"John told me something about an earring someone found."

"Yes, that was in the box, and something else. There was a stamp. A stamp attached to a letter. John told me it might be worth as much as fifty thousand pounds."

She blinked and sat up on one elbow. "Incredible! Are you sure? He never said anything to me about it."

That rather fit my impression that John and Fallon's

marriage had not been that close. There was the death of their child; did Fallon blame John for that? I was pretty sure that she and Tony Marsh were having an affair. Had John known? Did Fallon know what John had had in mind for the castle property? I wished I had an hour to myself, to think, but I didn't. I had an important man from Edinburgh waiting for me downstairs, probably slapping his watch by now.

"I have to leave again, Dotsy," Fallon said. "Tell Maisie I won't be here for dinner because I'm driving to Fort William and I'll be back late."

"Will do," I said, backing out the door. "The coin guy is downstairs, so I'd better go and face the music."

I WAS EXPECTING to meet a fusty old pettifogger smelling of mothballs, so I was rendered temporarily speechless when the gray-haired man who stood when I entered the great hall flashed me a heart-melting smile. He looked a lot like Cal Ripken, Jr., with his buzz-cut, thinning hair and cornflower blue eyes, and he had wisely chosen a royal blue polo shirt to wear with khaki trousers. The effect was devastating.

"Dorothy Lamb?" he asked, extending me his hand.

"Call me Dotsy," I said, "but you'll probably call me something worse when you hear my news."

Dr. Owen raised his eyebrows.

Might as well get it over with.

"I'm afraid the coin was stolen not more than ten minutes ago." I then spilled out the whole story, ending with, "Has anyone come through this room since you've been sitting here?"

"No. A young girl with short brown hair received me and suggested I sit here until she found you."

"That would've been Christine. She must have forgotten to give me the message, or gotten sidetracked. Things are in a horrible mess here today, Dr. Owen. You've heard about the death of Dr. Sinclair, I'm sure."

"No!" The look on his face was one of genuine shock. "What happened?"

I needed to do a lot of explaining about the coin, about John's death, about why John had given him my name, so I suggested we go to the library where we could talk comfortably. On the way there, Dr. Owen asked me to call him Kenneth and explained that he had dropped by today because he had to go to Fort William anyway to scout out a couple of badminton players he hoped to recruit for his team. They had a seniors' tournament coming up, he said, and one of their regular players had had a heart attack.

I thought it was a bit odd that, although shocked, he didn't seem to be tremendously upset about John's death or the loss of the coin, until I realized that he may have never actually met John Sinclair and that it was we, not he, who had suffered the loss of the coin.

"Did you know John Sinclair well?" I asked, leading him into the library. William and the woman he'd been talking to were gone now, and we were alone. I indicated a chair by the hearth and took the one on the other side for myself.

"I met him once, at a symposium in Edinburgh. I remember we discussed some recent Roman finds from London but, of course, we had no idea at that time that he'd be calling on my services for a find this far north." Kenneth settled into the chair and threw one leg over his other knee. His white socks and a bit of hairy leg showed above his Adidas. "John Sinclair was a young man, wasn't he? I mean, younger than I am?"

Our conversation turned to coins and to medieval history. "Based on photos John found on the Internet," I said, "our coin appeared to have been Byzantine, and minted in 1040 or thereabouts. Do you think that's right?"

"Of course, that's why I wanted to see it, but from the photo he e-mailed me last week, it appeared to be a gold tetarteron minted in Constantinople during the reign of Constantine the Ninth."

"I can't help but hope that it ended up here because of King Macbeth's pilgrimage to Rome in 1050," I said. "I have a keen interest in Macbeth."

"Ah yes. A pilgrimage to Rome. Very possible." In stark contrast to Kenneth Owen's gray hair and eyebrows, his lashes were jet black which made it even more impossible to avoid staring at his crystal blue eyes. "Have you heard of the Via Francigena?"

"It was a route through France and through the Susa Valley into Italy, taken by pilgrims traveling from the British Isles to Rome," I said. "I know they traveled on foot, and that a king like Macbeth would have gone with a large entourage, staying in monasteries along the way."

Kenneth raised his eyebrows again and smiled. "This is your field, I take it? I can't help noticing that you have an American accent."

"I teach ancient and medieval history in a junior college. Yes, this is my field, sort of." I shifted in my chair and folded my arms across my lap because I had held my stomach in as long as I could, and I wanted him to think of me as thinner than I really am. "I've heard that when Macbeth was in Rome, he threw his gold around like King Midas or something."

"Perhaps, but this coin had to have been picked up on the Continent. Trading activity along the Via Francigena was intense. Pilgrims from the British Isles often came from Canterbury through Flanders and across the Alps into Italy. Byzantine coins were traded frequently, and it wouldn't be at all unusual for some of them to be brought back home. What's unusual is to have found one this far north. This area was the boondocks in the eleventh century."

"Would anyone from this far north, other than a king and his entourage, have made such a journey?"

He shrugged. "Who knows?"

"If this coin has been stolen by someone who plans to sell it, Kenneth, how much could they get for it?"

"Not much. Whoever stole it will be sadly disappointed because with no provenance, no documentation at all as to where it was found and by whom, it's nothing but a Byzantine gold coin; fairly rare, but the thief won't get more than a couple hundred pounds for it."

"What a shame!"

"Don't be surprised if you get a ransom demand. The only way to make this theft worth the risk is to put the screws to someone who understands its importance."

I gasped. I hadn't considered that possibility, but it made sense. "They'll be wasting their time if they put the screws to me. I'm tapped out this month."

As we chatted on, I had an idea. Since Fallon wouldn't be at dinner, it shouldn't be any extra trouble for the kitchen if I invited Kenneth to join us. He got up to leave, so I guided him back to the great hall and on the way I asked him.

"I'll be at Fort William for a couple of hours," he said, "and that's about an hour's drive from here, right? Sure, I can be back here by dinnertime. Thank you."

"Come to the kitchen with me. I need to make sure it's okay." We found Maisie and Tony sitting at the big wooden work table as three women plus Christine dithered around them. Tony had a sheet of scribbled notes in front of him.

Christine turned and yelled at me, "Mrs. Osgood called a few minutes ago. She said to tell ye she cannae make the early train. She'll take the one that gets here at ten-fifteen."

"So Lettie won't be here for dinner, either," I said. "Maisie, Fallon said to tell you she won't be here for dinner and now I hear that Lettie won't be, either. So is it all right if I ask Dr. Owen and a friend of mine from the dig to join us?"

"Two less, two more? That's no problem."

Tony looked up from his notes. "Someone from the dig?"

I ignored the question and shuffled Kenneth Owen out the side door. As we walked through the little mud room at the side of the kitchen, the room where the game, the unwashed vegetables, the muddy boots were dropped off before they messed up the kitchen, I remembered Lucy's reaction to this spot. The little Border collie had gone crazy over something she heard, saw, or smelled here and, since she was a dog, I'd bet it was a smell.

I led Kenneth around to his car, still parked in front of the castle. "Would you do me a favor, tonight?" I looked at him through lowered eyebrows. "If my friend from the dig is able to join us, would you flirt with her?"

"What?" He laughed and jumped backward, as if he'd been hit.

"I assure you, she'll be easy to flirt with. She's very pretty, and by doing so, you may help someone else come to his senses."

"Am I likely to get beaten up?"

"Not at all. The person who needs to come to his senses is quite docile, I think, and if I'm wrong, I'll protect you."

Still laughing, he drove off.

TWENTY-FOUR

VAN HAD HOPED his visitor would be Dotsy, but it wasn't. The jail was too small to boast of anything like a visiting room, with Plexiglas shields and telephones, and newcomers were simply taken down the hall to the prisoner's cell where they could talk through the bars while an officer watched, a few feet away. Van dropped his year-old copy of *Fish Farmer* magazine, his sole source of entertainment since they'd locked him up, on the floor beside his bunk when he heard two sets of feet approaching.

"I want my money, asshole," the visitor said.

"Fine, thanks, and how are you?" Van stood back from the bars, both hands jammed into his pockets.

"I'm not in the mood for jokes. I want my money."

"Well, you got me there. I don't have any. I don't have a watch, or a comb, or a pack of breath mints, because they made me empty my pockets when they brought me in."

"Where is my money?"

"In Seattle, Washington, most likely."

"Okay then, I want my tickets." The visitor hissed out the words under his breath, his gaze darting to the guard and back to Van.

"The police have them."

"Holy shit. Did you tell them?"

"No," Van whispered, turning his face away from the listening guard, "and I can't change my story now, or they'll think I'm lying about other stuff, too."

"You better hope you get convicted. That's all I've got to say."

"What?"

"We don't have the death penalty over here anymore, so you'll live longer if they convict you than you will if they let you out."

Van's face flushed and his jaw muscles worked furiously. "When I get out, you'll either get your money or your tickets."

TWENTY-FIVE

I DROVE BACK TO AVIEMORE and to Ed Cross's office as soon as Kenneth Owen left the castle. Cross told me he had sat in on the police's interview with Van this morning and that it had lasted more than two hours. It had ended with Van being formally charged with the murder of Dylan Quale.

"Van insists that he knows nothing about these Super Bowl tickets," Cross said. "But it makes no sense. The police don't believe it, and I don't believe it, either. Two tickets, for two adjacent seats in a stadium, for a sporting event to be held in the U.S. next February. One found in the stairwell of Castle Dunlaggan, only a few yards from a dead body, the other found in Van Nguyen's desk drawer in a room that, coincidentally, he happened to share with the deceased! Van Nguyen is the only person in sight, other than yourself, who comes from America and has any likelihood at all of possessing such tickets. It strains credulity, you must admit, Mrs. Lamb."

"Did the police mention fingerprints?" I asked.

"Apparently, the ticket found on the stairwell bears the fingerprints of everyone but the Dalai Lama, and the one found in the desk drawer has Van's prints and some fuzzy ones they can't identify."

"I agree with you, Mr. Cross. Van isn't telling the truth about those tickets, but that doesn't make him guilty of murder." I kept my hands clasped together on my lap, tightly enough that Ed Cross wouldn't see them shake. "Could we go over to the jail together and talk to him?"

"I suppose so," he said, as he rolled his desk chair to the coat tree and grabbed his jacket.

We walked the short distance down the main street to the police station. Crossing the parking lot, I stopped Mr. Cross with a tug on his tweed jacket sleeve. "Oh, look, there's a student from the dig," I said. "Assuming he's here to visit Van, I guess that answers my question about whether the kids at the camp know about the arrest."

Proctor Galigher loped across the lot, pointing a keyless entry device at a silver Quattro. The car responded with a little tweet. I couldn't remember for certain, but I was pretty sure the Quattro belonged to Hannah Dunbar, the pretty endocrinologist from the dig. I vaguely recalled seeing her climb out of it in the parking lot at the dig. Of all the students, Proctor was the last one I would have expected to see here.

"Proctor!" I called out, too loudly for him to pretend he didn't hear.

He turned and waved, then opened the car door and started to hop in, obviously trying to get away without talking to me. But I was too quick for him. "Have you seen Van?" I asked.

"I was checking to see if he wanted me to bring him anything," Proctor said. He closed the car door and started the motor, giving me no chance to prolong the conversation.

Ed Cross was able to gain entry for both of us into Van's tiny cell, while an attendant waited for us in the hall. I sat on the bunk and wondered how in the world one could get any sleep on it. It was like a concrete slab covered with a thin, woolen blanket. Cross elected to remain standing, and Van started to sit on the floor at my feet but I stopped him. "Don't sit on that floor. It's filthy!"

"Hello, Mom?" Van said, cupping his hand to his ear. "That woman's voice travels halfway 'round the globe. Amazing."

"Sorry, I can't help myself. Here. Sit beside me. Is there anything you need, Van? Anything I can bring you?"

"Some clean clothes would be nice, and some better reading material." Van kicked at the magazine on the floor. "Do you think they'd let me have my MP3 player in here?" He planted his elbows on his knees and glanced up toward Ed Cross. Van's black eyes seemed to have lost their sparkle.

"I'll ask before I leave today," Cross promised, then cleared his throat self-consciously. "Mrs. Lamb and I are both concerned about those Super Bowl tickets. Neither of us believes that you have no knowledge of where they came from."

Van flinched at the accusation.

"Look at it this way," I said. "Regardless of whose tickets they are or where they came from, it doesn't matter. Compared to a murder charge, those tickets mean nothing! I don't care if you printed them yourself. I don't care if you stole them from an inner-city boys' club. You're better off telling the police the truth because they'll find it out anyway, eventually."

Van looked straight at me, his eyes level and steady, as if he was getting ready to lie to me again, but then his face sort of melted. He dropped his gaze to the floor. "I bought the tickets for Proctor Galigher."

"Why didn't you say that to begin with?"

"I got them from a friend back home who can always get you tickets for anything you want. They're real tickets; not counterfeit or anything. Just not necessarily obtained legally. Those tickets aren't supposed to be on sale yet. Proctor paid me to get the tickets for him, because he wants to give them to Tony Marsh. Tony's supposedly going to Florida in February for some conference or other and he's taking a woman with him."

"What woman?"

"I don't know and I didn't ask." Van looked up at Ed Cross who was standing in the middle of the cell, his arms crossed, his face grim. "I hadn't seen Proctor between the time I got the tickets in the mail and when Froggy was killed. So when the police questioned me that next day in the tent at the dig, Tony was standing right there and Proctor was behind Tony, waving and making signs like, you know." Van made a "zip it" motion across his lips. "When the police asked me if I knew anything about a Super Bowl ticket, I didn't know they'd found one at the castle. I thought the tickets were both still in my room. I didn't know why the hell they were asking about it, but with Proctor and Tony standing right there, I said 'No.' "

"And then you felt as if you had to stick to your story, when they found the other one in your desk," Cross said.

"Yeah."

"Why did Proctor care?" I asked. "Because he wanted to surprise Tony with the tickets? Under the circumstances, wasn't it more important to tell the police the truth?"

Van waited a while before he answered. "Proctor was going to let Tony think he had been given the tickets for free. He didn't want Tony to know how much he'd paid for them because then it would have seemed like an out-and-out bribe for a good grade in field studies."

"But it was an out-and-out bribe, wasn't it?"

"Proctor comes from a rich family. He has a lot more money than brains. He mostly gets along by doing stuff like that, but sometimes it backfires on him."

"Like that plagiarized paper that Froggy read?"

"Oh, you heard about that, did you? Yeah, like that. He tried to bribe Froggy not to turn him in, but Froggy wouldn't have it."

"Froggy told you this?" I looked at Van closely and saw relief on his face.

"Yeah, Froggy told me."

TWENTY-SIX

As I DROVE BACK TO the dig, I rearranged my thoughts about
the Super Bowl tickets. I felt sure that Van had at last told us
the truth, and when I put myself in the place of a young man
being questioned by police, not knowing at the time why he was
being questioned, I began to understand. Already suffering
from a guilty conscience because of his illicit procurement of
the tickets, he would have been sitting there in the spotlight
while the Scottish police, one of his superiors (Tony), and his
partner-in-crime (Proctor) all watched and listened. I could
understand that he might have said to himself, *I don't know
what the hell is going on, so I'd better play it safe and do what
Proctor is telling me to do: zip it.*

This was my fourth trip today between the castle/dig and
Aviemore, and I was beginning to feel the glow of competence. When I reached the side road where I had to make a left
turn and climb the hill toward the dig, my foot slid automati-
cally to the clutch in preparation for down-shifting. Wow. The
little Micra and I puttered smoothly up the hill, past the
MacBane farmhouse, and into the pitted parking area beside the
tent. I steered expertly around the worst mud holes and braked
to a clean stop alongside Tony's car without even killing my
motor. Wow.

Joyce Parsley had moved to a new spot on the other side of
the church wall and was drawing a grid of an excavated hole.
Her head bent low over the big pad of graph paper resting on
her knees, she sketched with her left hand, holding the pencil

at an awkward angle. Both her feet rested in the bottom of the hole she was sketching and, as usual, her camouflage hat was pulled down low, hiding her face.

"I've been to the jail to see Van, Joyce."

"What?" Joyce looked up with a start. Her hat toppled sideways. "Why is Van in jail?"

"They've charged him with Froggy's murder."

"Oh, no! He couldn't have done it!"

"I agree, but I'm afraid the police think he did." Joyce could be very difficult to talk to, I'd found. She had a dozen ways to avoid eye contact and to sidestep unpleasant subjects. That hat of hers. She used it like an ostrich uses sand. At the moment, I wanted Joyce to come clean with me and, to do that, I needed eye contact, so I pushed her grid drawing aside, stretched out on my stomach, and stuck my head into the hole. "What's this?" I reached in deep with one hand and flicked a small, shiny flake of mica. "Oh, it's nothing. Never mind. Ever since I found that gold coin, I think every shiny object I see is another one."

Now that I'd forced her to put the drawing aside, I turned to face her, propping myself up with one hand on the edge of the hole.

I said, "Joyce, do you miss Froggy? I do."

"I miss him a lot," she said, her eyes filling up with tears. She swiped at her nose with the back of her hand.

"Froggy was very fond of you."

"How do you know that?"

"He talked about you," I said. Here, I was lying a little bit. Froggy had mentioned Joyce to me once, but all he'd said was that Joyce followed him around. He thought she was almost a stalker.

I remembered Froggy telling me, "At school, I saw her walking past my flat at strange times of day and night. She'd happen to be walking past the biology building when I was going in or out, and here, gosh, I've seen her hiding in the bushes outside my window!" Joyce, I thought, didn't need to know that.

"He talked about me?" Her face reddened. "What did he say?"

I mentally crossed my fingers and said, "He talked about how he considered you to be a good friend and he said he felt comfortable around you."

Joyce beamed.

"So when Van told me what you said the other night, when you saw him outside the door of the camper and yelled, 'You killed Froggy,' I said to myself, 'I bet Joyce knows something.'"

"No! It wasn't like that!" She grabbed my arm. "I didn't even see Van. I was yelling at that old man behind him."

"Boots?"

"I don't know his name, but he's the creepy, old guy who's always hanging around with that black-and-white dog."

"That's Boots. He works at the castle as a handyman."

"Okay, whatever," Joyce wrinkled her nose and looked out toward the moor.

"You're saying Boots killed Froggy? Why? What makes you think that?"

Joyce ducked her head again and muttered, "No reason. He just acts creepy."

I knew that wasn't all. Not by a long shot. I gave her a minute to reflect on how inadequate that answer had been, then tried another approach.

"When was the last time you saw Froggy, Joyce? The last time I can remember seeing him was at lunch that day."

"I saw him after that. About two or three o'clock, maybe."

"And he was okay then?"

"He was running."

"Running where?"

Joyce paused a moment and squinted past the dig in the direction of the MacBane house. "About two o'clock, I got tired of working so I took a walk down the road." She pointed northward with her pencil. "I saw Froggy come running out of the house where he stays. The MacBane house. He ran down the drive toward the castle, but he didn't see me and I didn't see where he went."

"Did you tell this to the police?"

"Yes." She glanced toward me briefly. "Of course I did."

"What was he wearing?"

"Shorts. No shirt. He was carrying a shirt in his hand, but he wasn't wearing one."

"Did he go into the castle?"

"I don't know. I didn't watch him that far."

"And you're positive you've told this to the police?"

Joyce flashed me a defensive scowl. "Yes. I told you I did."

"So where does Boots come into this? You must have had some reason for yelling 'You killed Froggy.' That isn't the kind of thing you yell at somebody just because you think he's creepy."

Joyce mashed her hat down lower, over her eyes. She dug at the stitching on her boot with her pencil.

I waited.

"Later that night…after dark…I was walking down the road again. I was about to the place where…there's a concrete slab beside the road in front of the MacBane house…I was there when I saw the geezer—Boots—walking toward me…from the direction of the castle."

"Yes, I think I know the spot." I recalled seeing the slab. It was cracked and weedy now, encroached upon by rhododen-dron bushes and pines, but I somehow thought it may have once served as a milk pick-up spot. Joyce was obviously having trouble telling me this story. She was admitting to spying on Froggy. From that concrete slab, one would have a clear view of Froggy and Van's bedroom window and a convenient thicket of bushes to hide in. "Did Boots see you? Did he threaten you?"

"No, he didn't see me." She cleared her throat. "There was a moon out. When I saw Boots, I saw something bright flash in his hand. It flashed in the moonlight. It was a knife. A big knife." Joyce looked straight at me and held her chubby little hands out, about a foot apart. "A really big knife."

"And you're sure he didn't see you?"

"Well, he might have, because he turned all of a sudden and headed off toward the woods."

"Which woods? The one between the castle and the MacBane house?"

"Yeah. The one where they have that old cabin."

"The shooting hut. Did you tell this to the police?"

"No. They didn't ask me about it so I didn't tell them. All they wanted to know was when was the last time I saw Froggy, and I told them about seeing him running down the road."

"Joyce, you have to tell this to the police."

"No!" She wrapped her arms around her waist protectively. "They'll say I was perverting the course of justice, or whatever."

"I don't think they will. Do you want me to take you to the police station?" I stood up and took her by the arm. "Joyce, if you could see the pathetic little jail cell they've put Van in, you'd do anything you could to help him."

As it turned out, I didn't need to make yet another trip to Aviemore. When we ducked into the tent to retrieve my purse, Joyce and I got absorbed into a conference with Tony, Hannah Dunbar, and Graham Jones. Tony explained that they were discussing the long-overdue memorial service for Froggy, but now there were two deaths that needed to be formally acknowledged.

Hannah asked me if I thought it would be better to have one service for both of them or have two services. "John's funeral will be Wednesday. The police have indicated that Froggy's body will be released to his parents soon, and they plan to have his funeral back home, of course."

"Won't most of the kids want to attend John's funeral?" I asked.

"I'm sure some will, but most of them have brought no

clothes appropriate for a funeral, and the church is going to be full to overflowing with local folk."

"I see. I, personally, would vote for two services, but that might detract from the significance of both mightn't it?" I imagined all the kids filing into the tent, two days in a row, a marquee outside announcing whose life was being celebrated. "Maybe one service would be better."

Joyce edged over to Tony Marsh and, pulling on his shoulder, drew his ear close to her lips. "Dotsy is taking me to the police station," I overheard. "I have to talk to them. Is it all right if we leave for a couple of hours?"

"Sure, but I'm on my way into town myself," Tony told her. "Why don't I take you, and Dotsy can work out these memorial plans with Hannah and Graham while we're gone? Dotsy, you're better at this sort of thing than I am; I'm putting you and Hannah in charge. Graham, you do whatever they tell you to do."

Before I could protest, Tony had steered Joyce out, leaving Hannah, Graham and me staring at each other. We decided to have one service. Graham would recruit volunteers to read or speak, and we'd ask around to see if any of them had any talent, like singing or whatever.

"Robbie MacBane is a musician," I said. "He plays violin, bagpipes, and maybe some other things. John was his cousin and Froggy lived at his house, so maybe we could get him to play."

"Lovely," Hannah said. "Perhaps he could play 'Amazing Grace' on the bagpipes."

"I'll run over to his house and ask him," Graham volunteered.

Then I remembered. "He's not home today. He's in Inverness visiting his wife. She's expecting a baby soon, and she's staying with her parents so as to be close to the hospital when the time comes."

Hannah shrugged as if to say, "Okay, what's plan B?"

"But he'll be back tonight. We can ask him, then," I added. In only a few minutes we had our plans well in hand, and I had jotted notes to remind myself to 1) pick up clean clothes for Van, 2) leave a note for Robbie asking him to play for us, 3) invite everyone at the castle to come to the service, 4) check back with Robbie later tonight to get his answer.

Graham went back to work, leaving Hannah and me alone.

"Hannah, would you be my guest for dinner tonight at the castle?" I saw her tense up. Quickly I said, "There'll be hardly anyone there, because of everything that's going on, but they have several extra hands cooking so there'll be plenty of food. I know that Fallon Sinclair won't be there and my friend Lettie won't be there." It was important that Hannah know Fallon wouldn't be there. Otherwise, I knew she'd never come. "And the coin expert from Edinburgh will be there. I want you to meet him."

"Well, gee. I'm too dirty to go to a nice dinner."

"You can run back to the camp and do whatever you need to do. Wait. How would you like to take a nice hot shower in a real bathroom?"

Hannah clasped her hands beside her face and smiled heavenward in a parody of ecstasy.

"I thought so. Why don't you pick up whatever you need from the camp, and meet me here at five? We can go over together."

I slipped away from the dig and drove to the MacBane farmhouse, where I found Boots in the barn. I wondered if I should talk to him about what Joyce had told me. I decided not to. If there was anything to it, I'd be tipping him off too soon. Boots took me around to his own kitchen door and picked a ring of keys off a rusty nail over the door frame. Why did they bother with keys? The nail might as well have had a big arrow saying "KEYS" pointing to it.

Once inside Van and Froggy's now-abandoned room, I quickly grabbed clean clothes, allowing myself no time to choke up, which I knew I'd do if I stopped long enough to look around. Van's bank of electronics stood as cold as the instrument room of the Titanic. On Froggy's desk sat the microscope, the slides and cover glasses, the empty drinking glasses (minus the mushrooms that I'd seen beneath them the first time I'd been in this room) and a laptop. It occurred to me that this computer would have another record of Froggy's work and online research, different from that which I'd studied in the finds shack at the dig. I wondered why the police hadn't taken it. I thought they always took computers, as evidence. Mental note: *Come back soon and snoop in this computer.*

NEEDING A LITTLE TIME to think, I drove the car to the castle, left it, then walked back to the dig. At quitting time Hannah told me one of the students had borrowed her car so we both had to walk to the castle from the dig. Hannah carried a backpack full of clean clothes and toiletries. It was a pretty evening, with a pink sky in the west, but clouds thickening in the south warned of approaching nasty weather. As we left the dig, I turned and looked back at the whole dug-up-and-roped-off site. Iain Jandeson was standing, shoulders back, hat in hand, at the summit of a small rise south of the excavated area.

Hannah's gaze followed my own. She grinned and said, "Beam me up, Scotty!"

I deliberately led Hannah to the castle by a longer route that took us through the cow pasture because I wanted her to show me where she had found that earring which was now missing, along with the coin and the stamp.

"Hannah, if they tested John's liver and other tissues when they did the postmortem, would they find traces of poison, if there was any poison to find?"

"Whatever are you talking about? Do you think John was poisoned?" Hannah came to a sudden halt.

"I don't know, but most of us at the castle had a bout of trouble, probably due to some wild mushrooms we had in a soup. And with all the different kinds of mushrooms you can find in the woods around here, I'm curious." I resumed walking, backward, so as to keep facing her. "And you are a doctor, so who better to ask than you?"

"Well, John was first taken ill, when was it? Thursday? Friday? And he died last night. That's two to three days later. By that time, most poisons would have been reduced to their metabolites, but in light of the fact that his kidneys had shut down, some might still have been present in some of his tissues."

"So the bottom line is?"

"I don't know for certain, but I doubt they'd find anything."

The pasture was carpeted more thickly with grass than I remembered. There were bare spots and occasional rocky outcrops but, by and large, it was lush grazing land. It occurred to me that Hannah had been extraordinarily lucky to have spotted the earring at all.

"It was right about here." Hannah stopped and kicked a clump of grass with her boot. We were midway between the castle and the woods. Almost exactly in the middle of the field.

"Was it lying on top of the grass, or down underneath?" I squatted and picked up a clod of soil. It crumbled and poured through my fingers.

"It was on a sort of bare spot. As I recall, there was a hoof-print where, obviously, a cow or sheep had stepped when the ground was wet. The earring was partly exposed, but an inch or two below the surface."

"So it had been there a while." Given the fact that these pastures were virtually never plowed, that might indicate the earring had been there for years. On the other hand, it might have been lying on the surface and the hoof of the animal that made the print could have pressed it into the soil.

"How much do you think it would be worth, Dotsy? I know nothing about jewelry."

"The amethyst was a nice, deep purple, as I recall, but amethysts aren't expensive. The pearls wouldn't have been worth much, either. But the setting was either platinum or white gold, I'm sure. It was a well-made piece. For a pair, I'd say maybe three hundred dollars? But with only one, could you sell it at all?"

"I doubt it."

"Hannah, was it an earring for a pierced ear, or the clip-on kind? I only saw it once, and I can't remember."

"Pierced. It had a wire hoop at the back, you know, the kind that hook at the bottom."

Ambling toward the castle, Hannah slowed her pace as if there was something she wanted to talk to me about while we were still alone. She picked a blade of grass, shoved it between her front teeth, and cleared her throat. "Is Tony going to be here tonight?" she asked.

"I don't know. Probably."

"Tony and I had been seeing each other for two years prior to this trip. In fact, we had talked about getting married."

This wasn't a total surprise to me. They avoided each other at the dig, and more than once I had caught a fleeting glimpse of pain as it flashed across Hannah's face. Tony's face looked exactly the same when he saw Hannah. Whatever else was going on, Tony and Hannah loved each other…I thought.

"I would never have come on this dig if I had known how it was going to be," Hannah continued. "We planned it and I applied for vacation time early in the summer. Then I discovered that Tony and Fallon Sinclair were having an affair. I broke up with him, but he came back, swearing it was all over and begging me to go ahead with this trip. He said with me staying at the camp and him staying at the castle, I could get away from him any time I wanted to, so if it didn't work out, I wouldn't be stuck sharing a place with him. He promised that Fallon wouldn't be here. He told me she hated the Highlands, hated the dig, and would never consent to live for six weeks in that drafty old castle. But guess what? Sheeee's here! I guess Tony didn't count on the strong attraction of his own sweet self. She was willing to brave the drafts, the mud, and the absence of stores, all for a chance to grab Tony whenever John wasn't looking!"

"How awful! Why didn't you go back home when you found out?"

"Believe me, I'd have loved to, but I've sublet my flat for the duration, I have no place to go home to."

"I bet you'd like to strangle Tony. Do you want me to help you? I know some places in the castle where we could hide the body and it wouldn't be found for years." I glanced toward Hannah and smiled.

"At first I wanted to kill him, yes. But, stupid as it sounds, I sort of understand. Fallon made it clear to Tony that if he dumps her, she'd tell John about the affair. John would've immediately severed all ties to Tony, of course. I don't know what he'd have done about Fallon. And Tony considered his partnership with John to be his ticket to recognition in archaeological circles."

"But even so, that doesn't excuse it." We had reached the stone wall of the castle's parking area. I set my lunch bag on top of the wall and showed Hannah how to scale it by using the uneven stones for toeholds, but she pulled it off with grace, whereas I did it with a groan and an "Oof."

We trudged around to the front entrance. Kenneth Owen's car wasn't there yet, and I hoped he wouldn't forget his promise to come back for dinner. Before I opened the door, which at this time of day was left unlocked, Hannah whispered, "Fallon is a widow, now. I wonder how that's going to play out."

I didn't say it, but I thought, *If I were you, Hannah, I wouldn't give a flying rip how it plays out! I'd move on and let her have him.*

TWENTY-SEVEN

KENNETH OWEN'S PERFORMANCE was Oscar-worthy. Of course, as I had told him, Hannah was easy to flirt with but, without overdoing it, he made it obvious to Tony that Hannah was the most irresistible woman he'd ever seen. Hannah had washed her short wavy hair in the shower and it had dried, fluffy and shiny, all by itself. She wore a blue and magenta crinkle cotton skirt with a belted blue tunic sweater. On our way down to dinner, Hannah apologized for using up all the hot water. "It took such a long time to scrub off all the layers of dirt," she said, "I do hope I haven't clogged up the drain."

I now had several important pieces of information and I had to decide whether or not to mention each of them at dinner. I might, if I did, catch each person's reaction to the news and see if it was, indeed, news to them or if they already knew about it. If I kept my mouth shut, the dinner conversation would probably tell me something about who knew what and who had told them. Fallon had supposedly left for Fort William shortly after I had last seen her, lying on the bed beside the empty box. Had she told anyone about the theft before she left? I had told no one, as yet, about Joyce's story of Boots and the knife, nor had I told anyone that I now knew where the Super Bowl tickets had come from. I decided to say nothing, and to try to find out more about Boots from William and Maisie.

I made drinks for Hannah and Kenneth, signed the sheet putting their drinks on my tab, and drew Tony into the conversation which, naturally, was about medieval coinage. The actual words bandied about like shuttlecocks were scholarly and polite, but the glances, the body language, the nervous fiddling with soaked paper napkins wrapped around quivering glasses, was wondrous to behold. I loved it. I sneaked away and sought out Maisie and William.

"The Downeses are leavin' tomorrow," Maisie said. "I'll miss them. They've been a bright spot in an otherwise terrible week."

"Aye," William said. "I'll not soon forget Alf wavin' his spoon to Robbie MacBane's bagpipes. The rest of us were horrified, but he thought it great fun."

"And I'll miss bein' called Lady Maisie. Made me feel right royal, they did. But the Merlin sisters are comin' back, the morn. Comin' for the funeral."

Changing the subject abruptly, I said, "I saw Boots this afternoon and he seemed rather odd, as if he didn't want to talk to me. I thought perhaps he was grieving. Were he and John very close?"

William and Maisie looked at each other. Maisie said, "I dinnae ken I've ever seen them together, really."

"Boots and John were not close, not at all," William said. "When John and I were lads, Boots would take me fishin' and huntin', but John wasna interested. Boots used to make sport of John's bookishness. I had tae tell him, more than once, to lay off because he was hurtin' John's feelins." William paused and looked around the room. Then he leaned toward me. "And I can tell ye right noo, Boots hates that dig," he said, lowering his voice to barely audible. "Calls it a boil on the bonny arse of Dunlaggan!"

Tony, Hannah, Kenneth, and I made a foursome for dinner. I made a point of sitting across from Tony, the better to see his reactions. Kenneth did it right. Not too familiar and never crass, he teased, flattered, and extolled Hannah's charms, occasionally touching her hand across the table.

Tony told us he had spent the day on a rat's nest of red tape and paperwork. Worcester University, unfortunately, was updating payroll today of all days. He'd had to tell them of John's death, and of his own assumption of the duties of director, pending a permanent appointment by the department. Graham Jones, he had suggested, should be elevated to assistant director, a paid position, and Iain Jandeson should now be entitled to the assistantship formerly claimed by Graham. This, Tony said, would be a godsend for Iain, who was working his way through school with no help from home.

"And then, just to make things a complete mess," Tony said, "we couldn't find any record of Iain's being a student at all! I told the woman, 'Iain has attended Worcester University for four years; what do you mean, he's not a student!' It turned out that Iain has changed his name since he first enrolled. His surname used to be Jameson, and he spelled his Christian name without the extra 'i' "

"Why did he do that, I wonder?" I said.

"Iain is a strange bird," Hannah said.

Kenneth smiled seductively at her and Tony scowled.

AFTER DINNER, Kenneth volunteered to drive Hannah to her camp, but Tony butted in with, "I'm driving over there now anyway, Hannah. I'll take you." Hannah smiled sweetly at Kenneth as Tony scooped her into his old Renault.

When they drove off, leaving Kenneth and me in the darkening parking lot, I had a moment's pause. Was this really a good idea? Wouldn't Hannah be better off to stay away from Tony? Oh well, I had already meddled, hadn't I? I tapped Kenneth on the arm and said, "You were perfect! Now, don't try to tell me you haven't used those lines before."

"You were right, Dotsy. She was not hard to flirt with; she's a beautiful woman. Young enough to be my daughter, probably, but lovely. Do you want to tell me what that was all about?"

"Not really. It's simply that Tony Marsh needed a dose of

his own medicine, and I hope Hannah makes him drink about a gallon of cod liver oil."

"Unfortunately, flirting with Hannah kept me from flirting with you at dinner, and I'd rather have been doing that."

I was so glad for the darkness. I felt the blood rise through my neck and into my cheeks, "I'm sorry I couldn't show you the coin today, but if it turns up, I'll call you."

"Why don't you call me anyway? How long are you going to be here?"

"Lettie and I plan to leave here on Friday, and then we'll take two days driving back to London. We fly out of Heathrow next Monday morning."

"Could you plan to spend Friday or Saturday night in Edinburgh? There are a number of things at the museum that you should see, and I could take you and your friend out to dinner."

"Thank you, Kenneth." My heart was pounding so hard I was afraid it was fluttering my blouse. "I'll check with Lettie and give you a call."

I DROPPED OFF Van's clothes at the police station on my way to the train depot to pick up Lettie. The dashboard clock read 11:00 p.m. as the sleek ScotRail train whooshed in and stopped with a slight metallic screech. The doors on the platform side slid open and Lettie stepped off with a double armload of papers and shopping bags. I hurried around to the platform and past a few exiting travelers to help her with her burden.

"I got so much info, Dotsy! You owe me a month's salary for the photocopies I had to make."

"It looks like you also did a little shopping."

While I drove back to Dunlaggan, Lettie tried to show me some newspaper articles she had photocopied, but it was too dark in the car to see them so I filled her in on my visit to the jail, the disappearance of the coin, Joyce Parsley's claim that it was Boots, not Van, who had killed Froggy, and my evening with Hannah, Tony, and Kenneth, the coin expert.

Lettie said she'd found records of the marriage of Roger and Becky, the deaths of both, and of Fenella, mother of William and John. More interesting, she thought, were the newspaper articles she found, written after Becky's death in 1963.

"Some are tabloid articles, so take them for whatever you think they're worth; you know how the British tabloids are. But some of them are from regular newspapers." Lettie continued to shuffle through her stack of papers as she talked, in spite of the fact that she couldn't possibly read them, the dim glow from the dashboard radiating barely enough light for me to make out the outline of her face.

Before returning to the castle, I stopped off at the MacBane farmhouse to see if Robbie had read the message I'd left asking him to play for our memorial service tomorrow. Nothing doing. Robbie's car wasn't there, and, except for one lamp in the downstairs hall, no lights burned inside the house. There was a vertical row of small windows on either side of the door, and through them, I could see the note I'd left for Robbie earlier. It was still perched, tented, on the hall table. Returning to the car, I noted that there were no lights on in Boots's cottage, either.

LETTIE CAME TO MY ROOM and arranged her papers around the edges of my bed. "I'll leave you with the whole mess, but these are the ones you should look at first."

"Lettie, you're amazing. How did you find all this in one afternoon?"

"When you work in a library, you get good at it. I don't waste time looking in the wrong places."

She made it sound so simple. The first documents were simply the official records of the deaths of Fenella, Roger, and Becky. As William had already told me, Fenella died of breast cancer, and the death certificate gave the year as 1955. Rebecca

Sinclair, née Seton, died in 1963, but there was an interval of ten days between the time of death (10 September) and the date on which she was pronounced dead (20 September) The certifier had scribbled a note in the section dealing with cause of death, explaining that the corpse was found in a state of decomposition that precluded any determination of the immediate cause. There had been multiple broken bones and the body had been found at the bottom of a cliff. Under "manner of death," the box labeled "could not be determined" was checked, but another note stated simply, "Suicide letter found. Suicide probable."

Roger Sinclair died on September 10, 1968, five years to the day after Becky, but his death certificate was much simpler than hers. Cause of death: gunshot wound. Manner of death: suicide.

"It's pretty obvious why he chose that particular day to shoot himself," I said, returning the photocopied sheet to the array of documents on my bed. "But, honestly, I'm a bit surprised that old Roger would've been so torn up about it. If he couldn't get along with Becky when she was alive, why should her suicide have compelled him to do likewise, five years later?"

"Maybe it wasn't suicide?" Lettie looked at me, her head tilted to one side. "Maybe he killed her. Pushed her over the cliff. Then killed himself five years later because he couldn't live with himself any longer."

I thought about that for a minute. It was a reasonable idea, albeit an idea with no corroborating evidence. I wondered if Roger had left a suicide note.

"Now, here's where it gets really interesting!" Lettie fluttered her hands and wiggled her butt. She handed me a copy of a tabloid article.

London, 20 October, 1963.
A meeting last evening of the South Thames Actors Guild erupted in a shouting match during the reading of the minutes of the group's September meeting. The conflict

was over a tribute to the memory of Lady Rebecca Seton offered at the guild's September meeting, two days after the death of Lady Seton was announced in London papers.

An unidentified member shouted out, "Retract that tribute! We cannot honor liars!" It was a reference to the address Lady Seton made at the August meeting this year, in which she told the guild that, in her will, she would be endowing a scholarship fund with the bulk of her estate. Her estate has been estimated to be in excess of £2 million.

Guild president, Paul Davies, called for order and told the group that Lady Seton's will, currently in probate, makes no mention of the South Thames Actors Guild and leaves the whole of the estate to her husband, Roger Sinclair. Davies stated that there was, in his opinion, simply nothing they could do, since the will is undoubtedly genuine.

Another member of the audience shouted, "We can sue her estate for breach of promise!"

A general chorus of "Hear, Hear!" echoed round the hall.

Pounding his gavel for order, Davies told the group that he would ask the guild's solicitor, Daniel Eddington, Esq., to look into the matter and report his findings at the next meeting.

"Extraordinary!" I said, flopping onto a bare spot between the papers on my bed. "She must have changed her mind." I looked at the date of the article again. "Or maybe she intended to change her will, but hadn't gotten around to it. There was only a month between her speech to the Actors Guild and her death."

Lettie didn't seem to be listening. She was sitting in the wing chair near the window, swinging her feet, which in that chair missed the floor by a good three inches, and writing on the margin of her train schedule brochure. "Didn't you say that kid at the dig, Iain Jandeson, was sort of living in an Indiana Jones fantasy world?"

"It seems like that to me, but I can't read his mind. He dresses like Harrison Ford did in the Indiana Jones movies, though."

"I know why he changed his name."

On the drive back from the train station I had told Lettie about Tony Marsh's discovery that, according to school records, Iain Jandeson was supposed to be Ian Jameson. "Okay, I give up. Why?"

"What do you call those puzzles where the letters are scrambled and you have to unscramble them?"

"Anagrams?"

"Right. Look." She thrust her train schedule at me. "Iain Jandeson is an anagram of Indiana Jones!"

I checked it out and Lettie was right. "Joyce Parsley, another kid at the dig, told me Iain also believes he was abducted by aliens."

"Maybe so," Lettie said, "but an anagram of E.T. wouldn't be much of a name, would it?"

Lettie put both hands over her mouth, but I could tell she was laughing behind her hands. I refuse to laugh at Lettie's jokes unless I absolutely can't help myself, and Lettie refuses to laugh before I do.

"Lettie, what do you think of the idea that Boots killed Froggy?" I lay back on my bed and stared at the ceiling. "Joyce Parsley went to the police today to tell them she saw Boots coming from the castle that night with a knife."

"Piffle."

"Here's the main problem: Somebody murdered Froggy, and so far, the only motives I've found don't amount to much more than enough to start a good fist fight."

"Do you still think John Sinclair was murdered, too?"

"Yes, I do. So let's think about things from that angle. Let's suppose the principal target was John Sinclair and that

Froggy was involved somehow. Perhaps Froggy discovered something he wasn't supposed to know. Now we have a richer field to till because I can think of motives galore for killing John."

Lettie folded her hands in her lap and looked at me attentively.

I sat up on the bed and drew my legs around beside me. "First, there's William Sinclair. If he knew about John's plans to turn this place into a tourist attraction, he'd do whatever he had to, to stop it."

"But William owns the place. John couldn't do anything unless William approved it."

"Okay, but maybe there's some reason why William would be compelled to approve. Don't ask me what that reason could be, but John was horrible about belittling William in front of other people. Did you notice how William never said anything back? He sat there, stone-faced, while John insulted his intelligence.

"And then there's Tony Marsh. Tony's having a fling with John's wife and he also steps into John's position as director of the dig. That's two motives.

"Fallon Sinclair. Fallon is now free to ride off into the sunset with her lover and with John's money, if he had any, which I suspect he did. Fallon had reason to resent John after the death of their only child due to John's negligence. That's two good motives.

"Amelia Lipscomb. She hated John because she was there, on the scene, when John and Fallon's child was suffering from heat stroke in the car and John was preening for the camera. The last thing I heard Amelia say about John was 'the bastard.'"

"If Amelia poisoned John Sinclair, I doubt that she'd reveal her feelings to you by calling him a bastard. That way, if they find out his death wasn't natural, she would have already pointed the finger at herself."

"Good point."

"What about Brian Lipscomb? That story he told us about why the police searched him and his car. I believed him at the time, but was he telling us the truth? And he's incredibly jealous. Have you noticed?"

"I think it's protectiveness rather than jealousy," I said. It would've been simpler for Brian to let Amelia come here by herself since he was unable to take off from work. "Now, Maisie," I went on. "No motive that I can see."

"If she has a motive, it would be to kill Fallon, not John. I hate the way Fallon talks down to her while availing herself of Maisie's hospitality."

"Robbie MacBane. If John's plans come to fruition, he loses his farm and his hundred-year lease. Bad news with a baby on the way."

Lettie didn't know about the MacBanes' expected progeny, so I told her about my conversation with Robbie that morning. I held up seven fingers, although, at this point, my count of suspects was probably off by as much as twenty percent. "Boots is as devoted to the preservation of the castle and its grounds as William is. He's lived here his whole life. If he thought John was ruining the place he'd do anything he could to save it, and William told me, tonight, that Boots and John never got along."

Lettie held up eight stubby fingers. "Iain Jandeson."

"What motive would Iain have?"

"He doesn't need one; he's nuts."

After Lettie left my room, I sat for more than an hour with the papers she had brought me. Several of them were about the career of Lady Rebecca Seton and about how delighted Central Scotland was to have her living in their midst. One article was accompanied by a photograph of her but, other than the fact that she had nice cheekbones, I couldn't tell if she was pretty or not. She had one of those awful late-fifties hairdos that made every woman look bad. If the photo had been in color, I could have seen what those violet eyes looked like. I thought again about the portraits of Roger and Fenella that hung in the ground floor room of the square tower and wished I could see a portrait of Becky. Why was there no portrait of Becky? Probably because, once she and Roger were both dead, Roger's sons would have been eager to retire any portrait of her to the... where? To the cellar, maybe? I cast my mind back to the foray Lettie and I had made to the cellar and remembered the picture frames stacked against the wall. Some of them had been nice frames, similar to the ones in the portrait room. Did any of them have paintings still in them? I hadn't paid any attention when I was there before, but now that I thought about it, I'd have bet money that a portrait of Becky was, or had been, in one of them.

On my dressing table, the little science fair experiment I had started the night before still waited for me to examine it. I lifted the shoe box off the mushroom caps, removed the mushrooms, and found that each of them had left a beautifully distinct pattern on either the white or the black paper. Most of the spore prints were some shade of tan or russet, but what good was this information? I laid the caps and the papers inside the box and stashed the whole thing on top of my wardrobe.

I dressed for bed and stood at my window, brushing my hair. The wind flung invisible needles of rain at the panes and, beyond the reflection of my own room in the glass, the world outside was pure black. There was no way sleep would come to me in my current state, so I grabbed my robe, sneaked down the hall, and rapped on Lettie's door. She opened it, squinting at me through sleepy eyes.

"I really need to pop down to the cellar for a minute, Lettie. Will you come with me?"

"No," she said, swiping green goo down the bridge of her nose.

"I didn't think you would, but I thought I'd ask anyway. What are your plans for tomorrow?"

"I'm going to Inverness."

"Before you leave, will you go to the cellar with me?"

"I'd rather do that than go with you now. What are you looking for?"

"A picture. A picture of Becky."

TWENTY-EIGHT

IT WAS SO SIMPLE WHEN it hit me. How the Super Bowl ticket had ended up on the castle stairs, why there was no knife slash in Froggy's shirt, indeed, why he was wearing Van's shirt to begin with. I lay stiffly in my bed, willing my body to relax, and revised my mental picture in light of what I'd learned today.

Van purchased two tickets for Proctor Galigher and they arrived at the MacBane house by mail. Van would have looked them over, tucked them into his desk drawer, and probably showed them to Froggy or to Robbie, both of whom would have been interested to see tickets that cost more than some cars. Van might well have dropped one and picked it up, stuffing it into the breast pocket of his shirt (his Hawaiian hibiscus shirt), planning to put it back in the drawer with its mate.

On Tuesday, a slow day at the dig, Froggy left his bench in the finds shack and walked back to his room. Joyce Parsley followed him, keeping well out of his sight. Once inside his room, Froggy would have made himself comfortable, taken off his shirt, perhaps taken a shower. Then something happened. Something drastic. Something urgent.

He dashed out of the room, grabbing the first shirt he found on his way out the door, which, naturally, would have been one of Van's hanging on the peg on the inside of their door. I had seen as many as five of Van's shirts piled on that peg at one time. Running out and down the road to the castle, shirtless, but carrying the shirt with one Super Bowl ticket in the pocket, he was seen by both Joyce Parsley and by the weird sisters who had been hiking along the road to the north. They had told me of seeing a shirtless man that they only knew wasn't Robbie. They wouldn't have seen Joyce because Joyce was skulking around in the bushes.

So Froggy, donning Van's way-too-big shirt as he ran, might not have buttoned it but simply stuck his arms through the sleeves. Did he go to the castle? To the field beside or the lawn behind it? It seemed to me that if he had been stabbed in the parking lot, the field, or the lawn, the police would have found blood. Even if the killer had had time to work on the site with a garden hose, there would have been some left.

Might he have been killed inside the castle? If so, how would that mess have been cleaned up? We had all been there at dinner.

Lucy! The mud room off the kitchen! Lucy had gone crazy, snarling and yelping, as soon as she and Boots had walked in. I had to count backward to that day; it would have been on Thursday. If Froggy had been killed in there, the blood would have been thoroughly washed away and quickly, because the evening meal had been cooked there. The bench in the mud room was used for cleaning fish and game so there might already be enough traces of blood—on the bench, on the stone floor, in the nooks and cracks in the stone—to light the place up like a carnival with a spritz or two of Luminol from the bottle of a crime scene investigator. Would animal blood react with Luminol the same way human blood does? I was sure it would. Although there are differences from one species to another, all blood is basically a carrier of oxygen and it's that capacity, I had heard, which makes Luminol emit light.

But Lucy would not have been fooled by lingering traces of animal blood. Lucy would have been able to detect not only the human blood, but also the fear, the terror of poor Froggy when he knew he was about to die.

By this time, it was after 2 a.m. and I was too keyed up to even think of sleep, so I made a mental list of things to do tomorrow: 1) go to the cellar and check out the picture frames, 2) ask Fallon to show me that box again, 3) check with Robbie and see if he can play for the memorial service, 4) get chairs set up in the tent, get some flowers, make sure there's a fresh pot of coffee before the service, 5) find an excuse to go into Froggy and Van's room and attempt to check Froggy's laptop for recently accessed documents and Web sites.

By 3:00 a.m., I gave up, switched on my bedside lamp, and read some *Macbeth*. How far off course I was! I had come here to learn more about Macbeth and eleventh-century Scotland, but now I was engulfed by two nasty murders, a tragic family history, and an urgent need to spring a nice kid from a cold jail cell.

Macbeth, act 2, scene 4:
'Tis unnatural,
Even like the deed that's done. On Tuesday last…

At that point, my dream picked up where the text went blurry.

MACBETH SWIRLED INTO my dream on a windblown mist. He wore a bullet-shaped helmet with horns, and a tartan shawl over a shirt of chain mail. He moved smoothly but he had no feet, his lower body tapering off into a spiral of fog as if he'd come out of a magic lantern, but beneath him was a sort of chessboard, with squares, and the one he hovered over was labeled "Thursday," so it might have been a big calendar rather than a chessboard. On Thursday stood a big black cauldron, and two weird sisters, possibly Winifred and Wanda, ladling out soup very sloppily into camouflage-patterned hats.

"Should I have some of the soup?" I asked Macbeth.

"I'd be wary of it if I were you."

"Are you the real Macbeth or are you Shakespeare's bad boy?"

"A friend."

He led me onto the previous square, which, although not

labeled, was logically Wednesday. On Wednesday there was sunshine, rolling hills and ridiculously cheerful birds that twittered all around our heads. Alf and Eleanor Downes skipped past us, both dressed as garden gnomes, picking gold coins from the throats of flowers. I looked at Macbeth and said, "Is this what you wanted me to see?"

Instead of answering, he turned spookily to the next square, clearly Tuesday because it was labeled as such in flashing lights, and pointed to the large dagger, dripping blood, which dangled above the letter "s."

"Is this a dagger which I see before me, the handle toward my hand?" Macbeth recited, a bit too melodramatically for my taste.

"I'm confused," I said. "What does all this mean?"

"Is't known who did this more than bloody deed?" Macbeth swirled around the square, and as he spun, big red mushrooms with white spots popped up all around.

"No, I don't know who did this more than bloody deed," I said.

"The deed was done on Tuesday last."

With that, Macbeth whooshed around the red mushrooms, ripping off chunks of them as he went, then whooshed right away.

I raised my fogbound head from the pillow, opened my eyes, still gritty from fitful sleep, and saw the first light of dawn at my window. It was Tuesday.

AFTER SHOWERING in the round tower, I had to wait on the narrow stairs above the second-floor landing before I could go down the rest of the way because William, the weird sisters, and their luggage were coming up. He conducted them into the same room they had shared on their last visit. We exchanged brief pleasantries and I hurried past them and down, being not yet completely dry or adequately covered by my robe.

As soon as I had dressed, I slipped down the hall and knocked on Lettie's door. She wasn't quite ready for breakfast, so I trudged on to the dining room alone. Tony Marsh and the

Lipscombs, already drinking their coffee, asked me to join them, but I took an adjoining table to save a seat for Lettie when she came in. Tony seemed to avoid eye contact with me, and I wondered if he was wise to my busybody meddling in his and Hannah's affairs. His eyes were puffy and red. Was it from lack of sleep or from crying?

The Downeses popped in to say good-bye. We had all grown fond of them, strange as they were. I, for one, almost envied their ability to keep the real world out of the one they created for themselves. This morning they both wore flat black tams with red pom-poms on top. Alf swished a long tartan shawl over his shoulder and Eleanor carried a clean-smelling bouquet of heather tied with a green ribbon. "Eleanor and I have taken rooms in Braemar for a few days, and from there it's on to Sterling Castle for the weekend."

Eleanor touched my shoulder for attention. "Have you heard of Kindrochit?" she asked. "We found it quite by accident, but it's the ruins of an old castle in Braemar, built by Malcolm Canmore, at one end of a bridge, to keep people from crossing the river without his permission."

"Malcolm Canmore?" I was amazed that I didn't already know about this. Malcolm Canmore, son of King Duncan, killed Macbeth and succeeded him as king. "I'll definitely have to go there."

Eleanor said, "It was built not long after he killed Macbeth at Lumphanan, which is a few miles down the road."

With kisses tossed around to all of us, the Downeses were off.

Maisie came over, bringing me a rack of warm toast. "The funeral will be the morn at ten o'clock. Noo, you and Lettie can sit in the part they'll have set off for the family because our family is verra small and the church will be crowded. I doubt ye'll be able to find a regular seat unless ye get there an hour early."

I started to protest that I wouldn't dream of insinuating myself into the family seats, then realized that the Sinclair family, sadly, might consist of Maisie, William and Fallon. And Robbie MacBane. It might actually be nice if we castle guests plumped up their numbers for them. That reminded me of the memorial service so I said, loudly enough for everyone to hear me, "The kids at the dig are having a service for John and also for Dylan Quale today. You're all welcome to come, but don't feel obligated. I know most of us have more than enough to do, before tomorrow's funeral."

Lettie joined me, breakfasting on porridge and milk. She was avoiding acidic, scratchy and hard foods because of the stitches; her mouth was still recuperating from the attack of the killer pencil. Afterwards, we went up to Fallon's room together.

We paused outside Fallon's door, and I put my ear against it. I could hear nothing at all. "If she's still asleep, I certainly don't want to wake her up, poor thing," I said. "Let's go to the cellar. I can come back here later."

THE SMALL RECTANGLE that had been freshly dug in the cellar floor and loosely refilled the last time Lettie and I were down there had been tamped down and smoothed over. The picture frames and brass head- and footboards still leaned against the walls, as far as I could tell, exactly where they had been before. In this little room, we needed our flashlights in addition to the overhead light, but before we attacked the rows of stacked frames, I walked through the doorless opening into the adjoining room where the only illumination was a weak fluorescent grow light. The shelves on which I'd found bits of the dark musty-smelling material were still empty and the other walls in the room, still littered with junk. I tried to remember what I'd done with the material I'd picked up and stuck in a paper bag.

Lettie had already started leafing through the stacks of frames when I returned to her. "I'm going to need another bath after this," she said. "These frames are filthy."

They weren't all picture frames. There was a plywood

square that looked as if it had been sawed from a paneled wall, a couple of nice, probably mahogany, boards which may have been dining table extenders, and the hands-down ugliest fox hunt picture I'd ever seen. I lifted it out of the stack, knocked some dust off, and showed it to Lettie. She opened her mouth and poked her forefinger in.

I found what I was looking for in the next stack. In a frame that, as far as I could tell, was identical to those holding Roger's and Fenella's portraits, was a grime-encrusted oil painting of a woman in a 1950's pageboy hairstyle, pulled back on one side with a tortoiseshell comb. From the photo I'd seen in the newspaper article Lettie had brought me, I knew it was Becky. I dragged it out and lugged it over to a vacant space along the wall. It was so dirty and dark, it looked like a Rembrandt. I dug into my pocket for the paper napkin I had swiped from the breakfast table and pulled it out. Before I could spit on it, I caught the disapproving look on Lettie's face and said, "Well, how do you suggest I wet this? I want to see what's under that muck."

Lettie pointed to the exterior door at the base of the stairs we had recently come down. "There's a puddle on the stone out there, it must have run under the door in last night's rain."

With a loud sigh of irritation, I plodded out and found some water that had collected at a low spot in the stone and dipped in the napkin.

I stroked gently at the face and cleared off a spot on a smooth, ivory cheek. Then the eyes—oh my! They were indeed a pure violet, so startling that Lettie gave a little gasp. I cleaned off the only ear visible on the slightly turned head and found that Becky had chosen to have her portrait done wearing amethyst earrings that exactly matched her eyes. Large brilliant amethysts, surrounded by little seed pearls.

The same pair whose lone survivor, until yesterday, had lain in the little box with my gold coin.

"That's the earring, Lettie. Hannah Dunbar found that same

earring in the field last week. She gave it to John, and he was keeping it in the box with my coin."

"So it's been stolen, too?"

"The coin, the earring, and a very rare stamp."

"How can you ever expect to find them? They're so small, you could hide all three under your tongue."

I chuckled, still staring at Becky's portrait, still not quite believing. "Not the stamp; the glue would come off."

"Clever of old Becky, wasn't it?" Lettie said. "Wearing earrings that play up the color of your eyes is—"

She was interrupted by two loud *thunks* coming from the direction of the stairwell. It sounded as if someone had fallen down a couple of steps. I dashed out and across the landing to the foot of the stairs, but I saw no one because only the lowest four steps of the winding staircase were visible from the bottom. Did I really want to catch whoever it was? What would I say if I did? I glanced back to make sure Lettie was behind me and then climbed to the first floor, where I found absolutely nothing in the west wing hall, the portrait room, or the great hall. I even checked the side door leading to the west lawn. Nada.

But someone was spying on us.

Lettie and I slipped away to our respective rooms to wash off the cellar dirt. Wedging my forearms into the basin until the tap water reached my elbows, I tried to remember the details of my early morning dream. Those red mushrooms with white spots. They had been so vivid. They looked like mushrooms you'd see in a children's book, always with elves or gnomes under them. I dried my hands and pulled the mushroom book out from under the bed. There was, indeed, a real mushroom that looked like that, the *Amanita muscaria* or fly agaric, called the fly agaric because it was once used, mixed with milk, to stupefy houseflies. A skull and crossbones in the margin of the page identified the *Amanita muscaria* as poisonous, but, as I read further, I found that it wasn't actually deadly and has been used by some cultures in religious rites for thousands of years. But since it was dangerous, inducing delirium, disorientation, sensory alterations, and visions, the authors of the book cautioned readers to stay away from it. Apparently there were differences between the *A. muscaria* that grows wild in the United States and varieties found in other parts of the globe. Some of the American varieties were particularly potent.

I tucked the book into my backpack. The next time I saw Joyce, I intended to ask her if these photos looked like the magic mushrooms they ate Saturday night. It wasn't as if she wouldn't have noticed if they were bright red with white spots.

TWENTY-NINE

A SECOND TRIP UP TO Fallon's room yielded no better results than the first; she was either elsewhere or sleeping late. So I caught a ride with Lettie as far as the MacBane house and wished her a successful day in Inverness. Spotting Robbie's car in the driveway, I strode up to the door and knocked.

The fishy aroma of frying kippers swirled around Robbie when he opened the door. "Ah, there ye are. I telephoned to the castle a few minutes ago; they said you'd left." His red curls were in rare form this morning, as he had obviously neither shaved nor combed his hair yet.

"How's your wife feeling?" Politeness dictated that I ask about her first.

"The doctor's makin' her stay off her feet, so me mother-in-law is waitin' on her hand an' foot. Noo, what will I do wi' her when I bring her back home? She'll be spoiled rotten." Robbie led me into his kitchen and offered me breakfast. I declined, but took a seat at the kitchen table across from Robbie's plate of kippers and eggs. He flipped a paper napkin across one knee and said, "I think she's doing well. If she can hold on to the bairn a few more weeks, the doc says it'll be all right even if he comes early."

"He?"

"Aye, it's a boy," he said with thinly disguised pride. He attacked his eggs, scissors style, with his knife and fork. Then he said, "The memorial thing you mentioned in your note; it's today, is it?"

"At eleven."

"What d'ye want me to play?"

"Could you do 'Amazing Grace' on the bagpipes?"

"Aye, I thought ye'd ask that. Would ye like me to play something on the fiddle as well? Froggy liked 'Annie Laurie' when I played it on the fiddle."

"That would be wonderful," I said. I tried to imagine Froggy and Robbie sitting in the parlor, Froggy listening to the plaintive strains of "Annie Laurie" from Robbie's bow. Would Van have been there, too? Based on the CDs I'd noticed on his desk, Van's definition of traditional music would be Jimi Hendrix.

"Have you seen Boots since you got back from Inverness?" I asked.

"Oh, aye!" Robbie dropped his fork. "He came over late. Must ha' been midnight. The police were oot here before I came home, interrogatin' him aboot runnin' around wi' a knife or some such foolishness."

"One of the girls at the dig, a girl named Joyce Parsley, told me—"

"The crazy lass? The one that sneaked aboot, hidin' in the bushes? Don't tell me ye'd believe anything she'd say!" Robbie waved his eggy knife in the air.

"I don't doubt that she saw something, but of course, Boots might have had a reasonable explanation for the knife."

"Boots told me he was merely takin' a fish-cleanin' knife back to the shootin' hut in the wood. Said somebody had left it on the wall by the castle car park." Robbie lifted the coffeepot from the automatic drip machine to the table, first holding it up to me, his eyebrows raised.

I shook my head. "May I go up to Van's room? I need to grab a few things to take to him." I didn't really need to pick up anything else, but it was a good excuse.

Once inside the bedroom, I booted Froggy's laptop, pulled up a chair to the desk, and clicked on the Internet browser icon.

Something wasn't connected. It took my electronically challenged self a good five minutes to locate a cable that was attached to something only on one end, and to reason that it might bc good to find a place to stick the other end. I found several wrong places to stick it.

At length, a window opened on the screen and asked for a password. I typed "froggy," but it didn't work. The user name on the display read "dquale," the same as at the dig site, so I tried *qualed, froggy1, froggy123, frogman, pollen, spores, mushroom, fernman,* and *fungus.* The thing cut me off.

I closed that window and walked to the real one that overlooked the castle and woods. Boots and Lucy were heading toward the castle, Lucy's heavy fur bouncing left and right as she trotted along. Back to the desk. I slid open the drawer under the computer and found a slip of paper, near the front where I could hardly have missed it, that said: "PW, doctorquale." So Froggy had been dreaming of the day when he'd have his PhD. If he'd been allowed to live as he had every right to do, he'd have had that PhD.

I typed "doctorquale" and I was in. I should have known Froggy wouldn't have used an imaginative password like "fernman."

Being computer-literate enough to know how to check the history of Internet usage, I did so and found that the sites visited were listed by date. The last time anyone had been online at this computer was last Wednesday, the day after Froggy was killed. Van would've had no reason to use this machine because he had his own, but he might have done so, anyway, for the same reason that I was doing it now. More likely, I thought, the police had done it while combing through his room on the first day of their investigation. I still wondered why they hadn't taken the whole computer in, as evidence. Perhaps that was one more stupidity committed by Chief Inspector Coates.

The last Web site visited on Tuesday was "All about

Amanitas." The one immediately before that was "Veiled mushrooms." So Froggy had started with veiled mushrooms and
proceeded from there to Amanitas, as he would have done if
he'd had an unknown specimen he wanted to learn about. My
hands were shaking so badly, I had to make two fists until they
calmed down.

I clicked on "All about Amanitas" and read what may have
been the last words Froggy ever read:

> Amanita phalloides *is easily distinguished from other*
> *pale-colored mushrooms by the veil which leaves a ring*
> *or a cup (volva) in the mature fruiting body. Also called*
> *the Death Cap, it causes death due to liver or kidney*
> *damage if treatment is not started almost immediately.*
>
> Amanita phalloides *is responsible for a large percent-*
> *age of mushroom poisonings worldwide, the first*
> *symptoms appearing after a 6-24 hour latent period and*
> *including vomiting, diarrhea, and abdominal cramps.*
> *This is followed by a period of apparent remission,*
> *lasting about a day, followed by the return of the*
> *symptoms. It is in this last stage that liver failure, kidney*
> *failure, coma, and death (often in 5-10 days) may ensue.*
>
> Amanita phalloides *is widespread across North*
> *America and Europe and is typically found under conifers*
> *and hardwoods. Like all the Amanitas, phalloides is dis-*
> *tinguished from other genera by a white spore print.*

I sat back from the screen and pressed my hands over my
eyes. What was it? Something was pushing at the edges of my
conscious brain. I drew my hands back a bit and opened my
eyes, staring at my palms. That was it! It was as if I were back
at the stone wall, standing guard over Froggy's body on the blue
tarp. I saw him lying on his left side, his right arm bent in front
of him so that his thumb was close to his face, his left arm

extended behind him, palm upward. The writing on the palm of Froggy's left hand: "halloi," wasn't it? Put a "p" in front and a "des" after it and you got phalloides!

Froggy had studied this Web page, grabbed a ballpoint pen, written "phalloides" on his hand (probably because no paper was handy) and took off down the road toward the castle.

But John Sinclair, if he was poisoned, was "done for" on Thursday, wasn't he? That's when we had the mushroom soup for dinner. I looked at the second paragraph again. There were four stages to *Amanita phalloides* poisoning. What if John had been in stage three, the period of apparent remission, when the soup was served? Then he would have gotten sick like the rest of us, but unlike the rest of us, he would not get better. He couldn't get better because he wasn't simply suffering from a sick-making mushroom. He had already been condemned to death by a deadly mushroom.

John had been sick that Wednesday and hadn't gone to the dig that day. But how in the world could this have been worked out beforehand? Who could have done this, and how was it done?

I grabbed a couple of things and stuck them into a plastic bag so that Robbie, if he was still here, would see me leaving with something, supposedly something Van sorely needed. My trek from the MacBane house back to the castle was both too long and not long enough. Not long enough to settle in my mind all this new information: Becky's picture, the scribbles on Froggy's hand, the seemingly impossible theft of the contents of the box, the timing of an intricate and evil scheme. Too long, because I had to get to Fallon's room before she left, and it was already close to nine.

FALLON OPENED HER DOOR when I was almost ready to stop knocking and break the door down. A half dozen loud raps separated by decently long intervals, long enough to have allowed her to slip on a robe and creep to the door at a snail's pace, finally paid off. She looked terrible. Fallon had that sort of thin, baby-fine hair that had to be washed and fluffed every day or it would go limp and stick to her head. Add to that her high forehead that almost qualified as a receding hairline, and Fallon, an attractive woman in normal circumstances, had the potential for looking like a baby orangutan.

Today, she resembled nothing so much as a Mexican hairless. Her eyes were swollen, her nose was red, and her face, blotchy and wan, received no cover from the thin sprigs of hair that hung dully around her ears. I swallowed my first impulse, which was to gasp, "Ohmigod! What happened to you?" and said, "I was concerned because you didn't come to breakfast this morning. Is there anything you need?"

"No, I…come on in, Dotsy. Find yourself a chair." Fallon's voice sounded as defeated as her hair looked. She wrapped her robe more tightly around her, gave the tie belt a tightening tug, and crawled onto her bed, covering her bare feet with the sheet.

"I can't say I know what you're going through," I whispered, unsure whether to sit down or not. "They say there's no life crisis as traumatic as the death of a husband or wife."

"Huh?" Fallon reached toward the box on her nightstand for a tissue. "That's right. I don't know what I'm supposed to do now," she mumbled. "It's as if everything I normally do serves no purpose now. It's all perfectly meaningless."

I stood silently, wondering how long I had to wait before I could ask about the box.

"Was Tony at breakfast this morning?" Fallon asked.

"Yes."

She's not grieving for her husband, she's upset about Tony! I recalled Tony's red, puffy eyes at breakfast and made a simple deduction. *Tony must have talked with Hannah when he drove her back to camp last night. Maybe he wants a second chance with her. If so, maybe he promised to break it off with Fallon, immediately. Maybe he's already done it.*

"Did you talk to him?"

"Not much. I reminded him, and everyone else of course, that we're having a memorial service for John and for Froggy Quale this morning. In the tent."

"Why wasn't I told about it?"

"I'm so sorry, Fallon. I should have told you yesterday, but I'm afraid I...well, I didn't see you after noon yesterday, did I? Anyway, we're having this service, especially for the kids who won't be able to go to either John's or Froggy's funerals. We'd love for you to be there, but don't feel obligated. If you're not up to it, don't go."

Fallon swung her feet onto the floor and wobbled over to the mirrored dresser. "I don't know if I could possibly get myself in decent shape by...what time is it? The service?"

"At eleven."

"Oh, dear, that's not long from now."

"Fallon, where's that box? The one that got emptied right under our noses yesterday?"

Fallon looked confused. "It's around here somewhere. Didn't you say John kept it in the big suitcase?"

"We took it out of the big suitcase. Did you put it back in?"

"No, I don't think so." Either Fallon hadn't given a second thought to yesterday's grand theft, or she was stalling for time.

"May I look around for it?"

"Help yourself."

I checked the closet, glanced around the sitting room, and opened the dresser drawers, feeling like a horrible snoop, but I found the box lying on its side under the bed, where Fallon had apparently kicked it. Dragging it out, I set it on the bed and looked at the back, where that hidden lever was. The one John had had so much trouble with, he'd had to work on it with a screwdriver. The screwdriver had slipped and gouged the wood rather badly, I remembered, but there was no scar there now. The wood around the hinge was as smooth as the day it was lacquered.

"Fallon, this isn't John's box," I said.

"But of course it is." She sat up and blew her nose into yet another tissue.

We both heard a definite *thump* that came from the wall behind and to the right of her bed. Fallon's head jerked around toward the noise. She turned back to me, wide-eyed.

"Someone's in the laird's lug," I said, as I dashed to the wall where I knew the little secret door had to be, based on the view I'd had of this room on the evening I'd been hiding behind it myself, and also based on where I thought the thump had come from.

"How do you open it?" I said. The wall from this side was just a flat, paneled wall.

"The laird's lug? I knew there was one, but I didn't know it was here. Oh, no! People could have been listening to everything we…for years!"

"So you don't know how to open it, I guess." I ran my hand around the edges of the panel. A section of the paneling, about two feet square, was set off by a knife-thin gap all around but there was no handle, no visible hinge, no finger hole against which one could pull. I tried a firm push on both sides of the square, but my only reward was a momentary and ever-so-slight budge. I put my ear to the panel, but the source of the thump had slipped off down those narrow stairs or was lying low until we left.

"Fallon, hide this box before you leave," I whispered. "Not back in the same suitcase. Find a new hiding place."

THIRTY

On my way out through the great hall, I ran into the weird sisters and Scarborough, the ferret. They were taking Scarborough's soy milk to the kitchen to be refrigerated, which reminded me of the mental note I'd stuck in my head on the way back from Robbie MacBane's house. A note to check on the sort of cutlery they used here. Robbie had mentioned bone-handle knives being kept at the shooting hut, and I recalled Boots using an old, wooden-handle knife on the one occasion that I'd been in his cottage. Of course, that didn't mean that all his knives were of the same sort, but kitchens often do have sets of knives.

Three women I didn't know were busy at the sink, counter and stove when we came in, and I used the distraction caused by the entry of a ferret in a red harness as a chance to sneak open a couple of drawers. In one, I found several of those nice resin-handle knives that last a lifetime and I spotted two more of the same type lying in the sink.

Now I needed to take inventory of the knives at the shooting hut.

Hiking across the field toward the woods, I took a northerly route, sticking close to the fence that gradually rose to the cliff from which Becky Sinclair had plunged to her death. I had no particular reason to feel I had to sneak around to the woods rather than simply walk boldly across, but I didn't relish having to explain, to anyone, where I was going or why. I followed the fence to its northeast corner and looked across. I could still see the bare spot that my body had cleared off the rocks the day I'd slipped and William had caught me in the nick of time. Moving along the fence, I found a low spot in the wire mesh and climbed over.

The leaves and pine needles crunched under my shoes and stirred up enough dust and pollen to launch me on a sneezing jag. Between sneezes, I thought I heard a rustle, like a single footstep, but when I looked around, I saw a squirrel skittering up a tree trunk. It lost its footing and fell *kerplop* into the leaves below, making the same sort of rustling sound. In a wood like this, there are all kinds of sounds. I paused for a minute and listened.

At the shooting hut, I first checked the fish-cleaning bench attached to the outside of the hut. This was where William had picked up a knife and taken it inside. I couldn't recall what sort of handle it had. There were plenty of dried fish scales in the cracks between the planks, and a fish hook, still attached to a length of line, had been jammed into the wood. But no knives.

I found a rock large enough to allow me to reach the key they kept over the door, rolled it into position, and climbed onto it. The door opened easily. I left the key in the lock and walked inside; it didn't look as if anyone had been here since my last visit. Diffused light from the grimy windows cast pale rectangles on the wood floor, and bare pillows still sat atop the navy bedspreads.

I walked to the sink. A knife lay on the drain board. Almost certainly the same knife that William had placed there. It had a black resin handle, like the ones in the castle kitchen. Of course, I thought, this doesn't prove anything. Knives have a way of getting moved from place to place. I opened each of the drawers under the drain board and on the other side of the sink. There was a set of stainless steel tableware, including knives with stainless steel handles, and several more serious knives, all with bone handles. But only the one with a handle of black resin.

I looked at that knife again. Would it have been large enough to have done the job on Froggy? Undoubtedly it would have.

Whose fingerprints would be on it? William's of course, but perhaps other, earlier prints as well. I remembered that William had swiped the blade clean, but not the handle.

"It's a mite chilly in here, dinnae ye ken?"

I jumped.

William stood inside the door. Silhouetted against the sunlight, he looked huge.

"I didn't hear you come in." My voice seemed to catch in my throat. "I was just exploring around the woods and I—"

"Thought you might find the treasure box here? The box with the coin?"

"You have a box like John's, too, don't you? John told me an uncle had given each of you one for Christmas when you were boys." My voice rang hollow in my own ears. Why had William asked that? I was afraid I knew.

"Aye. I still have it."

"Did you know the police are questioning Boots about a knife he was seen with about the same time Froggy was killed?"

"No, I hadnae heard that." He walked around me to the sink and picked up the knife. "Is that why you were studyin' this one when I came in?"

I couldn't answer him.

"Did you know that Becky, my stepmother, was found at the bottom of that cliff you and I nearly went over, ourselves, the other day?" He leaned back against the sink, but he still held the knife in his hand. "Of course you did. You know a lot about Becky and my father and that whole time of trouble, don't you? You know the earring that woman found in the pasture was Becky's, don't you? And you know the box in Fallon's room right noo isn't the one John showed you, so bein' the clever woman you are, you've probably figured out whose box it really is."

I felt, very strongly, that it was time for me to leave. I began edging sideways toward the door, but meanwhile I had to say something.

"Was Froggy killed in the kitchen of the castle?"

A veil of incredible sadness fell across William's face. "Aye, I fear so."

I couldn't bring myself to ask the obvious question: Did you kill him? I watched him, silently, afraid to make any sudden movements.

"Becky didn't kill herself, did she?" That, too, was a dangerous question, but this was no time for small talk. "Did John kill her? I'm told they never got along."

William began pacing. From the fireplace to the window on the opposite wall and back again, but (was it my imagination?) always staying closer than I was to the door. He carried the knife casually in his right hand, swiping the blade across his thigh from time to time.

"Nae. Our father did it."

He said it so simply, so matter-of-factly, I almost missed it. He was telling me that his very own father, old Radge Roger, had killed the beautiful Lady Rebecca, their stepmother. Why was he telling me this? Because, I feared, he didn't expect me to live long enough to tell anyone else.

I took a couple of small steps toward the door, but William paced across in front of me, uncomfortably close. I retreated. He was breathing hard and fast. Working himself up to say something more, I imagined.

"I have both those amethyst earrings, noo," he wheezed, his nostrils flaring. "I've had one since the day they found it on the body. The dead, rotten body that lay at the bottom of yon cliff for more than a week before they found her! I wanted so badly to tell them where she was. The searchers. They must have had fifty people oot lookin' for her, but me father was deliberately confusin' them. It wasnae right, him lettin' her lie there for ten days, covered with leaves, gettin' eaten up by rats and maggots. But he wouldnae let me say anythin' to them.

"He killed her, throttled her, at the castle and then he

couldnae figure oot how ta' get rid of the body, so he called on me, big strappin' lad I was, at the time. Carryin' dead weight is bad business, ye ken? I threw her over my shoulder and carried her across the field to the cliff. The one earring must have fallen off on the way.

"I dinnae want to have anythin' to do with it, but what could I say to me own father? Pardon me while I call the police?"

William stopped and looked at me intently, his gaze darting left and right, as if searching all parts of my face for clues to what I was thinking.

"Did John have anything to do with it?"

"Nae, but unfortunately he saw me traipsin' across the field with the body. He never let me forget aboot it. My whole life." William's face was inches from my own. "Every bleedin' time I'd get a bit ahead on money, John'd be there with his hand oot. 'I need money for this, I need money for that,' he'd say, and I'd say, 'John, the castle needs repairs. Maisie and I haven't been oot ta' dinner in a year,' and he'd remind me that I was an accessory to murder and, if he wanted to, he could ruin the Sinclair family name. Crazy as my father was, I dinnae want him remembered as a murderer!"

Somehow, I had managed to back my way around to the door. I slipped my hand behind my back and turned the knob. The door was locked.

William saw what I'd done, and a dark shadow passed over his face. "I locked the door when I came in," he said. "But, Dotsy, I willnae hurt ye if ye'll only listen and understand that I havnae done anythin' I dinnae have to do."

"Tell me about Froggy."

I'm certain that what I saw on William's face was genuine sorrow. His shoulders drooped and his head fell forward. "The puir lad was in the wrong place at the wrong time. He saw the mushrooms I was choppin' up for John's omelet, that day. Maisie was gone to town. It was just John and me there at noon.

"The lad would have ta be the one person in this part of Scotland who was an expert in spores and mushrooms and such. After we'd eaten and John had gone back to the dig, this lad comes back. Comes in through the kitchen door screamin' scientific stuff and screamin' murder."

"So you grabbed a knife and killed him, used one of the blue tarps that was already lying in the parking area, wrapped him up and dragged him across the back lawn. Dumped him on the other side of the wall."

"I dinnae do anythin' I dinnae have to do."

Did William honestly expect me to agree with him? That cruel fate had made him kill two people and conspire in the cover-up of a third murder? What rotten luck! I stood, dumbstruck, staring at him with both my arms hanging awkwardly at my sides. In the distance I thought I heard a call. A few seconds later I heard, "Scarborough!"

The weird sisters! They were in the woods and not far away from the sound of it. How could I let them know I was here? That I needed help? I was afraid to yell.

"Scarborough!" This call sounded farther away.

Damn. They've gone past the hut. They're leaving.

William looked at me, rather pathetically. "I'm thinkin', Dotsy, that in a few days ye'll be goin' back to America. Ye won't have to worry aboot that lad, Van Nguyen, the one they've put in jail, because I'll make it straight with the police. I can give him an alibi; maybe point them in another direction."

"What other direction? Toward Boots, maybe? If you think I'm going to let you spring Van by implicating Boots or anyone else, you're nuts!"

William lurched toward me, grabbing me around the waist so quickly I had only enough time to glimpse his transformed face. After the sorrow and regret I'd seen and heard an instant ago, I now saw rage. Unreasoning, primal rage. The knife whipped up to my throat.

"And if you think I'd let you leave here and run your mouth off to all and sundry, you're nuts!" His hot breath poured down on the top of my head.

A thump and then a series of bumps and scratches emanated from the general region of the fireplace. William's left arm, around my waist, jerked me forward. I felt cold steel against my collar bone.

From outside the door, I heard, "Scarborough?"

Perched on the hearth, his tiny paws raised to his chin, was Scarborough, ferret extraordinaire, covered in cobwebs and soot. He looked at us with his little black peppercorn eyes as if to say, "Am I interrupting something?"

Thank God, Winifred and Wanda had seen him fall down the chimney, so there was no way they'd leave before gaining entry to the hut by whatever means necessary. When they rattled the door, William tossed the knife under a bed and drew the key from his pocket.

I helped them chase Scarborough around the room, under the bed, across the sink, and behind the pillows and it was wonderful! To be free to chase a ferret with no knife at my throat! I could have happily chased him for hours. When Winifred (or maybe Wanda) at last snaked out from under a bed with Scarborough tucked firmly to her breast, Wanda (or maybe Winifred) said, "Where's William? Wasn't he here?"

I dashed out of the hut and past the little loch, picking my way upslope through a rhododendron thicket. I didn't bother looking out across the field toward the castle or eastward to the road that led to the MacBanes' house or to Aviemore and Fort William. I knew where William had gone.

To the cliff.

"WANDA, DO YOU HAVE your mobile phone with you? Call nine-nine-nine."

From the way William's body lay at the bottom of the cliff,

it was obvious that it had been smashed like a bag of lightbulbs but, while Wanda walked to a clearing to get better reception on her phone, Winifred volunteered to make the long trek around and down to the bottom of the cliff.

She placed one end of Scarborough's leash in my hand and closed my fingers around it. "I'm going down there and feel for a pulse or something," she said. "I know it's futile, but when the police get here, the first thing they'll ask is, 'Did you try to help him?' We want to be able to tell them that we did."

"Of course." I found a rock to sit on, folded my arms across my knees, and buried my head against them. My brain swimming with the events of the last few minutes, I needed time to sort them out. Behind me, Wanda was speaking to someone on her cell phone, so once again I found myself watching over a body until the police arrived.

William's most startling revelation, to me, was that John had been blackmailing him all these years. That the castle and its lands wouldn't have been operating in the red but for John with his hand perpetually out for a payoff. I hoped there would be records at the castle that would either bear that out or refute it.

The earring, not the coin and not the stamp, had been the reason for the theft of the treasure box. With the one earring, found with Becky's body, fully described and included in the original postmortem reports, John's possession of the other one and, if necessary, Hannah Dunbar's word on where she found it, gave John hard evidence that Becky had been dead before she went to the cliff. I have pierced ears and I have never lost an earring of the latching-loop sort, which Hannah said that one was. To lose one would require a yank that would practically tear off your earlobe. Becky couldn't possibly have lost it while walking across the field on her way to commit suicide, but a body draped over a shoulder, perhaps even dropped into the brambles a couple of times? Yes. It could easily have been ripped off.

My top priority at this point had to be Van. Was there actually any hard-and-fast proof that Van was innocent? Without a confession from William, could I convince the police to let him go? That Boots was innocent, too? I had Wanda and Winifred to affirm that William and I had been alone together in the shooting hut and that William had dashed out and jumped off a cliff while we were chasing the ferret, but what did that prove?

Wanda came up behind me. "I got through. An ambulance and the police are on their way."

"Good," I said, handing her Scarborough's leash. "Wanda, I need to think. Would you deem it too awful of me if I sit here quietly by myself for a few minutes?"

"Of course not." Wanda took Scarborough back, a safer distance from the edge of the precipice, and left me alone.

The box. Where was the box now? Were the three little items still in it? Might William have stashed them away and put John's box in the place where he normally kept his own? Might he have put them in a safe, or a bank's safety deposit box?

This is the evidence that will free Van! I'll be able to tell them that there's a black-handled knife under the bed at the shooting hut with William Sinclair's fingerprints on it, but I can't tell them where the box or the three little items are. The police will have to find those things themselves. I'll be able to tell them that they can find William's box in Fallon's room and Fallon can tell them where she hid it this time. I don't even know that myself. I'll be able to tell them that, when they do find the other box, they'll find screwdriver marks on the back. Fallon can back me up on all of this.

I'll be able to tell the police that if they go to the cellar, they'll find a portrait of Lady Rebecca Seton Sinclair with a clean spot around the ear. I can tell them that if they can find the contents of the box, they'll see that the earring matches the one on Lady Rebecca's ear in the portrait.

All together, that certainly ought to do it.

The strange *thunks* in the cellar and those coming from the wall in Fallon's room had been William, of course. That's how he'd known that I knew about Becky and about the switching of boxes.

Finally, I saw how the theft had been pulled off. William, hiding in the laird's lug anytime he felt the need to do so, might or might not have known that John had put the box in the big suitcase in his closet. William could have stashed his own box, open or closed, inside the laird's lug at any time and waited for a chance to make the swap. He would've needed to wait until someone took the box out of the suitcase, because to have walked out of the room with that huge shiny metal suitcase (which, I was sure, was too big to fit down those tiny stairs in the laird's lug) would have been too conspicuous. His chance would have come when he heard the coin expert was on his way and he saw me heading up to Fallon's room, obviously to get the coin. The fact that the box was about to be opened made it imperative that he do something quickly. After all, Fallon or I might have decided to remove the earring as well as the coin.

So he had dashed through the library, up the secret stairs, and to the third floor where he could have waited behind the paneling until Fallon and I extracted the box from the suitcase, and, while we were looking for the key to the box, he popped out, switched boxes, and popped back into the little hole in the wall.

Wait a minute. How would William have known we'd have to look for the key? He must have hidden it himself. He'd have had plenty of time to find it and hide it during the two days Fallon had been at the hospital with John. Even if John had had the key with him when the ambulance carried him off, William would still have been able to retrieve it while he sat with his poor brother in the ICU, or from Fallon's purse while she sat with John.

"Mrs. Lamb?"

I couldn't believe it. Here we were again, Chief Inspector Coates and I—and another dead body.

I told him everything I knew. Surprisingly, he didn't seem

to doubt my story about William holding a knife to my throat, and that struck me as odd, given the fact that he was a friend of William's and he didn't like me at all. "I can hardly expect you to believe all this," I said, "but I'm telling you the truth."

"I believe you," Coates said dully. "There's blood on your neck."

I SNEAKED THROUGH the side door of the round tower to go back to my room because I didn't want to talk to Maisie yet. I wanted Chief Inspector Coates to break the news to her that her husband was dead. The stairwell, as usual, was dark because the bulb in the wall light, as usual, was missing. I found it somehow comforting to see that some things hadn't changed.

Once inside my room, I kicked off my shoes and plopped down on the chair at my vanity table. My own reflection in the mirror startled me. I looked a complete mess, of course, but that wasn't it. An angry red line slashed diagonally across the left side of my neck and ended in a trail of dried blood that ran down into my collar. That had been close! If only I could leave it that way until Lettie got back. I wanted her to see it. But I'd really have to clean it up and find a way to cover it before I dared talk to Maisie.

My gaze fell on the wastebasket and on a small brown paper bag in it. That was where I'd put that stuff I found in the cellar. I pulled the bag out and held my breath before opening it. It hadn't smelled good a week ago; I expected it to smell worse now. Strange, but the contents of the bag seemed to have expanded.

Inside, I found the black fibrous material, still damp, probably because it had been sharing the trash can with some wet napkins. Nestled in the center of the dark material was something new. Something that looked like an egg, but wasn't an egg, because it was soft. My finger made a dent.

I snatched the mushroom book out of my bag and frantically flipped through the color plates. I had seen something that looked exactly like this thing. It was in here somewhere. I found it on page 58. "Death Cap, button. *Amanita phalloides,* emerging from sac-like cup."

THIRTY-ONE

"MAISIE GETS THE CASTLE, of course."

I felt as if I looked good because, with the money I saved by only having to pay Van's lawyer for five hours' work, I had treated myself to a shopping spree up and down Princes Street in Edinburgh topped off with a visit to Penhaligon's Perfumers on George Street for some of their heavenly Eau de Toilette. I splurged on an amber bouclé knit dress that exactly matched my eyes. Now, where had I heard that recently?

Dr. Kenneth Owen took Lettie and me to the Queensferry Arms for dinner. Our window looked out over the rail bridge spanning the Firth of Forth, a name which becomes progressively funnier the more you've had to drink. Kenneth was wearing a dark suit and plaid tie in which he looked less like Cal Ripken, Jr. than he had in that blue polo shirt, but he was still handsome. I had promised myself another, more leisurely, trip to Scotland someday and was already agonizing over how I'd manage to let Kenneth know I was coming.

"Will she be able to take care of all that land on her own?" Kenneth looked up from his baked salmon with neeps and tatties.

"She's going to ask Robbie MacBane to co-manage it with her. He is, after all, sort of a Sinclair. By marriage at least. And she confided to me that if the partnership goes well, she'll leave the castle and all the land to Robbie in her will. Maisie had no idea that William had slipped another species of mushroom, a nonlethal but sick-making kind also from his little farm in the cellar, into the soup we all had for dinner."

"He made himself and everybody else sick in order to carry out his plan." Lettie shook her head and sighed.

"Maybe he didn't eat the same soup, himself," Kenneth suggested. "He might have dipped out a cupful from the pot for himself before tossing the bad mushrooms in. He could have been pretending to be sick along with everyone else."

"Ooh, that is possible!" Lettie said and then added, "Robbie and his wife are going to move into the castle after their baby is born."

"And a little MacBane means an heir for Robbie to leave it to. Had the castle stayed in William's hands, it might have been left to an elderly Maisie who wouldn't have known who in the world to leave it to."

I pulled a little enameled pill box from my purse and passed it across the table to Kenneth. "Your coin, sir, and may you discover that it was actually dropped by the hand of Macbeth."

"Thank you. I'll write you about my progress when I know more," Kenneth said. "Shall we exchange addresses? E-mail and otherwise?"

I wrote mine out for him and he gave me his card.

Lettie put down her fork and said, "Fallon gets the stamp."

"Of course," I said. "And the earring? Well, Maisie probably has both of them now, but I bet she never wants to see them again. I wouldn't blame her if she fed them to the geese."

Kenneth looked at both of us. "What sort of financial shape is the castle in?"

"Fairly good, I gather," I said. "William and Maisie had actually been operating at a profit all along. Good management on both their parts. But John's constant demands for money to keep his mouth shut ran them into the red."

"And the Super Bowl tickets?"

"When the police release them, they'll belong to Proctor Galigher, I imagine, and I really don't care what he does with them."

Lettie wiggled her shoulders and put her hand beside her

mouth as if she was telling us a secret. "Tony Marsh could still use them. He could take Hannah with him to America, and they could go to the Super Bowl."

"Aha! So my little flirtation worked, did it?" Kenneth said, his eyes twinkling.

"I believe it did," I said. "Van Nguyen is free to return to Cambridge, his parents none the wiser. Tony Marsh and Graham Jones are in the process of applying for grant money to finish the work on the dig. It would be a shame to stop now. But when they complete their work, Tony told me, they plan to cover it all back up and return it to the barley field it was before."

"Much better than a theme park," Kenneth said.

I noticed then that Lettie had gone silent. "Are you all right, Lettie?"

She nodded.

"How about your ancestor research, Lettie?" Kenneth asked. "Did you find everything you wanted?"

Lettie's face screwed up and reddened. "No! I found out what I didn't want!"

"What do you mean? Lettie!" I didn't know whether to steer her toward the ladies' room or offer her my napkin. It was an awkward moment.

"I found out...I found out that Ollie and I are related!" Lettie's eyes welled up and overflowed. "I was looking for information on Ollie's grandmother, who was from Glasgow. She was a Cruikshank. So I found her and discovered that her mother was a Hynd, daughter of Flora and Robert Hynd, the same Flora Hynd who was a Sinclair from Aviemore, and she's my ancestor, too! So there's no doubt. No doubt at all. Ollie and I are related!"

"Small world, isn't it?" I said.

"But, Dotsy." Lettie sniffled. "This means that our children are retarded!"

Kenneth ducked his face into his napkin. When he managed to wipe the silly smirk off his face, he said, "You have the same great-great grandparents? Or is it three greats, I lost count. That would make you and your husband no more than sixth or seventh cousins, however you figure it, and if that constituted in-breeding, we'd all be idiots."

"Lettie," I said, "if you marry your first cousin, your children may be retarded. If you marry your sixth or seventh cousin, the rule says, only one of your children will be retarded. Now, which one of your kids would it be? The one who's starting her residency after graduating summa cum laude from med school or the one who runs his own computer software firm?"

Lettie's face told me she knew I was teasing. She took a playful swat at me.

And Kenneth added, "But part two of that rule states that if the ancestors in question are Scottish, all other rules don't apply!"